THE BUICK STALLED ON RAILROAD TRACKS

Then Josh saw the light. Small, glaring, and unquestionably moving toward him.

He tried the engine again, with no result. He pushed at the driver's side door. It didn't open. Neither did the passenger door. And though the windows were open, an invisible barrier held him in the car.

The tracks rumbled and groaned; the heavy wheels of the train cracked over the gaps in the rails. The light grew brighter.

A scream for a whistle, and Josh spun around to stare in fear: the engine was a locomotive, coal-bearing, not diesel. Where had it come from? The cowcatcher was painted bright red, the bulging sides of the engine sleek, black, spouting brilliant white steam.

He swallowed, wondering how it would feel when the locomotive stopped an inch from the door, wondering how he would explain his predicament. Then he stopped wondering.

And the locomotive didn't stop.

Also by Charles L. Grant
published by Tor Books

AFTER MIDNIGHT
DOOM CITY
GREYSTONE BAY
THE HOUR OF THE OXRUN DEAD
THE ORCHARD
THE PET
THE SOUND OF MIDNIGHT

Charles L. Grant

The Glave

A TOM DOHERTY ASSOCIATES BOOK
NEW YORK

THE GRAVE

Copyright © 1981 by Charles L. Grant

A TOR Book
Published by Tom Doherty Associates, Inc.
49 West 24 Street
New York, NY 10010

ISBN: 0-812-51843-8   Can. ISBN: 0-812-51842-X

First Tor edition: December 1988

Printed in the United States of America

0 9 8 7 6 5 4 3 2 1

For QUINN,

who knows as much as any of
us about the dark side of midnight;
and who isn't averse to a little
gore now and then.

1

The end of April in Oxrun Station, and the dying was reversed with the temperature's slow rise and the week's worth of rain that added to the thawing. Pavement and blacktop were washed to a shimmering, storefronts were polished, streetlamps seemed taller, and the air lost the melancholy that had turned it November grey. A faint green haze—still a promise, though no longer a winter's dream—appeared as a cloud among branches and twigs, while lawns once brown showed heartening signs of struggle. Pedestrians walked instead of shuffled, smiled instead of grimaced, and automobiles slowed for passengers and drivers to examine the change.

The bench in front of the Centre Street luncheonette was repainted a pale blue—for the newspapers stacked there and for those who used it to wait for the bus. Patrolmen leaving their headquarters down on Chancellor Avenue tugged more confidently at their tapered tunics, set their caps at a slight angle just this side of rakish, did the same for their grins as if they had just had a raise. And in front of the Town Hall (across from the jail) the first circle of crocus broke stiffly through black soil.

It was a stretching, smiling, we-made-it-again time

when only the deepest of the snowfalls was remembered and made worse.

The evenings were still destined to be chilly, the afternoons not quite June, and there were already muttered complaints about all the rain; nevertheless, the past was done for another nine months, and New Year's was no longer the first day of the year.

Over the farmland valley beyond the village, however, cupped in a bowl of low and rounded hills, the greening was more prominent. Acres of it, square miles of it, blended into a freshly bright carpet; slopes of it and orchards of it luring the birds back from the South. There were newly energetic prowlings at night —small creatures looking for a leisurely meal, larger ones that refused to be driven away by progress. Motors were tuned with an ear cocked and listening, implements sharpened, gutters cleaned, cellars and attics aired without screens. For those who had lived for a time in the city it was quiet, an almost numbing silence only temporarily shattered by the passing of a train; and for those who had lived in the Station and the valley for more than one year there was no silence at all: the streams hissed, trees groaned, birds stalked and chattered, the ground itself shifting to accommodate the pattern.

Josh Miller listened.

He did not pretend to be a man of the soil or a huntsman more at home in the woods. He preferred, much preferred, to sit in the front of his television set and watch an old movie with Greenstreet and Lorre, or read a travel book or locked-room mystery, or do some quiet entertaining in the small house he owned down on Raglin Street (near Quentin Avenue, a block and a half south of the town park). Or even better—to find himself either here in Oxrun or in some other small community rummaging through houses and old shops at the whims (and the pocketbooks) of his old and new customers.

On the other hand, and truthfully, he would never

deny that he enjoyed Connecticut's spring and the voices it brought back after a long and hard winter, and he took a few moments to identify what he heard.

He was sitting on a low bulbous rock just outside the first rank of trees that marked the surrounding hills' thick woodland. Behind him was the forest, ahead and sloping down nearly two hundred yards to the flatland was an open area of low shrubs and hidden rocks; beyond that was the untilled and sparsely treed acreage belonging to Donald Murdoch. In the middle distance, a mile or so away and barely seen now because of all the green, was the black streak of Cross Valley Road; and farther on, an abrupt density of trees—on the left and right the hills again, and in the center those same trees marking the small estates of the Station's wealthy, estates that stopped at a hill (better called a rise, though no one would admit it) that signaled the back of the village's huge park.

Green no matter where he looked, and he knew that by August he would be praying hypocritically for autumn and some new color.

For the time being, however, it would suffice, it wasn't white.

Absently, then, he scratched at the back of his neck, the side of his jaw. He was wearing a deep blue windbreaker he had kept from the Air Force, a blue-plaid flannel shirt open at the neck, and dark blue denims tucked into high boots that had seldom seen a shining. His hands were gloved, his white-blond hair flattened over his ears by a sun-bleached baseball cap whose emblem had been torn off more than a decade ago. His face was somewhat rounded, eyes deepset and black, his nose sharp-angled and threatening to hook. Not a handsome man, nor plain; intriguing because of the thin-lipped mouth that twitched and quivered, a consistently sardonic semaphore that added a dimension to his speaking, was somewhat unnerving when he listened.

He sighed loudly then, and stretched his arms

slowly over his head, back, clasped hands, up and
around and into his lap. A grin, broad and self-
mocking, at the unchallenged indolence that pre-
vented him from leaving his perch on the rock. This
was unquestionably no day to be working, he thought
as the grin softened and his shoulders drooped into
comfort. There were women strolling in the park with
their heavy coats and sweaters off at last, and a silver
Rolls at Station Motors he wanted to dream over from
all possible angles. Not to mention the coeds spilling
over the quad at Hawksted College, the naps he could
take beneath the willow in his backyard, the short
drive to the Cock's Crow on Mainland Road where he
could listen to Gale Winston play her piano and
conjure dreams of a past that never was. Any of that
(or any of a dozen other things) would be infinitely
better than sitting on a cold rock at the end of a cold
April, hoping that a damned stupid plow would show
itself miraculously so he could go home (or to the
Cock's Crow, or to the college, or to the park) and
count his fee for the finding.

Any of it would be better . . . and none of it would
pay the bills.

He fished clumsily in his breast pocket for a cigarette and, after fighting a breeze that had crept up on
him from behind, lit it and coughed.

He could also stop smoking and add thirty years to
his life.

Listen, his mother had told him once, *if you absolutely have to smoke, at least smoke a pipe. You don't
inhale. You know that, of course. You don't inhale a
pipe. Your father smokes a pipe. Why don't you ask
him how it's done? He won't bite you, you know. Why
don't you ask him, and get rid of those filthy things*.

He had asked, and he had tried, but he could never
get the hang of reading at his desk without all that
tobacco tumbling onto a book and burning a hole
through to the end.

Then quit altogether, you'll live longer, she'd said.

His mother would not have been his mother if she did not have an answer for every problem life gave him.

A fly buzzed toward his eyes and he swatted it away, ducking, shuddering, thinking it was a wasp.

He wondered what his mother would say about that.

Not, he told himself quickly (as though she were listening and shaking her head), that he had any real gripes worth mentioning. After all, he said silently to the assembled weeds and thickening brush spread before him, I have managed to create a decent life for myself, one that doesn't tie me down to an office with someone else as boss. And I certainly have enough money squirreled in the bank so I can live reasonably well for a fairly long time in case it all falls apart. No mortgage, no loans . . . what more could I want? He crossed his fingers immediately, a childhood reaction for warding off a jinx, but he knew full well (and sometimes frighteningly well) how lucky he was, certainly more lucky than most people he knew in that he was able to do exactly what he wanted . . . and was getting paid for the pleasure.

In her letters his mother stopped just short of calling it sinful. His father merely shrugged, smiled, and looked wistful.

The breeze picked up, and he hunched his shoulders against it, a cold breeze suddenly that made him squint and turn away. And found himself looking back into the woods, as though someone behind him were breathing shadows at his back. It wasn't the first time he had felt it—here, even in town—and the reaction disturbed him. He wondered, then, if perhaps he wasn't trying too hard this time to get the commission. It wouldn't be the first instance he could remember when he had driven himself too hard.

But he knew that he hated almost too much to fail.

Just eight years ago—almost to the day, he realized with a start, and a reminder for a celebration—he had completed his hitch in the service and had decided (as much from laziness as any deep, compelling desire) that there had to be a way he could combine his love for mysteries in book form with a way to make a living. He had once considered a try at archeology—the perfect life, it seemed, to be able to roam the world in pursuit of ancient civilizations, to find a Rosetta stone of his own or the whereabouts of the true Atlantis or the untrammeled remains of Carthage in the North African desert; Stonehenge fascinated him, and Napoleon's real death; how had Rasputin actually died, and what had really happened to those poor souls at Roanoke.

Nothing original, nothing spectacular or insightful about the way he perceived it, and he had learned rather quickly that he hadn't had the talent. But he did have the patience—and he did have what retrospect proved to be an incredible stroke of luck. The right place, and the right time, and a reception for a challenge.

Shortly after his return to Oxrun, his parents had decided they had had enough of the Puritan work ethic. They sold their small business, gave him the house when he insisted on staying behind, and moved to Colorado. A month afterward, his conscience informing him unmercifully that he could not live forever on his discharge pay, he attended a cocktail party where, during the course of the evening, an acquaintance mentioned she was trying to locate one of the original theater posters for a Broadway show that had lasted exactly ten performances back in 1927. *The Marvelous Kings*, she'd thought it was called. Or something like that. But she had no idea of the playwright, the actors, or even the subject involved.

A week later he recalled the conversation, and the title; and he could not get clear of it once remembered no matter how hard he tried. He thought about it, cursed at it, worried at it, lay awake nights and muttered about it, finally trained into New York because it was growing impossible, like shards of popcorn, to get it the hell out of his teeth.

During his first day he sat in his hotel room and called himself stupid. Read the Manhattan Yellow Pages. Saw a movie. Read the Yellow Pages again.

Then, the following morning, he told himself to either fish or cut bait; but the popcorn was still there, more firmly lodged than ever.

So he bothered Equity, the Shuberts, City Hall, and the archives of the Metropolitan. He talked with doormen, ticket takers, stagehands, and old actors. He prowled museums he didn't know existed. He hunted agents and studios and theaters and bars. Within four days he had a name. In two more he was in Boston. A day later he walked up to the woman's house in Oxrun and asked her how much she was willing to pay for the poster he had found.

She was willing, as it turned out, to pay quite a lot.

In less than a month he had turned half of the Raglin Street house into an office, found a lawyer and incorporated himself, and began leaving word at parties, at the post office, at the shops, that he was open for business. The only things he wouldn't find were lost husbands and strayed children.

The house, however, became too uncomfortable. There were too many other people moving through the rooms, commenting with their eyes on the furnishings, his living. A year ago, then, he arranged to take over an empty office on High Street, just off Centre, with rooms above that he used for storage. Miller's Mysteries, and the business grew, easily turning a steady and comfortable profit as word continued to spread about the curious, white-haired young man and the items he unearthed. Billboards, like the first one. Butler's tables edged in filigree silver. Letters. Gowns. A manuscript in Maine, a derringer in Natchez, a signed crock in New Hampshire, a photograph in New Jersey; and more than a few things were uncovered right in the Station.

He hated telephone answering machines and services, and he hated working with numbers, and he hated doing anything but his job; so he took on Felicity Lancaster to keep the books and dust the shelves, fend off the unwanted and entice the hard-to-get.

And it had taken him quite a while to realize that he was, without question, excited . . . and content. There were just enough challenges to keep him from getting stale.

The breeze swirled again, pushing at the fringe of hair around his cap, slipping down his shirt to tighten his chest. He frowned as he stared at the agitated foliage around him. It felt as if there were a storm in the offing, but the sky was still blue, no clouds to be seen. He zipped up his jacket and lit another cigarette.

The weather, he thought glumly; one day it's warm and summer, the next you'd think it was February and snowing. His mother called it pneumonia time, the weeks when summer colds came ahead of schedule and stayed through September, never really dying. Whatever it was, it was distressing. He didn't care for things that changed on him without warning.

The breeze stiffened.

He squirmed and told himself he had better get moving. There were shadows here in broad daylight that he did not like to see.

But as soon as the thought surfaced he shook his head and dismissed it. Considered a quiet visit to a friend, Lloyd Stanworth, who would doctor him away from this unnatural reaction. And that too, he thought, was pushing the imagination.

But he did not look behind him when he heard the leaves whisper.

2

When the damp from the rock began to penetrate to his skin, Josh grunted and decided it was time to move on. The solitude here was taking chips from his sanity, and all he needed now was to see monsters in the woods.

I've seen some things here, his father had whispered once, while his mother was out shopping and they were alone in the house; *you can't live in the Station all your life without knowing the place isn't what you call your normal town.*

Josh had never believed it, never seen evidence that his father was right. But it wasn't the words that had bothered him, back when he was twelve . . . it was the sly look in his father's eyes, the wry quiver of his lips, and the fact that the afternoon was the afternoon of Halloween. It had frightened him more than seeing the masks on the children and hearing the wind in the trees; and it was almost a month before he knew he'd been kidded.

Nevertheless, he did not look around when the breeze kicked again.

Go, he told himself instead; go and have a drink.

But he hesitated, hating to admit to another round of defeat. What had brought him out here had begun two weeks ago, just after he had returned from a frustrating and ultimately fruitless journey to northern Vermont after a child's wicker rocker supposedly rare, one of a kind. He had not been in the High Street office more than five minutes, had barely been able to take off his coat and put his feet in his desk drawer, when Melissa Thames called in. She was over six feet tall, and well over sixty; the money she had Josh never dared dream of, and she wanted him to find an eighteenth-century plow.

"A what?" He looked up from the receiver to Felicity, who was rummaging through some old picture files for a portrait of Errol Flynn. She knew it was the old woman, and she studiously ignored him.

"A plow, Joshua," Mrs. Thames told him patiently, her voice slightly nasal, her manner friendly and brisk. "You know what a plow is—you make long holes in the ground with it. I'm redoing, you see, and I need to have that plow. That's not all that hard, is it? I must have a plow."

Mrs. Thames was the only steady customer he had who was still able to shake him.

"Mrs. Thames, I really don't think I follow you. A plow, right? Did you . . . what I mean to say is, did you buy a farm out in the valley or something?"

"Don't be an ass, Joshua," she had snapped, though he could sense her smiling. "What would I do with a farm at my age? I've just redone the maid's cottage out back—you know what it looks like, you've been in it a few times—I've just redone it in what I fervently hope is genuine Colonial. I've heard that some farmers used to keep their smaller plows by the threshold, for luck as it were. So I want a plow. For luck."

He had nodded as if there were nothing unusual in the request. "A plow. An authentic plow."

"Authentic, Joshua. Absolutely."

"Okay. An eighteenth-century handplow in good shape, not rusted away or anything like that, so you can put it in—"

"The maid's cottage. Yes."

"Mrs. Thames, you're crazy."

Felicity had gasped.

"I'm rich," said Mrs. Thames. "I can afford it. The question is: can you do it?"

At that point in the conversation Felicity had come over to stand beside his chair, her curiosity piqued by his protests and her inclination to worry stirred by his accusation. She was short, bordering on the plump, her face the gently hard-edged facade of old-fashioned farmers' daughters, complete to the perpetually red cheeks and the full red lips. As far as Josh was concerned, for the time he had known her, her only major fault was her stubborn insistence on wearing (no matter the season) brightly colored sweaters that served only to accentuate her weight rather than hide it. And he had convinced himself without substantial proof that it was only the painfully soft violet of her large eyes that kept her from spending every night at home, alone with a cat that hated everything about him, especially his shins. He had in fact tried just once (and as tactfully as he could) to explain how those beloved sweaters of hers tended to detract from her pleasant looks, and he had received in turn a stern lecture on sexism, employee/employer relationships, and if he was so damned concerned why the hell hadn't he ever taken her out for more than an occasional lunch.

He remembered he had never given her an answer as she'd listened intently while he explained what Mrs. Thames was after. And when he was finished, one hand smothering the mouthpiece, she had looked to the ceiling and shook her head slowly, as if she were a judge reluctant to pass sentence. Then she'd sighed loudly. "It gets muddy out there this time of year, Miller. I hope you have boots." She looked down at him and grinned. "There's rats and snakes in the barns, too. Have a good time. Charge her a fortune."

The mud he had found readily enough; the rats and snakes he had not, and for that bit of luck he was grateful Felicity wasn't as perfect as she'd like him to believe. But neither had he discovered anything that even remotely resembled the implement he was hunting. From sketches Felicity had copied from texts in New Haven he knew the handplow was constructed of two thick bows of wood joined at the base by a single huge blade, joined near the top by a crossbar of iron easily removable if either of the handles split or wore out.

But knowing what it looked like hadn't helped him thus far.

Suddenly, as he was crushing the cigarette out under his heel, the breeze exploded into a stiff violent wind that pelted him with dust and dead leaves. He covered his eyes instantly with his forearms and ducked his face toward his chest, holding his breath and waiting, thinking for no reason *my god it's a tornado* until the air abruptly stilled.

The silence made him realize the wind hadn't made a sound.

Cautiously, counting slowly to ten in case there was a resurgence, he lowered his arms and looked around him, frowning. Saw nothing amiss except a faint swirling of dust that hung darkly over the slope a dozen yards away. It hovered, scattered a moment later, and he was hard put to believe he had seen it at all.

The sky was still blue, untouched by clouds.

There was no breeze; the leaves were still.

"Nice," he told the air then. "How about the next time you bring me the stupid plow."

He pushed himself off the rock and dusted his jacket, brushed fingers through his hair. A brittle brown leaf clung to one knee, and he flicked it off, watched it fall, kicked at it and missed. Great, he thought; the wind was exactly what he needed to end one hell of a miserable day. The mud was cold, the woods were cold, in spite of the gloves his hands were cold. And all because of a lousy plow that's probably long since rotted into the side of the hill. It was, he told himself sourly, easily the dumbest thing he had ever agreed to find. If the request had come from anyone else but Mrs. Thames . . .

Home, then. It was time to head home when even the wind didn't want him sneaking around.

The faint sound of a siren wafted from the west. A downed tree, he guessed, or a branch through someone's front window.

As he started down the slope he glanced to his right, at a thick and rich stand of maple that protruded from the forest, a broad-boled and ancient stand that surrounded (and now concealed) a three-story clapboard farmhouse a quarter mile distant. He felt himself taking a step toward it, changed his mind with a warning whistle, and continued down through the brush, angling away from the homestead toward the car he had parked at the end of the flatland. He sidestepped a patch of sodden, sinking ground and jammed his hands into his jacket pockets, worked his face to a passable scowl.

Anyone else but Mrs. Thames . . .

He spat angrily. All he was doing was skirting the solution, and he hated it, especially when he knew, when he positively knew that the answer was right here in front of him, his eyes for the moment simply unable to focus on the clues he needed. Failure was not exactly a stranger to his work, and he could remember without half thinking about it worse times than this.

But it was just so goddamned frustrating! And so goddamned unfair.

After the barn lofts and the attic rafters and the stables of the valley's tenants had proved depressingly empty, he had made himself a series of maps of the land, blocked off and marked for quick identification. Then he had launched a series of excursions through the lower woods in hopes of coming across remnants

of foundations that signaled a forgotten farmhouse or
desolate outbuilding. Each time he returned empty-
handed he shaded the map, stared at it, at the others,
hoping the roughly drawn lines would suddenly join
in an arrow, an X-marks-the-spot that would save him
his temper, and Mrs. Thames' patience.

It had only been two weeks, he kept telling himself,
but the shadow of the Vermont trip refused to leave
him be. And today was the fifth day of trying, his first
in an area of briar and ash at the back of Don
Murdoch's place; and his feet, he thought sourly, were
rapidly turning to moss.

He kicked out in reflex, glanced back again at the
house he could not see.

Murdoch—a large man dark from his curly hair to
his constantly squinting eyes, from his spiked eyebrows to the ghost of a beard that made one wish he
would either grow it or shave closer—had purchased
the small parcel of land only the summer before. He
had made it clear he had no intention of working it
(other than tending a rather large, successful garden),
used the fields instead for the walks he claimed he
needed to write some of his books. Josh had never
heard of him or his work, and Nat Clayton at the
library had told him one afternoon that Murdoch was
not the most sought-after author she had ever encoun-
tered, apparently selling just enough to keep his
publishers happy and his readers from desertion.

"Let me tell you something," Murdoch had told
him, standing in front of the fireplace in the house, his
hands chopping at the air as though he were sculpting,
"I may not be the richest man in the world, but I know
damned well what I'm doing with my life. How many
others can say that, huh? So I don't win the Nobel
Prize, so I don't sell to the movies or TV . . . so what?
Who cares?" He had laughed, raucously, richly. "I got
what I got, Josh, and that's all that matters."

The man was, Josh had to admit, personable
enough, and had a proverbial beauty for a daughter; so

he listened politely to the stories of the agonies that eventually transformed themselves to books, and drank his cheap liquor, and laughed at his jokes, and spent as much time as he could stealing glances at the woman.

In December Murdoch brought him out to dinner, none too subtly leaving him alone with his daughter. But there had been an awkwardness he had been unable to surmount, and Murdoch had returned from the kitchen, scowling as if he had been eavesdropping at the door.

In January he came to the office.

"What do you have against my Andy?" the man had demanded.

Felicity was at lunch; Josh was too surprised to speak.

"Huh? What's the matter with her, Josh? Don't you like her? She's a good girl, a fine woman, I want you to get to know her better." There had been no leer, no wink. "She's a good girl," he said again. Softly. "A very good girl. It isn't right she should be out there all alone."

"Don," he'd said, just as softly, "what happened to her mother?"

Murdoch sighed and slapped his hands to his sides. "Died ten years, out in Arizona. We went there for her health, the clean air and all that. It helped her lungs, but it didn't help her heart."

"Oh. Hey, I'm sorry."

Murdoch waved the apology away. "It's all right, I'm over it. But I tell you, Josh, I'm not all that sure Andy is, you know what I mean? She's got to have people around her, and nothing I do will make her live on her own." He slapped his chest, his stomach, yanked at his hair untouched by grey. "I'm healthy as a horse, and she worries about me. Me, one of the greatest unknown writers in the known universe." He laughed again. "Josh, do me a favor and take her out once in a while, all right?"

Josh had been dumbfounded; a father who was trying to give his little girl away? To a stranger?

Murdoch suddenly lost his bluster, became nervous, almost jittery. "Do it for me, will you? She's driving me crazy out there with all her fool help."

No matter how often he replayed the scene, Josh could not remember saying yes or nodding. But he knew he must have given the man some sort of sign, because the next thing he knew his hand was being pumped and Murdoch was himself again.

"You won't regret it, Josh. I promise you that. She's got college, she's got smarts, she won't embarrass you or any of the rest of the damned snobs in this town. I tell you something, pal—I never would have come out here if I didn't have to. Give me the city anytime, that's what I say. Christ, it's miserable out here!"

"Hey," he'd said, suddenly defensive, "it isn't that bad, you know."

"Bad enough. Bad enough. Damn, I hate waiting." He'd stopped, frowned. "Wish I could just snap my fingers and the book'd be done, you know what I mean?"

Felicity had walked in, then, and Murdoch had left.

And Josh had taken Andrea to dinner, to movies, on rides through the country he had always thought lovely. Not often, but enough. And now he was wondering what he'd gotten himself into.

Just like the plow. Spending every available daylight hour covering himself with mud, dead grass, and stinging gouges from thorns that were plastered over with his name. He punched at the air. Only two things kept him going through this miserable weather: his pride, and the idea he would let the old woman down if he gave up so soon. It's only been two weeks, he reminded himself again; only two weeks. Give yourself a break.

He stopped at the car for a long, pensive moment.

Here. Damnit, it had to be somewhere near here, if it was here at all. Damnit, it felt right. The land

looked right. A farm other than Murdoch's had been
here before—the age of the newer trees and the
unmistakable signs of a land-clearing forest fire made
it almost a certainty. Here, goddamnit; he *knew* it.
Knew it so much he had already spent hours past
sunset checking through Oxrun histories, maps from
Town Hall, diaries held at the college; tall-tales and
folklore and old surveyor's plots. And though none of
them had aided him directly, neither had they been
able to prove him unarguably wrong.

Not only was it depressing, it was frustrating as
hell.

He didn't need this. Not now. Especially not now.

He shook his head sharply and yanked open the car
door . . . and threw up his hands when something
leapt at his eyes.

3

Josh yelled, as much in abrupt fear as at the sharp
pain that erupted in his shoulder when he threw
himself back and caught the edge of the door. He
dropped to the ground on his back, slapping at the air
in front of his face, at his chest, rolling over several
times before sitting up and staring. His mouth open
and gulping for a breath. His legs outstretched and
trembling. He was cold, and his teeth chattered, his
head jerking from side to side while he blinked away
unbidden tears to clear his vision.

*He was a child. He was stalking Big Game through
the night-infested jungles of his backyard, his shadow
clear and long from the hot burning sun overhead.
Drums sounded. Lions roared. He heard the unmistakable grumbling of an elephant herd wallowing at a
waterhole nearby. Sweat poured down his face, darkened his shirt under his arms, slipped into his boots to
make him feel as though he'd been trudging through
mud. He knew the jewels had been hidden somewhere within reach, came to a greybark dead tree and
dropped into a crouch. Listened. Tested the wind for
the scent of the enemy. A rustling in the foliage above.
A rustling in the shrubs that cut him off from the
plain. He examined the tree carefully, wiping a fore-*

arm over his face and laying his rifle on the ground beside him. There was a hole, a large one, just above eye level. He sniffed, swallowed, checked the area behind him and picked up his rifle again. Slowly, trying not to disturb the leopard sleeping in the branches, he poked the butt into the hole to test for obstructions. The jewels were there; he knew they were there; and when he felt something give he grinned, rammed the butt home . . . and screamed as the cloud swept out of the tree and settled over his head. There was a running, then, a shrieking, a thousand bombers buzzing in his ears. The jungle was gone, the lions were gone, the elephants and the leopard and the waterhole and the plain; only the wasps, and the fire, and the sound of his sobbing.

"Jesus," he whispered, reached into a hip pocket for his handkerchief. He flapped it out square, then rubbed it hard over his face. "Jesus." The cold slipped away, the trembling subsided, but he could still feel the race of his heart in his chest. And he thought he could still feel the fire of the stings that had stitched over him that afternoon, so long ago he wished he could forget it. Gingerly he pressed a finger to various parts of his neck, knowing he wouldn't find anything but doing it just the same. At the same time he scanned the air, the car, the shadows of the weeds he had fallen into. Saw nothing until he had pushed himself to his knees and was slapping at the dirt on his jacket with the bill of his cap.

It was a bird. A robin. It was lying just under the car, half in sun, half in oiled shadow.

He rose awkwardly to his feet and put his hands on his hips, squinting though the sun was already westering behind him, staring blindly at the forest until he could convince his mind to start working again without all the remembering. Then he grabbed hold of the edge of the car door and knelt again, poking at the dead bird with a stiff forefinger. Its neck was broken, eyes glassed over. He frowned, scratched his cheek, turned, and dug a shallow trench in the soft earth with his heel. When it was done he shoved the bird in and covered it. With his boot, not his hands.

He knew it hadn't been his flailing that had done it; he had already started falling backward before he had made first contact. Then it must have been that windstorm. The bird had been slammed into the car, its neck was snapped, and he had been so immersed in thought that he hadn't seen it lying on the roof, partway over the door.

His imagination had done the rest.

And once he had figured it out to his satisfaction he immediately looked around him, realizing what an idiot he must have looked like to anyone happening to see him. His grin was sheepish. A faint warmth spread momentarily over his face. The hunter of plows and the finder of Time's secrets undone by a robin. It was a good thing Fel hadn't been with him; she would have laughed all the way back to the office, laughed the next morning, laughed for a week. After that, she would only grin now and then.

A grunt for a laugh, and he slipped in behind the wheel. Both front and back seats had been encased by the cheapest terry cloth coverings he could find as protection against dirt. At least for the time he searched for the plow. He hated them. They were green. But his car he considered close to a national treasure—a twenty-five-year-old Buick, deep maroon, complete with the air holes on the sides of the hood, the rocket ornament, and the weight that made him feel as if he were driving a tank. It was the only thing he had gone looking for entirely on his own, a whimsy that became an obsession until he had found it a year after he'd started.

Now it was his trademark, and he protected it with a jealousy usually reserved for lovers.

But why, he thought wryly, should this car be any different from what he did for a living?

Sometimes, as now, he could not help stepping back and looking at himself, seeing what he was doing, thinking that the people who had first settled this part of the country would have thought him a lout, if not directly engaged in some of the devil's own work. As he backed carefully toward one of the potholed spokes that poked off of Cross Valley, he tried to imagine another man of thirty-three spending his beautiful spring days on the hunt for a dumb plow. No, he decided; he was probably the only one in the world fool enough to try it.

He considered, then, stopping in at the Murdochs' for a drink and a free dinner. Decided against it when he remembered with a wince the paperwork waiting back at the office. He had promised Fel that morning he would spend at least part of the day there, before she rebelled and started screaming at all his work she was doing. A promise, he realized, already two hours late in the keeping.

Cross Valley Road extended from a handful of abandoned iron mines on the slopes of the northern hills to an abrupt dead end on the slope of those to the south. It was straight, well maintained, and from it extended any number of spurs poking into the farmland, spurs that were known only by the houses and homesteads they passed. No one knew why it didn't carry on over the hills, why it stopped where it did, why it didn't curve to encircle the rest of the land; and no one (save newcomers who didn't know any better, and were taught quick enough once the issue was raised) ever proposed making additions or alterations. Cross Valley was Cross Valley; it was almost as though there were a Commandment to protect it.

Josh drove slowly, feeling now a delayed reaction to the imagined assault, and not wanting to leave the open space for the closeness of the village. There were also the potholes, which the Buick accepted with a minimum of shuddering, dropping in and out of them with remarkable disdain. He grinned at the power he gave himself behind the wheel, scowled at a streak of dust he saw on the hood, then told himself that if he didn't watch out he would be spending every sunny day for the rest of his life spread-eagled over the roof to protect it from the elements. He knew he loved the old bus, but it was hard not to fall into the role of fanatic.

Once on Cross Valley, his delays having run out, he turned right and headed for the intersection with Williamston Pike. From there it was a four-mile (and then some) ride to the village center, passing along the way the estates of those whose money was so old, so ingrained, they never even considered the possibility of its going. And that, in a large and small way, was one of the reasons why he had remained in the Station after his parents had left. The village itself was not large at all, virtually self-contained, and its population was generally more wealthy than the facade it gave to the world. Yet upper class or middle, the town as a whole took care of its own. Not like a family, but as protection against the world.

A horn blared at him suddenly and he shook his head once, saw up ahead a gathering of vehicles at the intersection he wanted. He stiffened and took his foot from the accelerator. On his right was nothing but barbed wire fencing and telephone poles, the fields sweeping beyond them. On the left, a space of woodland between the road and the railroad tracks where a few small homes crouched in the shadows. And at the corner a young willow that had been snapped in half and slammed to the ground. A yellow sedan was angled over the stump, bleeding oil and blue-grey smoke, its front end smashed to chrome and glass glitter. The windshield was gone, the passenger door jammed open and twisted almost off its hinges.

There were two ambulances idling on the shoulder, and as Josh pulled off to the side and yanked on the parking brake, one of them crawled onto the pike and darted away, silently, its red light spinning. A patrolman stood in the middle of the road, hands in his pockets and waiting for some traffic to direct around the scene. He lifted his head slightly when he saw Josh stop, but made no move to join him, eying instead the hesitant work of a second patrolman who was walking around the demolished car with an extinguisher in his hand.

A wasp settled on the outside mirror. Josh rolled his window up slowly and watched it slip around the curve of the chrome. A trickle of perspiration drifted down his spine. The car grew warm. When he blinked and the wasp was gone, he threw open the door without checking for cars, stopped only long enough to toss his cap onto the front seat before strolling over to the cop.

Fred Borg had been a policeman in Oxrun Station since before Josh's birth, had finally and beefily resigned himself to never making chief, or wearing anything more than the sergeant's stripes on his arm. The only time Josh could recall the man rousing himself was a year or so ago, when the present chief, Abe Stockton, had the uniforms altered from blue with grey piping to the opposite. Fred had protested the change simply because it was change, had lost, and Josh had never understood why Borg had been so adamant in his opposition. Probably, he thought with a grin kept to himself, the new color showed the dirt too readily; right now, Borg was streaked with dust, with what looked like grease, and a few darker blotches he did not examine too closely.

"Josh," the man said, a short nod in greeting.

"Hey, Fred." He glanced over to the wrecking crew attempting with violent mime to attach a towchain to the sedan's rear bumper. "What's up?"

The second patrolman (Josh reached for his name, and failed) finally gave up stalking fire around the car and tossed the extinguisher into the back of the traffic patrol's station wagon. Then he leaned against the

front fender and fished a cigarette from his pocket.
Borg scowled, but said nothing.

"Fred? You there, Fred?"

Borg grunted and gestured vaguely toward the
wreck, out toward the hills to the north. "Tourists,"
he said; and from the tone Josh knew that was a
condemnation in itself. "Damned fools must've been
up at the mines. Seems they came down looks like a
zillion miles an hour and missed the turn to the pike."
He shook his head in saddened disgust. "Best I can tell
from what was left, they were young, too. Don't think
I have to go up there to see what they were doing. Just
dumb speeding is all that happened. Dumb, stupid,
halfassed speeding."

A half-dozen automobiles appeared at the intersection simultaneously, and as Borg popped a whistle
between his teeth to sort out the confusion and wave
on the rubberneckers, Josh wandered away, up the
center of the tarmac along the path the car had taken.
Absently, he fumbled in his jacket pocket and pulled
out a short-stemmed pipe that had never seen a flake
of tobacco. With the rough-sided bowl mouth down,
he bit on the stem and chewed it thoughtfully, every
few paces glancing up to imagine the car sweeping out
of the forest like a hornet from its nest.

Five minutes later he knew what was bothering the
police—there were no skid marks; it was as though
the driver had deliberately rammed into the tree, no
sign at all he had tried to dodge it.

He shuddered and returned to his car, waited until
Borg had a free moment to join him.

"Yeah," Borg said, seeing the expression on his face.
"Pretty sick, if you ask me."

"Drinking?"

Borg shrugged.

"How about drugs? Wouldn't be the first time
around here, you know."

"Couldn't tell you, Josh. They were all dead and

smashed when we got here. Got a call there was an accident out this way, but by the time everything got moving . . ." and he waved a hand wearily.

Beneath the driver's door Josh could see a pool of dark, viscous liquid; he hoped it was oil. "How many were there?"

Borg looked down at him and grinned. "You working for the *Herald* now, Josh?"

He shrugged, embarrassed. "Nope. Just nosy, that's all."

"Yeah, well, this one you'd like, pal, believe me."

One evening just over two years ago, Borg had come to Josh, asking if he could locate a one-of-a-kind photograph of his wife's mother. He had taken part of a short vacation in Seattle to locate it, had taken no payment for it after he'd returned, and Alice Borg had become his friend for life. She did not understand, or pretended not to understand, that there were still some things he liked doing for fun.

"Yessir," Borg said, rubbing his hands together as though he were chilled, "you'd love this one, pal, absolutely."

"Well, are you going to tell me, or am I going to have to guess?"

Borg cleared his throat and pointed. "There were five people in that car there, Josh. Every one of them was killed on the spot. Two got tossed through the windshield, landed fifty yards into them bushes back there; one got dumped out t'other door and broke her neck hitting the ground; one got smacked against the dash, nothing left of his face."

Josh felt slightly nauseated, but swallowed hard to keep it down. "You said five. That's only four."

"Yeah. Seems to me, friend, one of them got himself away."

Josh stared at the glass and slivers of metal, pieces of the car's interior strewn over the road and its shoulder, at the wrenched and fire-blackened metal, at the finally successful work of the tow truck's personnel, and he shook his head emphatically. "No, Fred. That's just not possible."

"Maybe," the policeman said, "but we got parts that don't exactly match up with what we got."

"What?" He looked up at the tall man, astonished, though he wasn't at all sure he wanted to hear it.

With a brusque nod Borg indicated a small, dark plastic bag lying near the rear wheel of the last ambulance. The attendants had just placed a much larger one inside, and one of them was reaching down for what was left. "That's an arm in there, Josh," Borg told him, waving at the attendant to go ahead into town. "Now I got a good look at all the others that were in there, they have all their arms and legs . . . or what's left of them, that is. That one there, my friend, belongs to somebody we don't know about yet."

He looked to the trees, to his hands, to the dim reflection of the ambulance's red light spinning over his hood. When he was able to look back, Borg nodded.

I suppose, Josh thought, it was just remotely possible. Shock, trauma, the miracle of escaping the death his friends had suffered. The body can do strange things when it's violently attacked; maybe this guy was thrown clear after the amputation, didn't know what he was doing. "Well," he said finally, "he couldn't have gotten all that far, right? I mean, he had to have more done to him than just losing an arm, right?"

"Wish I knew."

The other patrolman called out, then, holding in his right hand the station wagon's mike. Borg muttered something Josh didn't catch and lumbered away, nodding *all right all right I'm coming already* as he crossed the road and stepped gingerly around a gleaming ribbon of chrome.

The second ambulance left.

Josh hugged himself as the tow truck finally wrenched the sedan off the willow stump, the chain rattling over the winch, particles of rust flaking to the ground. One of the men, his coveralls slicked with grease and perspiration, wiped his hands on a rag and joined the policemen, nodding, laughing once at something the younger cop said, then punched Borg's shoulder lightly and returned to the truck. A moment later it backfired, gained traction, and trundled onto the pike. As the sedan straightened out behind it, a hubcap fell off; it didn't roll, it didn't spin—it just lay there on the black.

Nosy, he thought then. Ghoul. I should get back in the car and go home is what I should do. Go to the office and take Fel up on all her invitations. That's what the hell I should do, goddamnit.

Instead, when Borg came back, he pulled out his pipe and, with one finger wrapped around the bowl, he used the stem as a pointer. "They came right down here, right?" He didn't look up. "They didn't try to stop—unless the brakes weren't working—they just took off and did that tree in. Doors fly open, windshield blows all to hell, you have bodies squashed all over the place. Right? Am I right, or am I right?"

Borg spun his whistle around on its leather strap, the silver blurring to white in the sun. "I said the same thing to Karl over there. I must've said it a hundred times. He thinks I'm crazy."

"Karl," Josh said, "is a goddamned idiot."

"You don't even know him." The protest was half-hearted.

"I don't have to. I know what I see, Fred. What I don't see is a guy walking away from this thing."

"Yeah."

"Anyway, if he did there has to be blood, doesn't there? He must have been bleeding like a pig."

Borg nodded, ran a hand over sandy hair that was thinning and coarse. "Trouble is, Karl and I have been all over this place, Josh. We didn't see a thing. The only body we found . . . the only bodies we found were right there where I told you before."

Josh shaded his eyes, inhaled, blew out the breath as slowly as he could. "Fred, I will say it again—a man, or a woman, is not going to be in that wreck, lose an arm, and walk away. Or at the very least, Fred, walk away without leaving a trail of blood, for god's sake!"

"Yeah," Fred said. "Tell me about it."

4

The drive back to the village was something more than a little unpleasant. Though he ordered himself several times to think about other things—Mrs. Thames, for example, and her damned handplow—he could not help an occasional guilty glance to the verge of the two-lane road, to the heavy concentration of trees beyond, could not help straining to catch a glimpse of a telltale gleam of fresh blood, or the unquestionable sprawl of a mangled body at the base of one of the high stone walls that encircled an estate. It was ridiculous, and he knew it, and he once almost drove off the road because his mind wouldn't connect to his hands on the driving.

At one point, nearly a mile in from Cross Valley, his throat contracted suddenly and his mouth filled with cotton when he spotted a glare of red in a thicket of high weeds. The Buick swerved as he braked, bucked when he slammed the gears into reverse and backed up swiftly. He rubbed a hand on the seat beside him, prayed he would see the police station wagon in the rearview mirror. Then he slid over to the opposite door, rolled down the window, and looked out. Cursed, laughed weakly, and returned to the wheel. It had been a sign, a small one, tipped by winter onto its side and weathered almost to the point of disintegration. On it, however, were the dull remnants of the words KRAYLIN CLINIC, lettered in a stubborn red that had thus far resisted the seasons. He had no idea what it meant, had no wish to investigate; he only drove a little faster, alternately swearing at himself and stealing swift glances at the speedometer's warnings.

A vacation, he decided then, thinking of Seattle and Alice Borg's mother. What he needed, obviously, was a break in his admittedly sporadic routine. How else could he explain his sudden nervousness? It wasn't as if this were the first accident he had ever come across, nor would it be the last. While he'd been in the Air Force he had seen two jet fighters splatter themselves in flames over the length of a runway, had seen the charred remains of the pilot inside. That was certainly much worse than a car wrapped around a tree. Definitely much worse.

But he could not shake the image of a one-armed man staggering through the trees, slowly bleeding to death.

That was the kind of mystery he wanted no part of at all.

At last, and none too soon, the trees fell away and the Station's heart was revealed.

The park and its tall, wrought-iron fencing appeared on his left, stopped at Park Street, was replaced by the library and its roof-high arched windows facing the pike. The next street was Centre and he turned left, an immediate right, and nearly sideswiped a motorcycle in a hasty U-turn that put him directly in front of his office. He sat for a moment, listening to the engine cooling. *An arm and no body.* He rubbed the side of his nose hard, yanked on his cap, shook his head, and snatched the keys from the ignition. Then, with a deep breath, he looked to his right and smiled.

The plate glass display window had been washed

only that morning, and still shimmered brightly over dark patches unevaporated on the pavement. There was nothing on the ledge inside but two broad-leaved plants in brown-and-white pots that completely masked the office beyond. But the quietly gold Miller's Mysteries in a crescent just above the center had always been sufficient to bring several outsiders through the door during a typical day, if only to discover exactly what he was selling. Most of these people listened to Felicity's spiel politely enough and left somewhat bemused, sometimes no further enlightened; others thought she was kidding and wanted to know where the camara was hidden; and there were a handful a month, seldom more than a half dozen, who called within a day or so with something for him to find.

Directly past the door was a broad area carefully defined by a multishaded brown hook rug upon which were arranged a quartet of club chairs in deep brown leather studded with gold, two small cocktail tables, and four ashtray stands in brass. There were no magazines, no colorful brochures, no price lists or catalogues to browse through or pick from. The walls held prints of Turner and O'Keeffe, movie posters, pen-and-inks and watercolors of the Oxrun Station a century earlier when the elms and chestnuts on Centre Street were still young and the road itself was wider and cobblestoned. It was not, then, a place for waiting, or a haven to pass the time while someone else in the family was wandering around shopping.

Past the rug and the chairs and also touched with artwork was a seven-foot walnut partition, open in the center and through which could be seen Felicity's desk, always neat, always with a clear glass vase and a single rose in the righthand corner. His own workspace was kept deliberately out of sight to the left, a virtually clichéd contrast to the rest of the office's orderliness.

Felicity was waiting for him when he came in, a

handful of pink message slips in her hand. Her hair was auburn and tightly curled, rounding her face more than necessary and accenting her huge eyes: her cardigan was buttoned to just below her breasts, her plain tan skirt hovering in folds about the center of her knees.

"Oh, Jesus," she said in disgust as he passed her and sat down. He looked to his boots and jeans and grimaced at the mud and the leaves and a few strips of grass. His knees were damp. The front of his shirt almost as filthy. He toed open the bottom drawer of his desk and hooked his heels on its edge. "That does it, Miller, I quit."

"No you don't," he said. "I'll clean it up later."

Her sour expression caught his tired lie, but all he could do was lift his hands to his shoulders and give her a shrug.

She grunted, then stepped back to lean against her own desk, left hand cupping right elbow, while she stared down at the messages. "They found an arm without a body out there on Cross Valley," she said flatly. She pointed to her cheek.

"I know." He took out his handkerchief, spat on a corner, and scrubbed at his face, just below his left eye. The cloth came away black. He dropped it in the wastebasket with a long silent whistle.

Fel looked to the ceiling, back to snare his gaze. "Damnit, Miller, how the hell did you find that out?"

He grinned at her unashamed. "I was there, m'dear. The question is, how did you manage to get the news so soon? Fred Borg was still out there when I left."

"I have a friend at the hospital," she said smugly. "He's one of the drivers. Called not twenty minutes ago with all the gory details." The right corner of her mouth curled almost to a sneer. "You going to look for it?"

"What?"

"The body. You going to track it down so they can sew it back on?"

"Come on, Fel, that isn't very funny." He thought of the sedan, the wind, the robin, the sudden cold. No, he thought; it wasn't funny at all.

"No skin off my nose," she muttered. Then she shook the messages at him to get back his attention. "Mrs. Hampton called just after you left. She's the one who's rebuilding the Toal mansion out there on the Pike?" She waited; he gave her no response. "She wants to know if you can get her a Victrola. She also wants to know if you can get her the dog that goes with it."

He cupped one hand to his cheek and leaned his elbow on the desk blotter. "Hell, no. She could find that in a dozen antique or collectors' catalogues."

"Good. That's what I told her." She stopped, frowned, tilted her head slightly. "You all right, Josh?"

"Yeah. Sort of. No, not really." He told her what had happened out in the valley, from his failure to come up with a clue to the plow, to the robin the wind had battered and left on his car, to the accident at the intersection and what he had seen there . . . and what he had not. "It has not been, dear Fel, the bestest of days." He nodded toward the slips before she could respond. "Go ahead. What else?"

"You sure you'll make it?"

He couldn't help a smile. She may use just a shade too much make-up, and she may not know how to drape her figure, and her typing wasn't perfect and her manner not at all, but when her voice softened and her eyes began to glitter as though about to cry, he knew he would kill if anyone tried to get her from him.

"Yes indeed," he told her. "I'll make it." He reached for a cigarette from the humidor on the desk.

"You smoke too much."

He snatched his hand back and wiped it against his jacket. Started. Pushed away from the chair and took the jacket off, dropping it on the floor in the middle of the desk-well. On his back and across his chest he could feel grains of dirt, a blade of weed or two, and he rolled his shoulders, arched his back to give him some comfort.

"You finished?"

He nodded.

"Okay. Frederick Thousman wants a first edition of *The Roman Hat Mystery*." She held up a palm to forestall interruption. "I told him. I told him. I also told him you'd strangle him if he got to it before you." While he laughed, she reached around behind her and picked up a thin, long package wrapped in brown paper. Tapped it once against her midriff and handed it to him. Inside was an angled pewter spoon whose handle was five inches long, its bowl deep and engraved with oak leaves and holly. It was lidded, the lid perforated where age had not clogged the tiny holes. "Sandy McLeod found this in that dead orchard in the field on the other side of Mainland. I gave him fifty for it and told him he could quit work in the bookstore and come work for us. He refused on the grounds that Iris and Paul would collapse without him."

Josh lifted it carefully from its shredded paper nest and held it high to the light, turned it, blew on it while dusting over it with one thumb. "Teaspoon. So what?"

"Mrs. Hampton might want it. It would keep her off our backs."

He replaced the spoon with care and dropped the box into his drawer. He seldom dealt with antiques such as that, and he had little knowledge of their worth beyond a layman's overview. That sort of thing he left to Felicity and the warren of catalogues she kept on a shelf along the rear wall. "You might as well write her about it. It looks ugly as sin."

"What would you know about sin?" Fel said. "Dale Blake dropped by. She wants to know if you can get her some sheet music from *The Blackbirds of 1929*, whatever the hell that is. Was it a radio show or something?"

"Nope. An all-black review of that very same year," he told her, interested for the first time since coming in the door. "Sheet music she wants?"

Felicity nodded.

"Sounds like fun." More, it sounded like the task that had gotten him started.

"I don't know," she said doubtfully. "I don't mean to knock your friends, Josh, but can she afford it? That's going to take time, and a lot of expense if you have to traipse all over the city, if not the East."

Dale Blake was the owner-operator of Bartlett's Toys, and he had known her since childhood, though they had never been all that close. He had been to her wedding to Vic Blake, and had been at the funeral of their adopted son, Jaimie, killed in a drowning accident in the park pond only the autumn before. Curious, he thought then, remembering the service; Dale was one of those women who seemed somehow better, almost relieved, when all of it was done and the last clod of dirt filled in the grave. Not that she was glad, of course; it was just one of those reactions that intrigued and bemused him. People, he'd long since decided, were worse than a jigsaw puzzle with ten pieces missing—every time you think you've got them, they hit you with a blank you can't fill in no matter how much you extrapolate from the picture around them. He laughed suddenly, and shook Fel's questioning glance off with a wave of his hand. A mixed metaphor . . . a mangled metaphor like that was prime ammunition for someone like her. Let it pass, Josh; she has ammunition enough.

"Hey, Miller, I asked you if she can afford it."

"She doesn't have to, Fel. Tell her I'll be glad to do a search the first chance I get."

"How," she wondered, more to the office than to him, "does the man manage to make a decent living?"

"I make it," he said quietly, firmly enough to bring a flush to her cheeks. "Anything else while I was out playing Natty Bumppo?"

Felicity sniffed displeasure and tapped the sheaf of papers against her chin. "A lady called."

"Oh?"

The smile was almost wicked. "I think she said her name was Andrea Murdoch. I could be wrong," she said quickly, "but I don't usually make mistakes like that. It was . . . yes, it was Andrea Murdoch."

He sat up quickly, damning her with a scowl. "Andy? Really? What did she want?"

"She wanted very definitely—and not very nicely, if you ask me—she wanted to know why you didn't stop at the house when you left." The wickedness prevailed. "She sounded awfully mad, Miller. I think you blew that one, but good."

"There is nothing to blow," he told her, dropped his feet to the floor, and turned away, staring at the blank wall next to him.

The office grew silent save for the muffled scratchings of Felicity's pen over hastily grabbed paper. He knew he should apologize to her, though he didn't know why—or even if—he had offended her. She was young; perhaps too young even for her ripe old twenty-four. Everything to her was the makings of a soap opera; a grand one, and convoluted, and perhaps self-mocking . . . but it was a soap opera nonetheless. She was, in fact, very much like his wife. Ex-wife. Both of them had been little more than children when they had married during the early part of his second year in the service; and when they had grown in California, in Tokyo, in Ankara, they had somehow grown apart. The divorce had been a simple one—though not all that painless—and they continued to keep in intermittent touch, through calling or writing, ironically more friendly now than when they'd been married.

"Miller?" Soft. Apologetic without knowing why.

He grunted, not turning. The grain in the walnut paneling was soothing, a balm; he used it sometimes to force his mind to drift when he was sorting clues from the dross. Or when he wanted to cut off the world from the embarrassment of his self-pity.

"Miller?"

She never gives up, he thought, not unkindly. Soap opera or not, she's saved me too often. "Yeah?"

A hesitation. A wondering. He could almost feel her make up her mind about the state of his mood.

"Just after you left Dr. Stanworth called. He wants to know if you'll have lunch with him tomorrow. I guess he wants you to invest in something."

He couldn't remain aloof, knew she'd done it deliberately to bait him, and draw him. "Now how in hell do you know that?"

"Doctors are rich, right? These days the only way you get rich is by investing in something. Like gold. So, you'll have lunch with him?"

"Sure."

"That's what I told him."

A rush of heated, irrational anger was doused instantly by his laugh and a bemused shake of his head. "Fel," he said, "what makes you think . . . whatever gave you the idea that I need a mother here, as well as in Colorado."

"You didn't wipe your feet when you came in."

"I own the place, remember?"

She scoffed, and tossed a folder across the narrow aisle, placing it squarely between his hands. "This is Mrs. Thames' latest gem. Something about a genuine Mohawk tribal bowl. I don't know. She came in just after Dr. Stanworth, while you were out stalking the Great Oxrun Handplow with gun and camera."

He didn't open it. In one corner, near the green tab with the client's name, was a doodled sketch of a robin on its back.

5

"Josh?"

The bird in shadow, waiting on the car for him to return; the bird in shadow, lying beneath the car with a broken neck.

A man, in shadow, without an arm.

"Hey . . . Josh?"

There was no doubt about it, he was cracking up. It had to be the answer. Why would something like this bother him so? Unless it was the accident, the blood by the wreck, the wind that had nearly knocked him off his feet. Too hard; he was working too hard, trying too hard; thinking he could run free in the world, chasing other people's rainbows.

He groaned; he knew he needed a vacation when he started getting maudlin.

"For god's sake, say something!"

He tapped at the sketch; he had to know. "This thing," he said, fighting to contain the sudden disgust he felt. "When did you do this?"

"Just before," she said, puzzled. "While you were telling me about what happened out there." Her eyes widened. "Oh, Jesus, Miller, I'm sorry. God, I'm sorry."

"It's all right."

"Hell, it was an unconscious thing, that's all. Really it was." She slammed a palm on her desk. "You're an idiot, Lancaster. You deserve to be boiled."

He said nothing. He pushed the folder to one side and stared instead at the curved back of the partition. A moment later, the muscles in his thighs and the small of his back began demanding a long hot bath and a long uncomplicated book. One with pictures, perhaps, so he wouldn't have to think.

Pop, have you ever had one of those days?

Son, when you get to be my age, every day is one of those days.

What do you do about it?

I go to bed and pray tomorrow will be different.

Does it work?

Sure. Unless it turns out to be one of those days.

He grinned broadly, suddenly, for the first time in months the absence of his parents making him ache. It was, however, a pleasant feeling, filled with the snippets and runs of nostalgia that glossed his childhood and made the world sane.

Until he thought again of the man with one arm.

He was chilled, then, and sand began to gather behind his eyes. "Why don't you take off, Fel," he said quietly. "There's nothing else that has to be done today, I guess. Nothing that can't wait, anyway."

"But Josh, it's only three-thirty!"

He gave her no response, waiting patiently until her stirring told him she had taken the hint. And when she finally realized what he wanted, she was in her spring coat and out the door with only a faint, whispered *see you tomorrow* left floating in the air.

A man and his wife strolled past, fragmented by the plants. A group of teenagers laughing fresh from the high school and heading for the luncheonette. A gaudy red delivery truck. A black-and-tan limousine that seemed to drive by forever.

Across the street the wooded lot that reached up to

the post office shimmered, darkened, gave up four
small boys carrying paper sacks in their hands. They
were looking in them intently, and Josh couldn't help
wondering until one of them pulled out a flower and
held it up to the setting sun. A school project. Every
kid in the town seemed to have a school project that
required them to hunt as he had in his backyard
jungle.

He began tapping a finger, looked down and saw he
was striking the folder. He turned it over quickly,
shuddering, and set himself to concentrate on the
messages Felicity left him. Concentrated, and centered, and cupped his hands under his chin.

Andy.

All right, he told himself, let's get down to basics
and stop this bullshit about men with one arm.

Andy. Andrea. Andrea Murdoch. Take her out, Don
had asked him; take her out and help me get her out of
my hair. He wondered if Murdoch had really known
what he was doing.

Andrea. Andy. A woman he had never taken into
the fortress of his arms, though he instinctively knew
she would fit there without strain. Hair of the
blackest, most radiant kind that swooped to her
shoulders in a cascade of midnight. Eyes and eyebrows
the same, just the same, framing and marking a face
neither magnificent nor dreamlike; a face, however,
that made you look twice to see what it had that made
you look the first time. A smile that was private, and a
slight tilting of her head as though the angle would
reveal a new dimension.

She had no job, and did not want one. As Don had
told him, she remained on the farm with her father to
coddle him in his moods, type his correspondence,
copy-edit and type the final manuscripts of his books.
She also ran his errands when he demanded his privacy, kept visitors away to keep him from wandering.

She was, he had discovered, wonderfully taken with

walking through the woods and across the fields, the wind permanently, it seemed, tangling her hair and blessing her cheeks with a gentle weathered glow. She haunted the orchards and exclaimed over the new fruit, kneeled in the garden and hacked at the weeds that threatened her children.

Andrea. Andy.

The first time he had seen her he had ached to bed her; the second time, she had consented to go with him (Don lurking in the background and winking his approval) while he traced what he had hoped were the outlines of an old farmstead not mentioned in the records. Silently watching as he crawled through the brush. The questions she asked few and pertinent. Not once drifting close enough to hold his hand if he wanted, yet not drifting far enough to warn him of exclusion.

When he dreamed of her it was conscious; when he spoke with her alone he could not help but stutter. And the idea that she might actually be, might honestly be annoyed just because he hadn't stopped by this afternoon excited him so much he couldn't think straight for an hour.

But the hour finally passed, and his ex-wife was remembered and Felicity's sometime longing violet eyes. He coughed loudly, forcedly, rubbing his face as hard as he could and deciding he had best not find some stupid excuse to get involved. Once burned and twice shy; but it didn't mean he couldn't be a fool if he gave it half a try.

The teenagers ran by again, and he suddenly realized just how he'd been behaving. And when the telephone rang he had nearly convinced himself it was time to head home and remember his age.

It was Melissa Thames.

"Joshua Miller, were you lucky out there for a change?"

He grinned at the receiver. "Now, if I were, I'd be

out at your place, right? And what's all this about a Mohawk bowl?"

"Oh, I don't know," she said airily. "It was just something that popped into my head. You know how I am, Joshua. And I honestly think that Miss Lancaster of yours was ready to laugh in my face."

"No," he said, hearing the lie. "Fel wouldn't do that to you, Mrs. Thames."

"The hell she wouldn't. She's done it before."

"I'll remind her to be more thoughtful."

"Much good it'll do you."

He frowned, then, and put a finger to the side of his nose. Rubbed it. Passed it under his eye and dropped it to push once at her folder. "Mrs. Thames, is there . . . it's none of my business, but is there something the matter?"

"No . . . not really," she told him, a cross between annoyance and the first stirring of a martyr. "Well . . . yes. It's just as well you didn't come out here, Joshua. I've had a tragedy today, and I'm just not in the mood."

It occurred to him that to ask about it might be tantamount to inviting disaster. Her last tragedy had been a stray and perverse strip of wallpaper in the maid's cottage that did not quite match the rest of the wall. He had offered to stop by and take a look, had done so before he'd known what he was doing, and ended up spending the next three days repapering under her less than expert guidance. If he hadn't enjoyed her company so much he would have been livid.

In spite of himself he asked her anyway.

"It's Thelma Saporral," she said; and he almost missed the tightness in her voice that controlled her speaking.

"I . . . I'm afraid I don't know her, Mrs. Thames. The name isn't familiar, anyway. Is she one of your ladies?"

Mrs. Thames' "ladies" were a group of women who met regularly at her home on the pike, a self-proclaimed and unabashed gossip session they would not dignify by calling a club, or a society, or a charitable organization. Though they had in fact done a great deal of work at the hospital, at the schools and college, raised funds after hurricanes and fires and such, their primary purpose was the passing of news (the worse the better) from one home to another. The telephone had been eschewed for all but emergencies; face-to-face gossip was much more exciting.

"Mrs. Thames, was she? One of your ladies, I mean."

"I'm afraid so, Joshua."

"I'm sorry to hear that."

There was pause, a rustling. "I don't mean she's dead, silly. Though she very well might be, for all I know, for all those idiots will tell me over there. She's . . . well, she's gone, Joshua. Just . . . gone."

He leaned back in his chair and wrapped the phone cord around his wrist. "I don't understand. Gone where?"

A clearing of her throat, a distant whispering from the radio. "She's been in hospital, you know . . . well, of course you wouldn't know, would you. Well, she has been. She had a seizure last week, her heart or her spleen or whatever it was that wasn't kicking around in there properly. And she was in the Intensive Care ward the last I heard.

"Well, I was feeling awfully chipper after I left your office today, and I recalled it was her birthday— seventy if she was a day, though she said sixty-five—so I thought I would drop by and let her know how the last meeting went. And would you believe it, Joshua? She was . . . she was gone." The brusque snap of her fingers. "Just like that." She snapped them again.

He frowned, somewhat bewildered. "Now wait a minute, Mrs. Thames, hold on a minute. You just said . . . do you mean—"

"Gone, Joshua, gone! My lord, aren't you listening over there? Have you got potatoes in your ears? She was gone! Gone from her bed. I walked up there and her room was empty, her clothes gone, and when I checked quickly with the telephone . . . I mean, when I called her home there was no answer at all."

"Ah," he said, grinning at last. "She walked out."

A loud, nearly wailing sigh made him take the receiver from his ear, stare at it, bring it back cautiously.

"Joshua . . . love . . . Thelma Saporral was hooked body and soul to one of those ugly little machines with all the lights and the beeps and things like that. She looked like she was on a television program, one of those true-to-life things. She couldn't have walked out if she tried."

"You asked the nurses, of course."

A clear tone for tolerance now, for understandable, but lamentable, stupidity. "I spoke very sternly with them, yes I did. But it was change of shift or something foolish like that, and the girls didn't even know Thelma at all. Well, one of them did, but she was worse than useless. The trouble is, I'm not family so I couldn't really let loose, if you know what I mean. In fact, Thelma, for all her talk, doesn't have any family left at all as I recall. It's all very upsetting, Joshua. Very upsetting."

He nodded. "I'm sure it is, Mrs. Thames." But, he thought, you should have heard what I heard today; old ladies walking out of hospitals don't hold a candle to dead men leaving an arm behind at an accident.

"She'll turn up, of course."

He did not miss the plea. "Sure she will," he told her as gently as he could. "I assume she wasn't as well . . . she wasn't in as good health overall as you are, Mrs. Thames, so she couldn't have gotten very far. Don't worry, believe me. And if you want, I'll call my friend, Sergeant Borg, at the police station and ask him to—"

"Done," she said, abruptly business again. "I have done my duty, Joshua. Thelma always was a bit nuts, you know. Thought she was the reincarnation of Joan of Arc. She heard voices all the time."

"Yes, but did she smoke?"

"Joshua!" But the laughter was there, and the relief, and when she finally rang off with a promise he would come to dinner one night the next week, he felt considerably better. The oppression that had filled the office had been lifted, the air outside less hazed with memory's shadows.

He knew what his problem was—or a major part of it, at least: Andrea Murdoch. And his life was filled enough as it was without complicating matters with affairs that promised more than he might be able to deliver. And though his seeing Andrea could scarcely be called an affair (except of and in the mind), the potential was there, and it was making him increasingly nervous.

Which in turn . . . in turn . . .

He rose quickly before his confusion overwhelmed him. As he reached for his jacket, however, he realized that emotional backpedaling powered by rationalization was getting to be an art with him, an art he would just as soon not bother to master. One of these days (and if he kept it up, it wouldn't be in the distant future) he knew he was going to slam into a wall he did not see coming, or drop over a cliff.

On the other hand . . .

"Stop it, damnit!"

He closed his eyes tightly, held his arms rigid at his sides. If there were any sure way of driving himself over the brink, this was it. This, and the dead man, and the bird, and the shadowing.

He paused, then, with one arm halfway through a sleeve and stared at the telephone. Call now, call later.

She might be waiting. You haven't eaten all day. His stomach muttered, and he decided to call later. Then he flipped over Mrs. Thames' folder and took an eraser to the sketch of the robin.

One of those days; tomorrow would be better.

But as he walked out the door his fingers were crossed.

6

Once outside, with the door locked behind him and his cap pulled firmly down over his hair, Josh decided he did not want to head home right away. The place would be, today, too empty; rooms filled with his life and his living . . . and just too damned empty. And the thought of his having to stand by the stove waiting for a meal to coalesce out of chaos made him grimace. There had to be energy, and suddenly he didn't have it. Not after the plow and the arm and Andy and the look in Felicity's eyes.

He stepped to the middle of the pavement and glanced west along High Street, narrowing his eyes against the red setting sun, half hoping he might catch Fel still walking the pavement; then east across Centre Street to the indented gates of the park a block away, smiling softly at an abrupt barrage of children bursting out of the shadows ahead of a trio of harried, hurrying adults. His laugh was more a grunt, and he moved over to the curb to check the Buick's locks. His left hand absently dusted a leaf from the roof. His gaze searched for the violation of a scratch. And when he caught his reflection in the passenger window— ghostlike, the shop blank behind him, through him— he grabbed the cap off and folded it, opened the door and tossed it onto the front seat, relocked the door, and tried to flatten his hair into a semblance of neatness. Brushed the dried mud from his jacket as best he could and walked away.

He moved slowly, then, his shoulders slightly hunched against the feathered chill that had settled with the day's dimming light. There was little vehicular traffic on Centre Street, even at this hour; most of the people who worked here lived in the Station and they preferred, as he did whenever possible, to walk from place to place. It had little to do with conservation or economics; there was simply too much to see at the change of seasons for those whose seasons were numbered by the score.

He nodded to those he knew, smiled at those he didn't, and by the time he had gone the two blocks south to Chancellor Avenue he realized he hadn't made up his mind where he was going to eat. He could always head back for the luncheonette, but the fact that he hadn't eaten all day made him decide in favor of something, if not better, then at least more substantial. Without the car, then, he had no choice: it was the Mariner, or home.

And that, he knew with a grin, was no choice at all.

The Mariner was a Monticello miniature divided into the Lounge and the Cove. The latter was essentially a family restaurant, the former a pleasant place for a quiet drink and an uncomplicated meal. Heads or tails, and again there was no choice. Despite all his years in the Station he had only once been in the Cove, with a family of young Scots fresh across the water who had somehow latched onto him during a walk through the park. The parents had been pleasant enough, but the children had been horrors, and he could not pass the Cove's white door without a shuddering memory of the smallest girl-child having a red-faced tantrum when the waitress suggested a vegetable instead of ice cream.

A quick look in both directions—and a glance at the police station behind him—and he hurried across the avenue, waved at someone who honked at him, and ducked through the righthand door.

A quiet, tall booth on the left. Darkwood wainscoting and posts. Silence. Deep wine walls textured and comforting. Amber lanterns. Curved mahogany bar. Carpeting so thick it was difficult to maintain a normal walking stride.

He sighed himself into place and gave his order at a whisper: Boston scrod and Irish potatoes, a salad, the house vegetable (he grinned suddenly and the waitress stared) and a bloody mary to start.

He took his time, eyes half closed, the conversations around him like the summer drone of sun-driven bees.

He had just about finished, ordering himself a Bristol Cream for dessert, when a shadow darkened his hands resting on the table.

He waited.

When the shadow didn't move he said, without looking up, "You going to stand there all night, or are you going to join me?"

It had been the aftershave that had warned him, a pungent and liberal application of spices that wafted ahead of Lloyd Stanworth no matter what direction the wind had taken. The surgeon chuckled appreciatively—as he always did at the same tiresome jibe—and took the benchseat opposite. He was, Josh thought without condemnation, the perfect, medium nothing; an unexceptional face, normal width to shoulders and chest, his clothes carefully apropos for the profession and the town. Only the scar tissue a dead and dull grey where eyebrows would have been made him memorable . . . if at all.

"Heard you had quite a day," Stanworth said jovially.

Josh didn't ask for source and page number; it was one of Stanworth's unnerving abilities—to know more about people's daily lives than the people sometimes knew themselves. Instead, he sat back and watched the sherry twist languidly in its glass. "You must have had a hell of a time trying to find a place to tack on that arm."

Stanworth shrugged. "A freak," he said, as though freaks were something he dealt with every day. "They'll find the body by morning, back in the woods. It happens, what can I say. The body's dead, but the mind refuses to believe it. The guy—it was a guy's arm, you know—was in tremendous shock, and he wandered. As soon as the pain, or the blood loss, makes itself known he'll collapse, and that's where they'll find him." He shrugged elaborately.

Josh was glad he had finished his meal. "But how far can he get?"

"Who knows?" The tone said: *who cares?*

The waitress drifted past to take the man's order and moved on almost without a pause, an effortless rhythm that Josh admired. Like lifting the brass ring on a slow-moving carousel.

"You have a purpose," he said then, and made a show of snapping his fingers in disappointment. "Oh, darn! You're here to tell me our date for lunch is off tomorrow."

"As a matter of fact, I am," Stanworth said, suddenly fascinated by the backs of his hands. "Josh, I'm really sorry, but a man's coming to town tomorrow I haven't seen in years. A good friend from med school who had the audacity to chose pediatrics instead of surgical research." He smiled hopefully. "I hope you don't mind."

"Hell, why should I mind?" he said truthfully. "As a matter of fact, I might not even have shown up myself the way things are going."

"Oh, really?"

Josh picked up his drink and sipped at it, saw a streak of sherry slip down the side of the glass and licked at it unashamedly. "Mrs. Thames," he said.

"Good god, Josh, are you still looking for that idiot plow?"

He nodded.

Stanworth clasped his hands on the table, leaned forward, closed his mouth when the waitress returned with his scotch and soda. After she'd gone, he sniffed once and closed his eyes tightly for a brief moment. "Josh . . . Randy and I were talking last night, and—"

Josh set his spine flat against the booth's wall. "Lloyd, do we really have to do this. Today of all days?"

"No, not really. But Randy is genuinely concerned about you, you know. She feels—"

"Don't you dare say 'responsible,'" he said flatly. "Randy is a lovely woman, and I commend you for being snared by her. But Lloyd, please . . . she isn't my sister, you're not my brother. The way I spend my life is my business." He held up a hand quickly to forestall interruption, saw Stanworth's disgust at the dirt still there. "Besides, it isn't as if I were starving, is it? I don't hang around the gutters, I don't molest little children, and I don't spend Saturday nights in the drunk tank. I do what I do best—I find things."

"But what's the purpose of it all, Joshua," Stanworth said, almost pleading. He blinked slowly, pushed a forefinger over the scar above his right eye. "And while it may be fine now, you know as well as I that the public can be awfully fickle. Here one day, gone the next."

"Eight years is hardly fickle, Lloyd."

"Well, if it was me," the surgeon said quickly, back-pedaling, "I wouldn't care, you know that. But you also know how Randy is when she gets a bug up her ass."

He did. He knew all too well. Randy Stanworth was a redheaded, surrogate parent for the world, if not the universe, a parent who knew precisely what her children ought to do with their lives, how they should go about it, and when they should start. She had also had an affair with him a half decade before, short-lived and tempestuous, emotionally draining and nearly

succeeding. When they'd parted; instinct had him
pull the telephone out of the wall so he would not call
her ten minutes after she'd returned home. He kept it
disconnected for a week. And he had stayed away from
the office for two. She was lovely, she was caring, she
was the perfect one to drive Stanworth on to his Nobel
Prize or die in the attempt.

In a way that was less disturbing than he would
admit, he loved her still.

"Listen," he said gently, to ease the man's embarrassment at a task obviously presented to him as a
no-win ultimatum, "tell Randy I understand and
appreciate her concern. Tell her too that I'm getting
pretty good at salting things away for my old age." He
grinned. "And I promise I will not die without her
express permission."

Stanworth bridled. "Hardly called for, Josh. That
was a low blow, a low blow."

"Yeah, I suppose it was." He did not offer an
apology, however, and was startled when the doctor
grabbed his glass, drained it without taking a breath,
and slid out of the booth with a strained farewell
smile.

Josh gaped after him, wondering in confusion what
he'd said that had driven his friend away. He must
have missed something, he decided, though it had
been a conversation well echoed in the past and one
they usually ended with a laugh and hearty shaking of
hands—conspirators against the familiar failure of a
well-meaning meddler. This time was different. This
time, somehow, something was wrong.

"Hey!"

Stanworth slowed at the door, though he did not
turn. Josh immediately scrambled for his wallet and
dropped some bills on the table, pushed out from the
booth, and caught up with him on the pavement
outside. They stood uneasily in the twilight, Josh
with his hands in his jacket pockets, Stanworth trying
not to clasp his lapels. Diagonally across the street

and to their left a trio of young men stalked angrily into the police station, a granite and marble copy of someone's idea of a Grecian temple. Behind them were three patrolmen, laughing among themselves. The pedestrians on the sidewalk barely gave the scene a glance, not even when one of the men had to be eased none too gently through the doors.

Spring, Josh thought, is the prime season for fools and other children.

"Well . . ." Stanworth looked about as if expecting to be picked up. At that moment, however, there were no cars on the street.

Josh touched his arm, unwilling to let him go, saying the first thing that came to mind: "Hey, listen, do you know . . . have you heard of a patient down there at the hospital, a Thelma Saporral?"

"I have."

"Well, look, she's got a friend who's a client of mine. As a matter of fact, it's Mrs. Thames." He smiled at Stanworth's suddenly pained and comical expression. "She really isn't that bad, Lloyd."

"So you say."

"Anyway, she called me earlier this afternoon. Mrs. Thames, that is. It seems that her friend, this Thelma, apparently she took off without telling anyone. Mrs. Thames got herself all bothered about it, and though I don't know how close you—"

Stanworth quieted him with a look. "She was my patient, Josh. And she did not take off." He stared over at the police station, a palm smoothing his broad tie against his chest.

"She didn't? But Mrs. Thames—"

"She's dying, Joshua," Stanworth said, "and I'm sure Mrs. Thames is well aware of that." He took a long breath, thrust his chin up and out to stretch his neck. When he spoke again, the irritation was gone. "Dying. I wish I could tell you differently, but there was nothing I could reasonably do for her here so I had her transferred over to a place I know in West Hart-

ford. It's one of those cases where you pray for a
miracle—some guy in a cellar lab with toy test tubes
and the like—and I really didn't feel like watching her
go."

"Oh . . . brother," Josh muttered. "Open mouth,
insert foot."

Stanworth clapped him on the back. "Don't be silly,
you weren't to know. It's just that . . . well, I see it all
the time, Joshua. These old women tend to be clan-
nish. Anything that affects one of them manages to
affect them all. I don't know her as well as you do, but
I'd bet Mrs. Thames is that way, right?"

Reluctantly, Josh nodded, and barely kept from
wincing at the sudden, professional tolerance the
doctor slipped over him.

"It's no secret about Saporral, her dying. I imagine
Mrs. Thames was rather flustered and just didn't ask
the right people. You can tell her everything I've told
you, I don't mind, but it might be a good idea to go
easy on the death part. They all know it, you see. They
sense it. But they'll be damned if they'll admit it. In a
way they're just like kids, teenagers—they think
they're immortal because they've lasted this long. It's
almost like a bit of self-hypnosis that only gets jarred
when one of their own betrays them. The time you
really think about dying is . . ." His grin was as
mischievous as he could make it. "Your age, Josh. Just
about your age."

He laughed deeply, explosively, and walked away
shaking his head. Josh watched him for a long moment, shrugged without moving his shoulders, and
headed across the road, back up Centre Street toward
his car. He wasn't at all sure the elderly actually did
view death in the manner Stanworth described; it
certainly wasn't the way Mrs. Thames thought of it.
She wasn't at all resigned to her eventual passing; and
if she had anything at all to say about it, she would go
on forever, if only because her house was never quite
complete, the lawn never quite right.

He paused, then, and stared at his reflection in a jewelry shop window. What would it be like, he wondered, simply not to *be* anymore?

He shuddered and moved on, shifting his hands from his jacket to his trouser pockets, realizing how the sun had left him while he'd been eating, how the streetlamps in the new foliage were still bright enough to cast double shadows on the sidewalk, flatten the brick and clapboard fronts of the stores, the banks, deepen the mouths of the alleys between. It was the middle of the week, shopkeepers gone home early, leaving behind them blind plate glass and a curious sense of desertion. Shades had been pulled down on narrow doors, only a handful of neon displays buzzing like flies trapped in a paper cup. The turret clock over the First National's doors chimed the hour. Directly opposite, someone was forcing a grey sack into the night deposit slot of the Savings and Loan.

He could feel it, then, creeping up on him as he turned the corner and headed for the Buick: the temptation to begin a short bout of self-pity. Here he was, in the middle of a village whose day had ended without the world ending around it, where peace and not loneliness was the commandment bestowed, and instead of enjoying it he was using it to speculate on the depth of the misery he would feel when he got home.

It was not only sinful (he thought with a sardonic nod to his mother), it was ungrateful.

But he was nevertheless helpless before it, could not resist slamming a fist lightly against the Buick's fender as he jabbed the key into the lock and pulled the door open.

And froze. Stiffened. Looked to his left toward the park, to his right down High. There were trees, parked cars, lights, darkness. Sounds, not noise, of people in houses, of children still in backyards, of pets on the prowl. Scents, not odors, of new grass and young

leaves, fertilizer on lawns, polish and leather from the
car, earth on his clothes. The touch of the key in his
bare hand, the feel of the tarmac under his boots, the
denim against his legs, a straggle of hair across one
ear.

He frowned.

Everything was as it had been for the past thirty-
three years, and something was different.

He looked up over his office, to the blind windows
of the second floor. They once had belonged to the
apartment of a man who'd run a security agency,
whose office was where his was now. Before that a
psychologist worked there. Before that . . . he could
not remember. On the left a teen boutique, manne-
quins in the window blind and rigid; on the right a
shop that sold pianos and organs, a spinet on display
with a floral elaboration sweeping up its side.

Everything was as it had been.

Except the air had gone sharp, had gone clear, had
gone cold; except the angles and the bricks and the
shadows and the curbs had suddenly grown edges that
would have sliced him had he touched them. He put a
hand on the car's chilled roof, expecting at any moment to lose his balance. Listening. Sensing. Attempting to convince himself that despite the light meal the
two drinks he'd had had gone to his head.

He didn't believe it.

There were signs, familiar ones, when he'd taken in
too much liquor: he would feel tired, lethargic, falling
into a silence that more often than not led directly to
sleep. None of this had happened. The sudden clarity
of vision and the vague wash of disorientation had
nothing to do with what he had drunk.

Again he scanned the streets, the facades of the
buildings in front and behind; he peered into the
closest trees, into the doorways, moved sideways and
checked the car's back seat. Perspiration broke along
his hairline and his palms felt moist. Tension stiffened
the muscles in his thighs, across his stomach, made

him rub the back of his neck as though a cramp had lodged there.

An attack, he thought suddenly against an impulse to panic; he was having an attack of some sort. He stared down at his hands, spreading the fingers and watching them tremble; he swallowed hard and concentrated on his body, trying to take measure of his heart, his blood, an abrupt sullen ache blossoming at his temples.

An attack.

Slowly, he opened the door and eased himself behind the steering wheel. He gripped the beveled rim until his knuckles were bloodless, his elbows locked, his back pushed hard into the seat.

He waited. Staring blindly at droplets of sap on the windshield.

He waited. And in a minute he would have sworn had taken an hour he knew he was wrong. There was no attack, nothing wrong with his head or his heart. It was something else entirely, something outside. He jerked his head around toward the office—there was no one there; checked the rearview mirror—saw only the empty street pocked by houselights; looked straight ahead—two cars drifting by silently, a lumbering red-and-silver bus, two men in plaid hunting jackets with arms about each other's shoulders.

No attack. But someone was watching him.

And the hand that gripped his shoulder almost made him scream.

7

There was nothing Josh could think to do but laugh at himself. It was, he decided, about the only sane thing left to him after a day like today.

The house on Raglin was a small, white-clapboard and black-shutter saltbox on a piece of property nearly as tiny. The front porch was not much wider than the door, the triangle roof above it virtually no protection from any sort of weather, an addition made by his father in preparation for a project that was (as was his father's wont) abandoned just after the conception. Its saving grace, as far as Josh was concerned, lay in its privacy—a thick screen of poplar separated the house from its neighbors side and back, allowing him prowling rights through the rooms without having to pull the shades. Within, a livingroom to the right of the foyer, a study that had once been the diningroom on the left and extending to the back, and a kitchen behind the living room made up the first floor; upstairs were two bedrooms and a bath, an attic above that was too low for standing, too inaccessible for convenient storage.

The whole was furnished primarily Victorian, only because he had never felt the need to replace what his parents had left behind. Besides, having grown up with wood-rimmed couches and armchairs, sidetables with raised scalloped edges, and lamps with fringed shades, he knew and understood all the idiosyncrasies of each piece—to get rid of any would have been very much like fratricide.

Now, with the Buick safely bastioned in the garage, with the housekey in its slot and the tumblers already groaning over, he was struck by an image of his face as it must have been when Peter Lee had reached through the open car window and had taken light hold of him: mouth agape, nostrils flared, eyes wide and popping, flesh tight and pale across his cheeks as the blood drained down to his heart which, he was positive, had relocated itself somewhere in the vicinity of the top of his constricted throat. He had recoiled violently, had been ready to thrust himself across the seat and out the passenger door, and would have done so had he not heard his name called out through the sudden explosion of panic.

Lee, the new owner of the Chancellor Inn, had (he explained once things were calm and flight aborted) seen Josh sitting there at the curb, unmoving, rigid, and had thought there was some sort of cardiac attack in progress. Josh, unable to stop himself, had babbled, excuses and explanations tumbling out before he had a chance to expand or discard them. He had made little sense, if any, and Lee had been reluctant to leave. Finally, he managed to convince the man that he was, in fact, just fine, thanks, and I won't forget your kindness. It served. Lee moved on, though he had paused for a second at the corner to stare back suspiciously.

"Jesus," he said as he stepped inside and closed the door behind him. "Jesus H." He laughed again, giddy, relieved, stripping off his jacket and boots and leaving them at the foot of the mirrored coatrack; later, if he felt like it, he would brush them off and put them away where they belonged. For the moment, however, in the house's full and comforting dark, he did not want anything to stand in the way of a long hot shower, a tall iced bourbon, and the couch in the livingroom where he would attempt to figure out exactly what was coming over him.

The shower was perfect. Muscle strain and nerves loosened under the pummeling, the needlestrings, leaving him feeling as though he would survive until morning.

The bourbon was slightly less successful because he took too much in the first welcome swallow and choked so hard he almost dropped the glass.

The couch was a failure.

He wore nothing but a tattered, cowled tan robe with hanging sleeves, his uniform for relaxing when he had no expectation of the world intruding. It also served to soothe him, so soft it was even after all these years and familiar to the demands of his body. The couch, on the other hand, somehow managed to develop a perversity: lumps, depressions, pockets of concrete that had him shifting in irritation, standing, sitting, standing again and pacing the small room as if he were due to leave on a long, eagerly expected trip early the next morning.

Watched. How in hell did he get the idea that he was being watched?

And who would want to bother with someone as innocuous as he was?

Yet he could not deny the sudden heightening of his senses, the crawling sensation between his shoulder blades, the sucking in of his stomach in preparation for a blow.

It wasn't the drinks, and it wasn't an attack, and why the bloody hell would someone want to watch him?

He paused at the front window and held back the curtains, flicked a thumb at the shade's oval pull; he knelt in front of the television and clicked around the dial, images blurring and the color drifting close to black-and-white; the faded oriental carpet was large enough to appear wall-to-wall, and he sat cross-legged with his back to the foyer, trying to untangle a knot in the two-inch frayed fringe—a task, he recalled with a wry grin, that had been his father's single source of exasperated defeat.

When he realized he was seriously considering taking a pair of scissors to the problem and was no closer to an answer for the problem that beset him, he rose and strode into the study, switched on the overhead light, and stared at the walls now lined with glass-fronted bookcases that barely fit under the ceiling. He stood in the center of the room's worn brown rug, squinting at titles, at piles of magazines, at filing cabinets, at the rear window and the darkness beyond. He walked to the back, to the swinging door that led out to the hallway, past the back door to the kitchen, and shook his head: no food now, nothing more to drink. He looked down at a jigsaw puzzle half-completed on a cardtable (a polar bear, the Arctic, brilliant blue sky) and picked up a piece, turned it, aimed it, placed it back on the side for discovery later on. Then he walked slowly toward his desk, a massive oak trestle set below the room's only other window, facing the street. He touched a finger to the correspondence yet to be answered, to the envelopes, to the books scattered across the back, looked up to the window, suddenly leaned forward and pulled aside the curtains to stare at the red MG parked at the curb.

He almost made it to the· staircase before the doorbell rang.

Andrea Murdoch took the couch's center cushion, leaving him the option of either sitting beside her or using the armchair to the right of the window. He took the latter, not because he wanted to but because he was suddenly and acutely aware of his nakedness beneath the robe. He sat almost primly on the edge of his seat, legs pulled back, hands clasped loosely in his lap.

Andrea grinned at him. Her midnight hair was pulled back into a ponytail, her blouse dark and snug, her jeans the same. Her face was still windflushed from the ride to the village, and the color served to accentuate the deep red of her lips and the lines of her high cheeks. She nodded at the robe: "You were expecting me?"

He shook his head and squirmed. Annoyed at himself because he had no brilliant retort, no devastating explosion of Noel Coward wit that would be at once innocent and diabolically promising.

"You didn't come by the house." Almost an accusation.

"I wasn't hungry today." Something inside him winced, and would have kicked his ankles if it had had legs.

She leaned back and stretched her arms over the couch's back. "I would have fed you anyway, you know that. Dad missed you. He wants to ask you some questions about Oxrun."

"Is he writing a book about it?"

She shrugged, and looked slowly around the room. "He might. He doesn't like what he's doing now, so he thought he'd pump you for some local gossip. He figures, doing what you do you must know just about everything and anything that goes on around here."

Her voice was manlike: deep, resonant, smooth as the black that lines a nightcave.

"I missed you, too. You should have come."

Pulling the ties more snugly around his waist, he reached to the sidetable and took a cigarette from a monogrammed, cork-lined box. Picked up a silver lighter and stared for a moment at the flame. "I promised Fel I'd do some work in the office today. She threatened to leave me otherwise."

"You should marry her."

It was his turn to grin. "She has a cat. I hate cats."

"I don't. Have a cat that is." She stopped her tour of the room and let her gaze linger on his face.

He didn't know how to answer.

There were only two lamps in the room: a standing one behind and to the left of his chair, a table model beside the couch—both were tall-shaded and created fogs instead of pools of light. A bright enough glow to see by, a shadowed glow that deepened Andrea's eyes when she narrowed them.

"I take it you haven't found the plow yet."

He shook his head ruefully. "Nope. Not even close, I think. I was about ready to give up today, if you can believe it."

"I can."

He frowned, forgetting the robe as he leaned forward slightly.

"I mean, you always take on the worst cases, don't you," she said. "If you were a private detective, you'd be living down in Mexico, hunting for Judge Crater and Ambrose Bierce. By the end of the third week you'd want to commit suicide if you hadn't found them, but you wouldn't give up until you were either dead or someone else found their bodies." She took a deep breath, and smiled. "You never give yourself a choice, Josh."

He crushed out the cigarette, reached for another and changed his mind. "I've failed before. You know that, right?"

She nodded. "But only when somebody sits on you to stop. You've as much as told me that yourself."

"Yeah, well . . ."

Though it was flattering, he thought, that Andrea had taken such obvious pains to learn so much about him, he could not quite shake the feeling that he was being stripped, in the coldest way possible. And then she smiled, fully and brightly, and the stirrings of his objections were smothered, were forgotten.

"You came all the way in here to do a profile on me?"

"No," she said. "I wanted to know why you didn't come out to see . . . us. And to ask you if you wanted to come to dinner on Saturday. Dad'll be in New York for the next couple of days, and he definitely wants to talk with you when he gets back. You do know the gossip, don't you?"

"I don't know, I guess so."

"Is it good?"

He laughed and settled himself again. "I doubt it. At least it probably isn't the kind that your father would want to write about. You forget, Andy, Oxrun is a small town. A village. What scandals we have had don't run to very much when you compare them to bigger places."

"Really?" Her disbelief was evident, and her mockery soft.

"Really." He waited. She said nothing, nor would she shift her gaze away from him. This time, however, he met it with a ghostsmile he knew she would eventually find infuriating. "And why don't you tell me why you really came here. You could have called about both things, you know. And your father has a fit whenever you leave the house alone."

"I told you the truth."

"No, you didn't."

Her hands flopped palms up to the cushions, bounced, and came to rest on her legs. She rubbed her thighs slowly, thoughtfully, and she sucked her lower lip between her teeth. "I don't want you to laugh at me."

She'd said it so softly he asked her to repeat it; when she did, he was astonished. Laughing at Andrea Murdoch would be one of the world's greatest absurdities—everything she did, she did deliberately, intensely, never (as far as he knew) given to frivolity or whim. She was not always serious, but neither was she flippant; carelessness was alien to the way she took her living.

"You promise you won't laugh at me."

He almost laughed. As he had watched her, as he had listened, she seemed to shrink out of her age and back into her teens, when one of the pains of adolescence was the fear of behaving as though one were an adult. The fear of doing it all wrong, and being caught.

"I promise," he said, sketching an x across his heart with two fingers and kissing their tips. "Come on, what's the problem?"

"It's not a problem, really. Well, yes it is, damnit." Her expression hardened. "I . . . am . . . bored, Joshua. I am so fucking bored I could scream."

The announcement did not surprise him. He had never been able to understand why, exactly, she had allowed herself to be brought out to the Station in the first place; she was too much a city woman, an energetic woman who needed and demanded the time-consumers a metropolis afforded her. Not that she would be out every single night, to this nightclub and that gallery, this premiere and that quiet dinner for two in a booth behind a tacky beaded curtain . . . but it all had to be there for the asking, and for the taking, if she wanted it. It had to be at her disposal for the advantage to be taken. Eliminate even the possibility, and sooner or later she would be padding the walls of her room. Apparently, her father's work was not giving her all she had hoped for when she had agreed to stay with him.

It was then, as he watched her moisten her lips for whatever was coming next, that he wondered (with a start that almost had him out of his chair) if her interest in him had been all the time simply a way to forestall impending ennui. If he had been the least objectionable of those others she had met in Oxrun, the one to escort her off the farm to the glories of what passed for nightlife in the valley. If he were the surrogate, the temporary patch, the diversion.

"Joshua, I want to help you."

The tone answered his question for him, erased the doubts, and brought him close to blushing with guilt. The eagerness was there, but there was no pleading; interest, and the tenderest hint of fear at rejection.

But he said: "I don't know, Andy. Fel—"

"I don't mean in the office." She left the couch and knelt in front of him, folding her hands over his knees. They were warm. They were heavy. He couldn't help but feel the touch of a breast against his calf. "I mean outside." She gave him an exaggerated shudder. "If I have to stay inside one more day, I'll start doing something stupid, like redecorating."

"You should meet Melissa Thames."

"Who?"

He waved it away. "If you mean, coming with me on trips—"

She slapped his leg; it stung, but he did not rub the spot. "Josh, are you being deliberately dense?"

His smile was inane.

"I mean, fool, like going out to help you find that plow. The way I did the last time. Remember that?"

Only, he thought, two or three times a day. Mother, you have raised yourself one miserable Don Juan.

"Look, I've been doing a lot of walking since the weather broke, maybe I can help. I don't know the land around here that well, but four eyes are better than two, right? What you miss, I might be able to find." Her grip on his knees tightened. "Come on, Josh, what do you say? You don't even have to pay me."

"I should think," he said loftily, "my company would be ample pay enough."

"Oh really?"

"Oh really."

She shifted closer, her right forefinger tracing tight circles over his knee. The robe felt heavy across his shoulders, and he slipped a hand inside to rub lightly at his chest. Warm, he thought; I should open a window.

"Josh?"

"Yeah, I'm still here."

"I, uh, I had to go to the police today. Had to pay a stupid speeding ticket that was sort of overdue."

"Sort of?"

A shrug, a grin. "A little. Anyway, I heard . . . well, I heard some of them talking in there. They said there was an accident out near our place. Well, on Cross Valley, anyway. They said, someone said you were there." She looked up at him, though her finger did not stop. "It must have been horrid for you."

"It was," he said. There was nothing of the vulture in her eyes, though, no search for vicarious carrion; sympathy only, and he reached out to brush a thumb over her forehead. "It wasn't the accident so much. It was all over by the time I got there. But the way that poor guy—"

"All right," she said softly. "I heard about that, too."

"Christ, they talk a lot in there."

Her smile was deliberately wicked. "I manage a good vamp now and then, when I'm nosy and I can't get it any other way. What I got, though, was two attempted pickups and a slap on the ass. I think it was Stockton."

He grinned at the idea of the old chief turning randy, pleased too that the mention of the accident was less disturbing than it had been. "I'll feel a lot better, though," he admitted, "when they find the poor guy."

"They did."

He stared at her, frowning. "What?"

"That's what I wanted to tell you. I was just leaving, and some guy came in and said they found the body about a mile from the intersection. In the woods north of the pike."

He drew a hand hard over his eyes, pinched the bridge of his nose. "The blood. There was no—"

"I don't know," she said quickly. "All I know is what I heard—the body was found and it was already picked up."

"Andy—"

She straightened, her face drawing level with his.

"Josh," she warned, "it'll all come out in the paper, right? Someone, one of the doctors, will have an explanation, okay?" She stared at him. "Okay?"

He didn't want to nod; he did it anyway.

"Okay. Now. Your next worry, now that the crime of the century has been solved, is how to use me when we go out tomorrow to look for that plow. I'll have to know exactly what to search for, why, how, and all that good stuff."

"Hey," he said, palms up, "I didn't say you were coming, did I?"

The smile returned. "Sure you did."

"No kidding."

"Coffee."

"What?"

"Coffee," she said. "Aren't you going to offer me coffee?"

He shook his head, bewildered, did not protest when she pulled him from the chair and took him into the kitchen. He sat at the table and watched her, astounded and not knowing why, while she moved from stove to refrigerator to cabinets as though she had designed the old-fashioned room herself. Nothing missed her critical eye, not the arrangement of canned foods nor the floral wallpaper nor the double sink nor the fact that he didn't have a dishwasher.

"You really do that stuff yourself?"

She laid out cups and saucers, found the bread and made them ham-and-Swiss sandwiches, sat opposite him and had him talking about the business before he realized what he was doing. And when he did, glancing at the clock on the wall over the door, he pushed back from the table and swiped at a breadcrumb clinging to the corner of his mouth.

"The plow," he said.

"Sure. The plow."

"That's going to have to wait."

Her confusion was evident, and a slight hint of anger. "What is it? You don't want to work with me?"

"No," he said quickly. "Don't be silly. You've convinced me you'll be invaluable."

"Fucking right I will."

"And your command of the language will stand you in good stead with all my better customers." He laughed. "No, what I mean is—I'm going to take a short break from it for a while. It's driving me nuts, and I hate that. I don't think straight. That music I told you about, the sheets for Dale Blake? I've decided —right now, in fact—that I'll hunt that up first. It'll clear my mind so I can get back into mudwalking with a smile instead of a groan."

"Oh." She dropped her hands into her lap. "Oh."

"Andy, it's not you, believe me."

"I do. It's just that . . ." And she lifted her shoulders, lowered them; it wasn't a shrug but an admission of disappointment. "You'll be going away for a while."

He nodded. "I know I'm not going to find it here. I'll have to hit New York again, and who knows where the hell else. It shouldn't . . ." He stopped, tried again. "That is, I doubt I'll be gone . . ." Faltered. Licked at his lips. Said nothing when she pushed away from the table and picked up the cups to bring to the sink. He stared at her back, thinking he'd just destroyed whatever it was he had built over the past hour or so. "Andy, listen, as soon as I get back I'll—"

She turned slowly. Her blouse was undone, her bra parted in the center. A glimmer of perspiration shone hard between her breasts, shadows sweeping down over her stomach toward the top of her jeans. Her hands commanded the direction of his astonished gaze, dipped to the snap and unfastened it, yanked down the zipper to expose a band of laced white. She pointed at him.

"You're naked under that, right?"

Without thinking, he nodded.

"Good," she said. "We'll fuck first, make love later."

8

It was not quite dawn, not quite dark; a few birds in the hickory that overspread the front yard had begun to stir noisily, a milk truck had passed five minutes before, and a large white cat strolled down the center of the street, head high and tail arched. Josh followed it as far as he could without turning his head, his palms pressed to his cheeks, his elbows hard on the trestle desk. He had not bothered to turn on a lamp, and the pack of cigarettes lying within reach had not been touched.

It's all right, she had told him; *don't worry about it, it happens.*

Perhaps it does, he thought for the tenth, or the hundredth, or the one millionth time, but knowing that did not make the experience any less unpleasant, or any less unnerving.

And worse: it wasn't that he felt inadequate, or unmanly—he felt, simply, incredibly stupid. As if he had forgotten everything he had learned (or thought he had learned) since the night he had lost his virginity during the third month of his Air Force tour. As if his body had abruptly reverted to prepubescence, realizing that something momentous was about to happen and not having the faintest idea what to do about it yet.

Over the past two hours, after he had finally crept sleepless from the bed, he had lectured himself on the various important stresses of anticipation, on the way the mind sometimes worked when it was overburdened and suddenly overloaded, on the way the functions of sex were not always given to command responses. He went over it all a dozen and more times, and still he felt . . . incredibly stupid.

Don't worry, she had said, drifting off in his arms, *I'm here and that's what counts so don't worry about it there'll be other times now and you don't have to worry.*

A board creaked. He glanced over his left shoulder toward the staircase, waiting, breathing shallowly through his mouth. There was no other sound. The silence was so loud he put his hands to his ears.

He had trailed numbly after her, and the tantalizing shower of clothing, wondering if this weren't a dream he was having, an attempt by his subconscious to soothe the anxieties he had stockpiled during the day. It must have been, he thought, because he wasn't this lucky. He had stopped at the bedroom doorway, shivering, and watched her sink to the mattress, shadows rippling languidly across the planes and curves and angles of her figure; he watched her lie back and cup her hands behind her head to fan her soft hair out across the covers; he saw her right hand rest in the darkpool between her breasts while a greyghost arm lifted toward him and beckoned. He had found his robe on the landing afterward, not recalling the discarding as he'd walked, remembering only that he had walked stiffly to her, uncertain, nervous, stopping when he felt her foot run along the outside of his leg. His vision adjusted further to the dark, and he saw her eyes holding him beneath half-lowered lids.

When she smiled he'd dropped over her and embraced her and the shock of her cool flesh against his had made him groan aloud.

And his fantasies crumbled into little more than fancies.

The middle step protested wearily; he lowered his hands.

The square of the window slowly grew defined, the flocked pattern of the curtains gaining darker substance.

He whistled in a breath and there were hands on his shoulders, kneading, and the faint scent of lilac when she lowered her cheek to his from behind.

"Feeling sorry for yourself?" A gentle question, a whispering against his ear.

"No." He saw the white cat drift by again, something dark and squirming in its mouth. "Well, a little, I suppose. Mostly, I feel just . . . stupid."

"For heaven's sake, why?"

A shrug. "I don't know. I just do."

"But—"

"I know what you said." He reached for the cigarettes, felt her stiffen, and stopped himself in time. "I know. I just . . . " And he shrugged again, helplessly.

She kissed his cheek, the side of his chin, her thumbs drifting up under his hair behind his ears. "Am I ever going to see your face again?"

He smiled, and could not remember the last time he had seen dawn.

"Come back to bed," she said, feather-soft. "I'm not mad, if that's what you're afraid of, and I don't care. Just come back to bed."

"I . . . it's not your fault, you know."

He could feel her grin. "I know."

A light breeze began to tousle the leaves, stir the shrubs. A car sped past with its headlights on.

He offered the car a Bronx cheer and scratched at his nose. "I might as well stay up. It's Wednesday already. A couple of hours and I'll have to get to work anyway."

"Why?"

He opened his mouth, closed it. "Beats the shit out of me."

She patted his head. "Good boy. You're the boss, you can go in whenever you want to. Today, as of now, is a half-day holiday in honor of . . . that cat. Come back and get some sleep. If you don't you won't be worth a damn to anyone. You'll also start feeling sorry for yourself and ruin everyone else's day, too. Let Felicity handle things, she knows what to do. Come on, Josh, come back to bed."

He rose and her hands dropped away, palms sliding softly down his back. By the time they reached the stairs she had one arm around his waist, and he didn't mind it a bit. "You can tell me how we're going to look for the plow."

"You're kidding. You still want to do it?"

"Sure, why not?" She paused one step higher than he and looked at him oddly. "You don't think I wanted to sleep with you just so I could go walking in the woods, do you? Do you really think I'm that bored?"

"No, of course not," he said quickly. "That's stupid."

"Good answer," she said with a mocking pat to his cheek. "If you'd said yes, you know, I would have cut off your balls."

He walked into the office just a few minutes past noon and intercepted Felicity's explanation-demanding glare with a firm, and startling, kiss on the lips. By the time she had recovered sufficiently to begin questioning his tardiness he had already forestalled her by launching energetically into a series of dictations that, at the close of the second hour, had cleared up a substantial portion of the correspondence he owed both contacts and clients. And his good humor was such that he could not stifle an occasional laugh at the looks she was giving him when she thought he wasn't watching.

Beautiful, he thought; god *damn* but it's beautiful.

The next item on the mental list he had made on his way to High Street was a stop at Bartlett's Toys. With a jaunty wave to Felicity, then, he strolled briskly over and spent a comfortable hour with Dale Blake and her husband Vic, trying to unearth as much information as he could about the sheet music she wanted. That accomplished he rose to leave, and when they protested his refusal to accept a fee for the search, he told them he would have to start driving all the way to Hartford if they didn't stop pushing. They laughed. Agreed. Never once mentioning what all of them knew: that for all the money Josh spent in the shop, neither of them could have bought a single meal a month at the corner luncheonette.

As he left the store—grinning and feeling somewhat self-satisfied and smug—he was snared by young Sandy McLeod, who promptly dragged him into Yarrow's to introduce him to the bookstore's owners, Iris and Paul Lennon. While Josh stood there, shifting his weight from one foot to the other like an adolescent in the throes of a woman's effusive praise, Sandy told the elderly couple—in a rambling, rattling, gesticulating narrative—how he had discovered the pewter teaspoon in the orchard and how much Josh had actually paid him for it. The pride in their eyes (they had no children of their own), the excitement in the boy's voice (he was virtually supporting his own way through college by working for the Lennons), was almost too much, and when he was finally back on the pavement he felt as if he had just learned through proclamation that his middle name was Claus.

A glance at his watch, a double check with the bank clock, and he was ten paces down the street toward the Mariner Lounge before he remembered Lloyd had canceled their lunch date the afternoon before. Good god, the old man is cracking up, he thought as he

reversed his direction with a sharp about-face, cracking up at last, and loving every goddamned minute of
it.

He laughed aloud, nodded pleasantly to a startled
woman, and returned to the office thinking about
Andy.

He was barely settled behind his desk when Felicity
handed him a sheet of paper. He stared at it, at her,
back to the paper again.

"What's this?"

"Your trip, or have you forgotten already." She
jabbed with a red-nailed finger. "That's the hotel
there, you've been there before. This is an appointment tomorrow at three with that creepy guy from
Equity—the train leaves at nine-ten, by the way,
plenty of time for you to check in and wash up—and
this is one, at five, with a guy who used to do some
publicity for a few of the theaters and now he runs an
actor's school or something on the upper East Side.
You've already talked to him on the phone a couple of
times. I didn't make any arrangements for the day
after because you might get lucky and be home for the
weekend. If you don't, though, you'll have to change
hotels because the whole damned city is booked up. A
convention, three or four, though why anyone would
want to go there beats the hell out of me."

Josh took a breath, feeling as though he had just run
a fast mile.

"Something wrong?"

He shook his head in amazement. "Why? I haven't
said I'd be—"

She put her hands on her hips, changed her mind,
and took the paper back to fold it. "Because," she told
him, "whenever you do your letters like you did
today, it means you're going away again. You do it
every time. That's why."

He leaned back and stared up at her. "Felicity, can
you be honest with me?"

She nodded warily.

"Is there anything, I mean anything at all you don't know about me?"

"Yes," she said. "All this time and I still don't know why you don't take me out."

He reached out to punch her arm playfully in lieu of an answer he did not have, missed, and struck her breast instead. He swallowed and looked away quickly, but not before she had slapped his hand. Hard.

"I don't stuff tissues in there, Miller," she said tightly. "Keep your hands to yourself."

He could think of nothing to say, was grateful when Lloyd called him a few moments later to apologize again for having to back out of their meeting.

"Don't worry about it," Josh said, feeling marvelously magnanimous. "But as long as you're on the wire here, can you tell me if there was anything important, or was it because you just wanted to see my rugged face again."

"There was, uh, no. No, Josh, nothing important."

"All right, just so I know. I'm leaving town tomorrow anyway, and I wanted to be sure I had all the loose ends tied up."

"No loose ends here, Josh."

"Good. Tell me, by the way, what you hear about that woman. Saporral? Can you give me something I can give to Mrs. Thames. Just to keep on her good side, you understand."

"Well, Josh—hey, my friend's here, I have to go. Take care, have a good trip."

Some friend, he thought, and made a bet with himself that it wasn't a man at all. When he looked to Felicity to make a comment, however, she gave him clear signals she did not want to talk. Did not, in fact, speak with him for the rest of the day, responding to his increasingly strained and ultimately cross inquiries with nods, grunts, vague gestures that conveyed nothing. And when she left at four-thirty he was at once relieved and tempted to chase after her. Temptation won, but he stopped himself at the partition when he was struck with the idea that he had done more than inadvertently brush against her chest. Suppose, he wondered without knowing where the supposition came from, that all those coy stories of her uproarious nightlife were nothing more than that . . . stories. And stories that were intended to draw a reaction from him, prod from him the impulse to be alone with her socially. He blinked slowly, considering, knowing that after his nonperformance the night before and Andrea's gentle acceptance, nothing about the depth of his stupidity in the face of female psychology would surprise him anymore. And he knew damned well he wasn't enjoying the lesson.

"Dumb," he muttered. "Dumb, dumb, dumb."

Then he shrugged and returned to his desk to clean up for the day.

Andrea was gone when he returned home that night. There was no note. Only the faint scent of lilac clinging to the sheets and one of the bath towels.

He walked through the room for nearly an hour, turning on all the lights and switching them off again.

Four times checked to be sure he had Felicity's schedule in his pocket; packed and repacked until he had to order himself to stop it.

Stood shivering on the front stoop, almost wishing he could feel as though someone were watching him just so he could feel anything at all.

But the saltbox house with all its trees and flowers, its books and mirrors, seemed suddenly too empty, suddenly too large. He returned inside and reached for the phone. No, he thought then; don't press your luck. It was entirely possible she was having trouble, too. The notion did not please him, and he went to bed early, took a long time to sleep.

Dreamt of bees and wasps and hornets in a field, filling the air in dark clouds, filling his ears with angry snarling, filling his mouth his eyes his ears with sweet

poison; dreamt of a woman in a black masque who
walked through walls and loved him scorched him
promised him left him; dreamt of Felicity riding a
huge Burmese cat that clawed and howled its way
through his bedroom wall to trap him under the sheets
and flail his skin gouge his cheeks snare his testicles to
make him scream; dreamt of a darkness as soft as the
sweep of Andy's hair, a floating and a drifting and a
scent of cloying lilac.

Woke at dawn and stared at the ceiling.

Oh hell, he thought, I think I'm in love.

9

Despite Felicity's hope and his own expectations to be home before midnight, by Friday noon at the latest, Josh had no luck at all during his first day in the city. All the man from Equity did was fill an hour with complaints about scale wages and scabs, a traffic jam on Sixth Avenue made him late for the five o'clock meeting and the actor's studio was closed after he ran up four dingy flights, and when he got back to his hotel he discovered the room still hadn't been readied.

He slept badly, fitfully, awoke the next morning with a headache that took an hour to subside.

He ate breakfast quickly and remade the missed appointment for Saturday evening. Swearing, then, he called Felicity, told her of the delay, and was astonished (and delighted) to find himself involved in four more searches that had come in that morning. Manuscripts they were, and odd enough to make him smile.

"I don't suppose you've set me up for some meetings," he said after she'd given him the want-list and the clients' names.

"You're down there and I'm up here," she said. "And it's cheaper if you call. Do your own work for a change."

He laughed and rang off, and decided that this

would be the vacation he'd been needing. The weather was on his side, as close to perfect as it could have been without looking for miracles: cool mornings, comfortably warm afternoons, a breeze that only occasionally sharpened to unpleasant gusts as he walked to all his appointments, to all the shops and hideaways he usually frequented on such tasks, to the hotels (as Fel had warned him) he had to change three times during a stay that eventually stretched into two days shy of three weeks.

The sheet music remained elusive for much of that time, but the manuscripts he was able to garner without much trouble at all. It pleased him immensely; he hadn't lost his touch. And every other night he telephoned Andrea to report his progress, and grouse about his failure. At one point he threatened to head home as soon as he could until she soothed him out of it with melodramatic portraits of Dale Blake, heartbroken and despondent, and Vic muttering dire threats about bodily harm. He laughed. He stayed. He ignored with an aching grin Felicity's observation that she was not at all surprised at the trouble he was having. After all, she told him with a sour edge to her voice, it was always the free ones that cost him the most money, and the most days lost from searches that paid the rent. When he reminded her he had already completed a quartet of others she herself had arranged, she grumbled incoherently and told him they didn't count.

Midway through his stay, after wheedling his way into a suite at the Plaza and grinning at Felicity's screams over the expense, he decided to try to bring Andrea down with him. He had had plenty of time to relax, he thought, and plenty of time to rid himself of his confusions. And he concluded that it might not be a bad idea to see her outside Oxrun, in a place considered neutral while they worked at . . . while they worked at their new loving.

When she didn't answer his first call, however, he

headed across the street to Central Park, wandered the paths until it grew dark.

And by the time he returned he was almost running.

Again no answer.

He took a long shower and wrapped himself in his robe, hoping perhaps it would bring him good luck.

By the fourth time he'd dialed he was feeling his anger growing, in spite of his warning that they were neither married nor engaged, and besides she wasn't expecting this call tonight and she wasn't a nun so what the hell was his problem?

The fifth attempt was successful, and it almost killed him when she refused the invitation, pleading a mound of work for an unrelenting father.

"Well, hell," he said. Thought, then snapped his fingers. "Hey, I have a brilliant idea."

She said nothing.

"Look, as long as I'm here, and since I really don't feel like going through any of those manuscripts again, what's the chance of my meeting Don for a drink someplace? If he's still in town, that is. It'll be good to see him, maybe shoot the—"

"No," she told him abruptly. Told him again softly. "Josh, I don't think that's a good idea at all."

He frowned at his knees. "Why not? Your father likes me, doesn't he? And he still wants to know some gossip, right? This would be as good a time as any to start, I would think. No one in town would know we were seeing each other. All very clandestine and hush-hush." He waited, but from the silence he gathered she wasn't amused. "Andy?"

"I'm here, Josh."

"Well?"

"No," she said again, firmly. "He's there, yes. I talked with him this afternoon. But he's busy, really busy."

"You know that for a fact. He told you that."

"Of course he did." Her voice tightened. "Josh, you

don't know him very well, not as well as I do. You'll have to take my word that not even I can get through to him when he's working on something. I don't know what he's up to yet, but he made sure he didn't tell me where he was staying. He's like that."

"Ah," he said. "Perhaps it's a woman."

"Maybe. That's his business."

He shook a cigarette from its pack and lighted it, blew the smoke to the ceiling. "Andy, I agree that's his business, but have you ever thought about something happening? What if you need him?"

"Nothing will, and I don't, and it's never happened before so why worry about it."

He wanted to argue further, swallowed the temptation and said his goodbyes. If Don Murdoch had turned into a temporary recluse, or had decided to play the part of the temperamental artist, he wasn't going to lose any sleep over it. On the other hand, he *was* sure that Andrea had let herself in for a goodly amount of household friction once Don knew he had tried to get in touch with him and had been foiled.

He felt himself grinning at the idea, broader when he realized he also felt no guilt at all over it. Andrea in trouble, while not the most pleasant of images, was something he decided was perhaps her due. As much as he was drawn to her, was mesmerized by her boldness, it was that very same boldness he believed required a certain amount of judicious tempering, a degree of self-restraint that only situations like this could give her, and teach her. At the same time he wished he had a little of that bullishness himself; if nothing else, it would mean a different kind of trouble than he was used to getting into.

He laughed aloud and tugged at his hair, pulling at an earlobe. One of these days, he told himself as he rose from the bed, you're going to understand yourself perfectly, and brother, are you going to be one hell of a bore.

Another spate of laughter, a resurgence of energy,

and the following week passed too quickly to be remembered. A trail was unearthed. A foray into the stacks of the library on Fifth Avenue, another into the morgues of the *Daily News* and the *Times*, and he was led at last to a small theatrical museum in lower Manhattan where he discovered exactly what he was looking for in an abandoned display at the back of a basement room seldom visited, never cleaned.

When he shouted his triumph he was nearly thrown out.

"Marvelous," he told Andrea that night, sitting on the edge of the bed and staring out at the new green clouding over Central Park. "Just marvelous. They wouldn't sell me what they had, of course, but a little lady with the most godawful purple hair gave me the name of a guy who reputedly parts with nostalgia at the drop of an open wallet. I called him just a few minutes ago and I'll be seeing him in the morning. With any kind of luck I should be home before dark. Sometime tomorrow, anyway, for sure."

"You're not quite as dumb as you look, Miller," she said.

He scowled. "You've been talking to Felicity."

"Sure, why not? I got through with what I was doing for Dad and decided to drop in on her this morning, to let her know what I was going to do with you. The plow, remember? She's a nice girl, Josh. I think she loves you."

"*She* thinks she loves me." He paused, grimacing at the irritation that had stirred acid in his stomach. He would have much rather told Felicity about Andrea himself; this way, now, there was a chance the girl would get her back up and make his life miserable until he either fired her or she quit. It wasn't fair, he thought sourly, and with a dollop of self-mockery, that people insisted on doing things on their own, without his permission, without his knowledge. He had no opportunity to say anything, however; a sharp burst of static made him wince and pull away.

"Josh?"

"Here," he said, rubbing at his ear. "Sounds like you have a hell of a storm going out there."

"You should see it. It looks like something right out of Hitchcock." Another sizzling interruption, and what he sensed was an apprehensive pause. "Josh . . . you're not going to like what I did this afternoon, either."

He nodded resignation. "You went to see Mrs. Thames, too." The next hesitation told him all he needed to know. Curiously, however, there was no reaction. It was, he thought, only something that made perfect sense—seeing the old lady about the plow was something that would have had to have been done sooner or later; it was Felicity he still worried over . . . and astonished himself at the affection he discovered: big brother, little sister, hurt that kid and I'll push your face in.

". . . most incredible house I've ever seen. And that woman! God, Josh, she's beautiful! A character, a regular character, like in those old movies. We had a good afternoon, and I explained to her what you were doing in New York and why you needed the break, and she understood perfectly. I mean, perfectly! She wanted to take off right away and go into the woods with me. I almost had to sit on her to make her wait for you to come back." She laughed, high and clear and overriding the static. "No wonder you like her so much, Josh. She showed me all the things you'd gotten for her, even told me what she had to pay to get them. You're a thief, you know that? I didn't realize, I mean really realize what a thing you have going. Beautiful. Absolutely beautiful."

"So are you," he said when she finally took a breath.

"What? Huh? Did you say something, Josh?"

He wound the cord around his hand, snaked it off, and cleared his throat. "Nothing," he said. "Listen, Andy, I'm going down to get something to eat, then hit the sack. I'll call you when I get in, all right?"

"If you don't, you're a dead man."

He rang off and decided that everything would be all right. Andrea can take care of herself; Felicity would have to get used to her being around; and since Mrs. Thames hadn't tossed her out on her ear it was certain he was not going to have to spread calming oil over the maid's precious damned cottage. So thinking (and wondering, and not caring, if he were making all that much sense), he treated himself to a long, intoxicating meal at Trader Vic's, had a nightcap in his room and a full nine hours of dreamless sleep that had him striding cheerfully and purposefully to his promised morning appointment.

There was a clean, freshly washed blue in the sky and a young look to the brownstone facades of the timeworn city. It took him less than fifteen minutes to come to an agreement with the old man (who got the better of the deal, though he did not seemed pleased), tuck the sheet music safely into his attaché case, and grab a cab back to the hotel for his bags.

He whistled as he packed; the look on Dale's face would be well worth the effort; the look on Felicity's face when he brought home the manuscripts would take care of the bank balance; and the look on Andrea's face when he stepped into the house would be all the commission he needed for a job that started out as two days and lasted nearly a month.

By one-thirty he was pushing cheerfully through the caverns of Grand Central Station, even buying a carnation from a white-robed young girl who wished him peace and healing karma.

By two-fifteen he was aboard the train which would, with one changeover at Greenwich, take him home. And he could not help preening at the look the ticket agent had given him when he'd told the man, "Oxrun Station, one way." Amid all the cutbacks throughout the rail system's Eastern corridor, only the Station had been completely unaffected. Not that there were dozens of scheduled stops at the village's depot, but there was the definite lure (and allure) of wealth to be considered. There were people in Oxrun who could not be ignored, and he did not mind at all that the agent had mistaken him for one.

His fine mood lasted until the train passed a quarry landmark that told him he was only twenty minutes from home.

At that moment, seemingly instantly, a ponderous flotilla of greyblack thunderheads obliterated the sun and turned the air to a premature twilight. The wind found tendrils that penetrated the green-shaded windows, and the leaves turned rapidly to their pale undersides. The air in the coach staled. May's warmth became humid, became cool, became damply cold. Rain suddenly burst against the panes in exploding starfish patterns, stretched into quivering spiders that crawled fitfully across the glass and blurred the walls of trees that hemmed in the tracks. The train lurched sharply, seemed to stall, then swayed so violently he had to grab for the seat ahead of him to keep from spilling into the aisle.

When he recovered, he brushed a hand through his hair and over his sport jacket, looked around in mild embarrassment, and realized for the first time he was alone in the car. He frowned as he tried to remember when the last passenger had left. Told himself it didn't matter, there were hardly great crowds riding out to the Station; nevertheless, the frown deepened. In the shifting darklight, against the flails of crackling lightning, the seats that stretched behind him shimmered, rose, rocked from side to side. A loose shade snapped against a pane. Condensation fogged the doors that led to the other cars.

He looked outside quickly, to reaffirm the world, and the train stopped completely. Slowly. Like a weary old man who'd forgotten he can't run.

10

Josh cursed and leaned back against the cracked leather seat. He suspected a tree or large branch had fallen across the tracks up ahead, and had no sympathy at all for the man who had to clear it. Now that he was so close to home, so close to Andrea, he was impatient. He did not like sitting alone in the middle of nowhere, forced into inaction by something as mundane as an early summer storm. He had important things to do. He had decisions to make. The glimmer of what star-drunk poets called a new life was taking shape on the horizon, and once he had recognized it he could not wait to approach it. It may well be a mirage, as such things had been in the past, but he knew he would be as much a fool for ignoring it as he would be for taking it entirely on faith.

He shifted uneasily.

The conductor usually came through on occasions like this, soothing tempers and promising miracles and stumping through the connecting doors, but there was no sign of him now. Josh rubbed his palms together, rubbed them over his thighs, slapped the seat beside him once, and was about to stand up when the car jerked forward. Waited. Lurched again and began a slow crawl no faster than a man's brisk stride. The rain had eased, and he peered through the

streaked window, looking for something to indicate
the reason for stopping.

There was nothing.

Several branches had been blown down, but none
large enough to interfere with the train; a pile of
rotted ties seemed undisturbed; two small boys in
yellow slickers and floppy hats waved at him as he
passed, bright red bobbers from their tangled fishing
lines swaying violently in the wind.

Josh shrugged and sat back with a traveler's weary
sigh. Whatever it had been was no longer a problem,
and before he had a chance to relax the train eased into
the station amid a glaring fanfare of blue-white flashes
that made him shade his eyes as he rose and grabbed
for his luggage.

The thunder came later, like breakers against a
cliff.

The depot was small, but unlike the others along the
line it was kept in excellent repair, neglect a sin for
one's first view of the Station.

On the west, southbound side of the tracks squatted
the station building, of dark red brick with tall arched
windows and a five-sided peaked roof of new black
slate, topped by a chimney broad and low. Behind it
was a parking lot; in front a wooden platform nearly
seventy yards long, protected by an extension of the
roof that canted gently upward to cover half the train's
width and protect the passengers from whatever in-
clemency there was. On Josh's side, northbound, was
a simpler building, little more than a long, three-sided
shed whose roof, like the one opposite, reached over
the rails. There were highbacked benches, a newspaper rack, and in each of the rear corners a concrete oval
like the bowl of a pipe reaching up to the rafters—
through a swinging brown door broken only by windows shaped like St. Andrew's cross was the entrance
to a passenger subway that ducked under the tracks
and surfaced in the main building.

With his suitcase in one hand and attaché case in

the other, Josh stumbled up the aisle, yanked open the door, and hurried down the steps to the platform. Just as he cleared them the train moved on, and a quick glance around him showed him he was alone.

Rain cascaded through the gap between the two roofs; the wind had found a shrill, unpleasant voice. He shuddered and made for the lefthand subway entrance, hipped open the door, and started down the steps. His heels were loud on the grooved iron edges, their echoes sliding off the tiled walls. Bulbs in small iron cages made the flooring seem damp and hid the ceiling behind the protection of their glare. The swinging door behind him trembled. He stopped for a moment to shift his fingers on the grip of his suitcase, took a deep breath, and had gone a single stride toward the staircase ahead when he heard the scream.

He stopped and cocked his head. The wind, he thought.

The scream came again, long and shrieking, as if whoever it was was also trying to breathe.

It did not take him long to make up his mind; he ran. Slipping once on a slick pile of leaves, colliding with the slightly curved wall, stunning his elbow. He dropped the suitcase as he yelped, fumbled for it frantically, and shoved it under his right arm. The first step was taken at a leap, his free hand taking hold of the cold metal railing and hauling him upward, two steps at a time. The door at the landing was partially ajar and he took it with his shoulder, exploding into the waiting room, whirling to a halt.

He was standing in the building's left front corner, the large room before him, silent and empty.

He dropped his luggage and put his hands on his hips, his mouth open for air, his ears straining, his gaze trying to penetrate the storm's twilight shadows. All the windows, their shades halfway down, were sheeted with rain and softly fogged over. There was no one sitting on any of the pewlike benches that faced the tracks, nor was the stationmaster in his small, glass-and-wood office immediately to Josh's left. A half-dozen lights encased in large ivory globes hung from the surface, weakly glowing, flickering whenever lightning flared nearby.

Indecisive and frowning, he took a step forward, then hurried to the back and shoved open each of the restroom doors. Calling out. Receiving no answer. He returned to the front and wiped condensation from the double doors that led to the platform, but there was no one outside, no one across the way.

He grunted and walked to the southside subway entrance. Pushed open the door and hesitated before taking the first step down. When he reached the bottom he shaded his eyes unnecessarily and peered along the tunnel. Thunder muttered, and the nearest light winked out.

With one hand absently rubbing his still numb elbow he returned upstairs, and shrugged at the empty room.

How many times, he asked himself, have you been in a storm and heard ghosts groaning and people screaming and unmentionable things bellowing in the dark? His mouth twisted into what might have been a smile. Too many times, he answered with a grunt. It's what comes with living in a town that's too quiet.

Though his unease remained as a faint tingling at the back of his neck, he felt more than a little foolish as he retrieved his luggage and carried it to the phone booth by the side door.

There was no response at the Murdoch farm, Felicity wasn't home, and there was no one at the office.

Great, he thought. Just . . . great.

He pinched wearily at the bridge of his nose and decided to call a cab. And with the storm working as it was, he knew it would take at least an hour before he would be able to pry one loose to fetch him.

Into his hip pocket for his wallet, then, and a worn, creased card with the taxi company's number. He had to hold it close to his eyes to decipher it, dropped it before he was finished, and swore loudly while he doubled over in the confines of the booth to pick it up.

The first time he dialed it was the wrong number.

Lightning mocked him, and thunder rumbled so loudly he could feel the vibrations beneath his feet.

At his second try he was disconnected before he could give his location.

At the third he had only managed the first three numbers before he lowered his hand slowly. Someone was in the building with him. The receiver slipped from his fingers and cracked against the booth's glass wall. He took a deep breath and slapped open the door.

A shadow beyond the last row of benches, features hidden by the windows' backlighting.

"Hello."

There was no answer.

It was a woman, he thought, her hands clasped primly in front of her. A beret angled toward her right ear. In a suit well-tailored and dark, nearly black.

"Hello?"

He stepped away from the booth, sideswiping his suitcase with one leg. It fell heavily and he reached automatically for it.

"You need help, Josh?"

His eyes closed, opened, and he raised his hands to indicate his helplessness. "I was just trying to call a cab," he said, while Randy Stanworth came out of the shadows. "What are you doing here?"

She shrugged. "I tried to get you earlier today. Your girl told me you were coming back. Thought you could use a lift."

Her pale complexion was made almost translucent by the dark red of her hair, the dark of her eyebrows, the dark of her lips. She had gained weight since he had last seen her some months before, most of it seemingly settling at her hips. She picked up his attaché case before he could object and headed for the exit, her stride short, her back straight. He considered calling her back to demand an explanation, then thought of gift horses and the storm and followed her out to a drop-nosed Jaguar XJ sedan. Once inside, squirming against the cold brown leather, he thanked her for the favor and waited for the lecture.

There was none. She kept her hands firmly on the steering wheel and her gaze straight ahead. The ruffled white blouse beneath her tweedy jacket gave her a figure he knew she didn't have, and gave her a spinsterish cast he knew she didn't feel.

"So. How's Lloyd?"

Her lips were taut, her cheek hollowed. She flexed her fingers and cleared her throat. "He's all right, I guess."

"You guess?" He set himself into the corner and stared at her. Though he could still feel the rolling of the train, smell the damp that clung to his clothes, he ignored it all when he saw the glint of a tear in her too wide eye. "Randy?"

She sniffed. "Josh, I am so sorry. I simply couldn't wait for you to get home. I had to meet you before you saw anyone else."

He felt a chill, and a dread. "Lloyd. My god, Randy, is—"

"No," she said, though he detected no regret. "No, there hasn't been an accident or a murder, nothing of that sort. I'm just . . . how well do you know Andrea Murdoch?" She glanced at him quickly, looked back at the rain that smashed headlong into the windshield. She was driving slowly, the only thing, he thought, that she ever did with caution.

"Well enough," he said without committing himself.

"You're not having a . . . thing?"

He grinned. "We see each other now and again, if that's what you're asking." Damning himself for knowing exactly the opposite. "Why? Have you met her?"

"No." A cold word. A dead word.

A mile, and they passed the entrance to Hawksted College, began the two-mile stretch to the beginning of the town.

He reached out and touched her arm. She neither flinched nor looked at him. Eyes on the road. Feet placed just so, skirt barely topping the round of her knees. "Randy, are you saying they're having an affair? Lloyd and Andy?" He tried to put as much disbelief into their names as he could, as much for his sake as hers.

"I'm not sure," she said at last. "I wish I knew." Suddenly, she pulled over to the shoulder and turned off the ignition, set the handbrake and covered her face with her hands.

Josh did nothing. Weeping women unnerved him, and his mind was still trying to pull itself away from New York and his work, away from the screams he thought he heard, and back to the Station where an ex-lover was fighting not to believe she'd lost a man. When she fumbled at the clasp of her purse, he took it from her gently and opened it, handed her a tissue, and waited until she had blown her nose, daubed at her eyes. A truck passed, spraying them; it grew darker. He reached to the steering column and turned on the emergency flashers.

"I wish I knew."

"Are . . . I mean—"

"No," she admitted. "I'm not sure at all, to tell you the truth. It's just . . . well, you have to be married, Josh, to know what I mean. The little things that are different; the little things that change when you're not looking."

His voice was toneless: "I'm not married now."

She turned to him and laid a hand on his thigh: "Oh, Josh, I am sorry. I completely forgot, really I did." She braved a smile. "I'm just not thinking straight these days, I guess. It's really got me frantic. I don't know who to turn to."

"How about Lloyd?"

"Oh, he denies it," she said, waving her hand like batting at a fly.

"Well, for crying out loud, Randy, don't you believe him?"

"Of course I do. He knows damned well he can't lie to me. He blushes every time he tries."

He slumped back in his seat, passing a finger over his brow and shaking his head. "Randy, you've confused me. First you ask me if Lloyd and Andy are seeing each other behind your—and my—back. Then you tell me he denies it and you believe him. I don't get it."

A pearl-and-ivory compact was in her hand, a cotton puff repairing the damage done by tears. "You never like to think it's just you, you know. It's always easier when there's someone else to blame. A woman. The proverbial other woman. It's an ego protection, Josh."

"Where is Lloyd now?"

She looked at him, puzzled. "At the hospital, I imagine. He's overseeing the transfer of a patient."

"To West Hartford?"

"Why yes, how did you know?"

"It must be a racket," he said, grinning. "Maybe he knows the guy there—financially, I mean." When he saw the look on her face he held up a quick hand. "Just joking, Randy, don't be so shocked. He did it last month, too. To a friend of a friend. It was just a joke." He took a deep breath. "Look, I haven't eaten all day. Why don't you let me take you to the inn for dinner? I could use the meal, and you could use an ear, I think."

He sighed when he spotted the mother in her take over, however momentarily. She nodded, restarted the car, and pulled back onto Chancellor Avenue without checking the traffic. While she drove, silently, intently, he wondered why she had picked Andrea out of all the women in Oxrun. There were surely others he knew better, saw more frequently; why Andy? Unless all this was merely an excuse to see him alone for a change. He knew he wasn't flattering himself. She still managed to remind him of their time together, one way or another, still made small but unmistakable attempts to see if he were carrying an invisible torch. She had never believed he could be truly happy without her, at the same time not so much a fool as to believe they could have been perfect together. Yet she never begrudged him his liaisons with others.

Not, he thought then, until now, that is.

He laughed shortly, and waved away her questioning glance. Began instead a fervid and somewhat embellished account of his stay in the city, patting the case lovingly as he spoke of the treasures he had hunted down, used every trick he had learned about her to make her laugh with him. When she did he relaxed. And after dinner was over he sent her on her way with a kiss and walked home in the dark. Gallant, he thought as he struggled up the front steps, but incredibly stupid. His arms ached, his back ached, and it wasn't until he was soaking in a hot tub that he realized Andrea's name hadn't come up again.

There was a telephone on a narrow shelf by the tub. He grabbed it, dialed, and listened impatiently to the ringing.

With nothing but a towel wrapped around his waist he stalked through the house. Tried again; no answer.

When he found himself taking frequent peeks through the livingroom curtains he knew he was hoping she would drive up unexpectedly, to give him another chance to prove himself with her. The realization disgusted him; that was something an adolescent would do—wishing so hard for his dream that he deluded himself into believing she would happen. After that, when she did not show, there would be a period of mourning, of moping, of pouting.

A third time. It was well past ten and there was no one at the farm.

He sat on the edge of the bed and punched hard at his pillow. He would not give her the satisfaction of

calling all night. She knew, she had been told he
would get in touch as soon as he returned; if she chose
to spend her nights with someone else, that was her
problem not his. He had things to do in the morning.
There were the manuscripts to send out and be paid
for, the sheet music to give to Dale, Mrs. Thames to
be coddled by another trip out to the woods . . . the
hell with her. And damn Randy Stanworth for making
him think this way.

11

Your problem, Joshua," said Melissa Thames, "is simple—you look much too vulnerable. You bring out the A.S.P.C.A. in women."

Even sitting in an enormous Queen Anne wing chair she was tall, her height deliberately cultivated by the wearing of severely tailored suits done in pale greys and pale blues, vertical ruffles on her blouses, thin belts and thinner watchbands, her fog-grey hair cut short as a man's and combed back over her ears without the grace of a curl or a wave. Her face was long, lean, remarkably unlined, dominated above by ghostly blue eyes and below by a large mole at the left corner of her mouth. Handsome, Josh had thought when he had first seen her; she had never been beautiful, but always aristocratically handsome. She had been born into wealth and wore it like one of her favorite cardigans—casually, almost carelessly, but never without an appreciation of its worth.

Her back was straight, her legs crossed at the knee, her hands on the grooved arms as though she were perched on a throne.

"It starts with that smile of yours," she said. "You think it makes you look worldly, cynical, but it doesn't. Only bitter, Joshua, only bitter. Your hair, too. All that gorgeous white on a man your age." She shook her head slowly. "You should dye it. At least darken it. If you ask me—and you didn't, but that isn't going to stop me, you know me better than that—if you ask me, you resemble a man wavering between middle-age and childhood. Like a drenched Irish wolfhound puppy—so goddamned big and so goddamned young."

He was in a leatherette club chair, a thumb polishing an already bright gold stud on the arm. "What does any of this have to do with your plow?"

Her pencil-line eyebrows rose in regal surprise. "Nothing. Nothing at all. You asked me why you were always in trouble with women. I told you."

"It was a rhetorical question," he said.

She laughed, most of the sound slipping harshly through her nostrils. "You know me better than that," she told him again. "I never accept a rhetorical question."

In his left hand he held a slender glass of cream sherry. He sipped at it, swallowed, stared at the dead maw of a huge fieldstone fireplace. He could walk right in there, he thought, without so much as ducking his head; he could walk right in and immolate himself and no one would be able to tell his ashes from the pine. A hell of a note. A hell of a note. He sighed to himself and sipped the sherry again, knowing he did not have to speak if he didn't want to. Mrs. Thames was patient about things that concerned her deeply, and it hadn't taken him long to understand he was one of them. He did not know why, and he did not mind—outside of his own study, this was the only house in Oxrun where he felt completely comfortable.

And the size of it did not matter.

On the outside, behind the tall stone walls that enclosed the grounds, it seemed like more than a transplanted English Tudor complete with a roof designed to appear thatched. Inside, however, it had been constructed to the owner's scale: large furniture,

arched doorways, ceiling-tall windows, long and narrow rooms, all of it to a depth twice as long as the
house was wide. Granville Thames had been seven
feet tall, and after his death a decade before his widow
had kept everything the same, with one exception; his
portrait had been added to hers over the mantelpiece
—full-sized and in fox-hunting regalia. And rather
than being dizzyingly overwhelming, they were perfect for the room, for the house, for the woman who
lived there. It had not taken Josh long to forget they
were even there.

"Joshua," she said then, "you have been back from
your trip for exactly one week. I thought you would
have been out to see me before now."

"I had every intention of doing so," he said.
Shrugged. "I didn't get around to it."

"Or not much else, from what I can gather."

He squirmed under her stare, more so because she
was right. The day after he'd seen Randy he had slept
late. Woke with a headache he was positive would
split his skull in half if he should try to move off the
pillow. He'd called Felicity and told her he was under
the weather. She sympathized, came around before
dinner and picked up the manuscripts for shipment to
their new owners. He called Andrea; there was no
answer. On a whim for which he had no rationalization, he tried to get in touch with Lloyd, and could do
nothing more than speak with his answering service.

Andrea was still not home—or answering the
telephone—the next morning.

He dressed, then, and drove out to the Murdoch
farm. The house was a three-story overlapping clapboard freshly painted white, with a wide, screened-in
porch that girdled the building and made it seem
shorter than it was. There was no MG in the graveled
drive, the curtains and shades drawn. If he hadn't
known better, he would have sworn nobody lived
there.

After a slow U-turn he parked on the other side of

the road and climbed out of the Buick, leaned against the front fender, and lit a cigarette. Smoked for ten minutes. Chain-smoked for half an hour. When he began coughing, he walked into the front yard and circled the house, the two outbuildings behind, passed between two giant maples and into the untilled field beyond. No dogs, no birds, only the hushed chatter of insects. A closer look, and he could not find a newspaper, a bottle of milk, and the garbage cans were empty. The garage was locked, nothing inside.

An hour later he felt the first swirl of guilt and almost ran back to the car. Guilt. Not because he could have been discovered snooping around, but because it had occurred to him that something might have happened to her father in New York, and Andrea had rushed down there to help him. There wouldn't have been time, then, for her to call. Later. When it was all straightened out. Later she would call.

And a week had passed without a word.

"She's a very nice young woman," Mrs. Thames said. "Very bright. Very intelligent."

"Yeah."

"I suspect, Joshua, you would rather not talk about her."

His smile was automatic, and emotionless.

Mrs. Thames clucked her disappointment. "Not like you," she admonished. "It's not like you at all."

"I'll get over it."

"I know that," she said. "Now all you have to do is believe it yourself."

He grinned, finally laughed, and finished his drink. They spoke for several minutes more—mostly about Agatha West, another one of her ladies' group members who had slipped out of town without leaving a word.

"She's a tramp, of course," she said with a malicious grin. "I don't care how old she is, she's a tramp. She probably took her milkman with her."

This time his laugh was dutiful, nothing more,

because he could see at the corners of her eyes a slight tic, a trembling, and an enforced jocularity in her voice that yielded more than it hid.

"She certainly gave herself a hell of a birthday present, I'll say that for the old bat."

He turned away a moment and stared at her portrait.

"You noticed," she said quietly.

"Huh? What?"

"Not the portrait, Joshua, the coincidence."

"Yes," he admitted, memory returning. "Saporral. She walked out on her birthday, too." He managed a weak smile. "Maybe it's in the blood or something. You reach a certain age . . . and you . . ." He faltered at the pain that creased her face beneath the powder. "Melissa," he said, "don't tell me you're afraid."

"You have never used my Christian name before, Joshua."

He waited.

She nodded, finished her sherry, and poured herself another. "I think I am, yes." A hand lifted to keep him silent. "Thelma and Agatha you know about. I don't suppose you know about Esther and Mabel. No. No, you wouldn't. Esther left her house on Devon last November, Mabel her apartment on Steuben just after Christmas. Their . . . birthdays." She stopped, and he said nothing. "It all happened on their birthdays."

He noticed her hand trembling, reached over, and gently took the glass away. "Mrs. Thames—"

"I like Melissa. It's been a long time since a man called me Melissa."

"Melissa."

The smile she gave him was swift, a grimace.

"Melissa, you have to face something, you know. Your age. The ages of your friends. I can't tell you why they left their homes, why they left at all, but maybe I wasn't so far off when I said that thing about reaching a certain age. Maybe they didn't like the fact of facing—"

"Nonsense!" She glared at him in fury, a tantrum so tangible he had to back away. "I don't know who's been feeding you all that nonsense, Joshua, but we've long ago faced what's sweetly called the inevitable. When you reach our time, if you don't you're a fool." A finger, long and ringed with diamonds, touched the depression in her chin. "I read a lot, you know. There's a poem by that man from Baltimore, the one who always writes those silly doggerel things."

"Nash," he said instantly. "Ogden Nash."

"Yes," she said, nodding thoughtfully. "Yes, that's the man. Funny little verses. Granville gave me a collection of his works for our thirtieth anniversary. I still read it, though I don't find them humorous anymore. It's because, Joshua, he wrote a poem about old people in there, one that says that an old man knows when an old man dies."

The room, the house, filled with a silence that lifted the hairs on the back of his neck. Fear; he could feel now the fear she could no longer hide.

"My birthday is next Saturday," she said. "And I'm being watched. I know it."

He started, and she noticed it, snapping his head around to seize his gaze with a frown.

"Joshua?"

"I . . . I'm not sure, Melissa. I guess it's what you just said, about being watched." He left the chair and stood on the hearth, hands behind his back, twisting hard and rapidly. "Me, too. Except my birthday doesn't come for a long time. September, in fact." He faced her again. "I'm sorry, I shouldn't have said that. It has nothing to do with . . . with your . . ."

"My trouble? My problem?" She waved him back to his seat. "I tried to get in touch with Thelma yesterday, at that clinic Dr. Stanworth sent her to in West Hartford."

"Oh, for god's sake, Melissa," he interrupted, more harshly than he'd intended, "you're not going to tell me the place doesn't exist."

"Oh, it does," she told him, almost primly. "But Thelma doesn't. They never heard of her."

"Did you call Lloyd?"

"I did. Or rather, I tried. It seems he's making himself scarce these days."

"Well, that's no problem," he said. "I'll get hold of him and find out for you. Probably, either you got the name wrong, or he told it to you wrong." He spread his hands. "Unless you think he's involved in white slavery or something."

"Thelma? A white slave?" The idea touched her somewhere below her fear and she laughed, putting one hand to her abdomen while her head rocked back, then side to side. Josh grinned at her stupidly, inanely, until she had regained control and spent a few seconds wiping her cheeks with the backs of her hands. "Oh, Joshua, bless you, I needed that badly."

"My pleasure," he said sincerely.

"And you will find out that little thing for me?"

"Sure I will. Just leave it to me."

She sighed and made a show of fixing her hair. Then they speculated rather sadly on the diminishing probability of his locating her handplow, had still another drink, and agreed that Josh should relegate this search to a secondary position. Put it to one side while he continued his other business, returning to the hunt only when he thought he had a clear and absolute lead.

"It's not all that important, you know," she said as she walked him to the door. He kept his back straight as a matter of pride; Mrs. Thames never slouched, and she was a full head taller. "If we can't find it by, let's say the end of summer, then I'll just have to have a replica made. The more I think about it, the more I look at it this way—if you do happen to find one in the ruins of some godforsaken place, then it really wasn't all that much good luck in the first place, and I would be then well advised not to have it in my house."

"The maid's cottage," he corrected.

"It's the same thing, Joshua, don't sass me. Remember, I make more than you do before I get out of bed in the morning."

A step toward his car and she stopped him with his name.

"I . . ." She nodded toward the front room. "Thank you again for that, Joshua. Sometimes, living alone in this monstrosity, one's imagination gets the best of one."

"I'll ask Lloyd anyway," he said. "I'm curious, too."

"You're a good liar, Joshua." She smiled. "Thank you for that, too."

There were no messages from Andrea at the office by the time he returned. Felicity, huffing at her desk like a matron insulted, told him she was getting sick and tired of his asking about that woman all day, and if he wanted her so badly he should stop glooming around, making other people miserable, and go do something about it, for crying out loud.

Meanwhile, she continued without half taking a breath, there was a request here from a new customer he should seriously consider. He took the letter from her outstretched hand and read it through once—a saddle from a racehorse that had had some local notoriety around a small town in Massachusetts. His first impulse was to ditch it, it sounded too crazy; his second was to remind him that an eighteenth-century handplow could hardly be considered sane.

He nodded, and Felicity patted his head, telling him with a barely contained giggle that he was really a good boy, not to worry, and if she razzed him so much it was because she didn't like to see him in the dumps all the time.

He kissed her hand, squeezed it, and remembered his promise to Mrs. Thames. Lloyd, however, was in surgery when he called, and the receptionist told him the operation was expected to last at least another two hours. He left a message and rang off. Felicity tried the Murdochs; there was still no answer.

"Enough," he said. "Go home, Miss Lancaster, and get your beauty rest."

"You going to be okay?"

"If I'm not, it's only going to be my fault, not yours."

Once alone, however, he couldn't help thinking about Melissa Thames and her fears, and the admission that living alone as she did was something less than perfect. It unnerved him, but did not depress him, and he slept well that night because he knew that in the morning he was going to do exactly what Felicity had advised him to do.

12

He awoke at dawn and daydreamed for two hours. Then he rose and fixed himself a large breakfast he did not want and knew he should eat. For a while he worried over Mrs. Thames and her friends, then decided that was something he could not take time for right now. He had never been able to understand the elderly, knew that this was something beyond his province to explore without more help. Later, he decided, he would look into Thelma and Mabel and whoever the rest were later.

Now, however, there was Andrea to consider.

He cleared the table and went into the study where he pulled from one of the shelves the latest of Don Murdoch's books, from the complete set given to him by Murdoch last winter. He checked the publisher's name and called them in New York, telling the firm's operator he was a New England reporter who wanted to do a piece on the new arrival. After a bit of hapless dithering he was switched over to Publicity where he wasted fifteen minutes listening to what sounded like a programmed speech. When the woman was done, he thanked her profusely and told her he'd heard Murdoch was doing some important research in the city; did she know where he was? It was news to her, no one ever told her anything. On impulse, he asked about Andrea; the woman admitted she hadn't known Murdoch was married, much less a father. The man, Josh was told, never bothered to fill out the standard author publicity form routinely sent to all new house writers. He hadn't known there was such a thing, went back to the bookshelf and hunted until he'd located Don's second book. When he called that publisher, he was told all files were confidential, and besides, they hadn't touched one of his books in twelve years. Murdoch always managed to garner fair reviews, but none of his novels (he had done five for them) had sold to a paperback house, which was where most hardcovers recouped their monies. Maybe he should try the man's new publisher; she understood they were doing quite well by him. He thanked her, rang off, and stared at the dial for nearly five minutes.

He drove out to the house again, this time not at all reluctant to try as many windows and doors as he could reach. All of them were locked. There was still nothing in the garage, still no sign that anyone had lived there at all.

Which was foolish. The Murdochs did. He ought to know. He had been in that dark, cramped livingroom often enough, staring at Andrea when he thought she wasn't looking, listening to Don while he explained how he did not care if he never got rich, as long as people listened to what he had to say in his books.

It occurred to him rather abruptly as he was driving back down Chancellor Avenue that he had not read one of the novels.

Guilt once more.

So much of it that he didn't notice the flaring red lights in his rearview mirror until a siren spurted and died, and he pulled over to the shoulder. Before the patrolman had come to the door he was already holding all his identification, and swearing silently at himself for not paying attention to what he was doing.

When he rolled down the window Fred Borg grinned at him.

"No, I am not," Josh said, disgust at himself turning his smile down.

Borg tipped his cap to the back of his head. "No you are not what?" And he laughed.

"No, I am not going to a fire, late for an appointment, rushing to the hospital, or trying to catch the train. I'm guilty as sin and you've got me, copper."

"Great." But he made no move to take out his ticket book. "You all right?"

"Sure."

"You don't usually drive this fast. Didn't think you wanted to take a chance with this beauty."

Josh fumbled his license back into his wallet and shoved the registration into the glove compartment. "I was somewhere else. Thinking. I had my mind on other things, Fred. Sorry."

Borg waved it away. "No problem. I just wanted you to slow down before you hit town, that's all." The tone was friendly, concerned, and the warning was clear. He started to walk away, changed his mind with a snap of his fingers, and leaned his forearm on the window ledge. His face was so close Josh backed away slightly. "Hey, you remember that accident back in April? The guy what took off? With the arm missing?"

"Like it was yesterday," Josh said, his sarcasm heavy.

"Hell of a thing, wasn't it. Damn. Thought you'd like to know we got a line on him."

Josh didn't care. Remembering waking nightmares was not part of his routine. "Really."

"Yeah. Once we got the names of the others, we asked around, found out they was all from Hartford. This one guy, the one with the no arm, he was a student over to UConn. Beats all shit, but it was his birthday, too. They was celebrating, I guess."

Josh nodded his agreement with the irony of it all.

Borg slapped the car lightly and straightened. "You drive careful, okay? Don't want you bleeding all over my roads." His laughter trailed after him, and Josh thought sourly June was too lovely a month to have to put up with a sound like that.

When he opened his front door he dislodged a packet of letters and circulars that had been jammed by one corner into the mail slot. He almost stepped over them, stopping himself in midstride when he saw Andrea's name on a return address.

Dear John, the war is so long and I'm so lonely and I've decided to marry your best friend Harry and I hope you won't be too mad at me I love you Andrea.

He rubbed a hand briskly over his stomach as he reached down for the envelope, noting as he headed into the study the New York postmark. The date was blurred, but the month was June; since this was only the third, and Thursday . . . he sat at his desk and looked out the window. Remembered the dawn. The white cat. The hands that massaged his shoulders, and the voice that had told him everything was all right.

"I don't need this," he whispered, and opened the letter.

Joshua darling, forgive the scribbling but I'm in a hurry and I don't have the time to tell you everything you should know. Dad called the morning you were supposed to get back. I tried to get hold of you at the Plaza (boy, are you a snob. The Plaza, yet), but you had already checked out. Dad needed some help, so I grabbed a few things and took the first train out. He sounded pretty desperate, like he was sick or something, so I didn't even take the time to leave you a note. I'm sorry. I'm very, very sorry. I know I should have at least called—

"Goddamn right," he muttered.

—but I was so worried! You know how Dad is. He never lets on anything is wrong until it's almost too late. He almost killed himself once doing that, a long

time ago in California. I thought he'd gotten over it. But not Dad.

Anyway, I want you to know everything's all right. He isn't sick. He was worried. Some guy called from his publisher and told him one of the paperback people was going to make a fantastic (!!!) offer for the last book. Maybe a FANTASTIC (!!!) offer on the next three. He was so excited, and so worried he'd blow it (I keep telling him to get an agent but he won't listen) he made himself sick. Not really sick. Just really nervous. When he finally called he was a wreck, believe me. I've been holding his hand for a week now and it's almost over. His editor is going to run what they call an auction today and tomorrow. It's so confusing. I don't know all the details. But I do know I'll be home on Friday. I promise you I'll call.

Please don't be mad.

I love you.

So does Dad.

Cross your fingers and wish us luck.

OH!!! I almost forgot!! Dad's birthday is the Fourth of July. I want you to find something for him. I'll tell you all about it when I see you.

Forgive me? Please!???

I love you, Joshua Miller. Keep your hands off Felicity.

Twenty-four hours in a day, he thought with the letter still in his hand. Twenty-four hours filled with so much activity that she hadn't found a single free stretch of three minutes in which to call him. To jot something on a postcard and send it to him. He shook his head vigorously. He was being unfair, in spite of the fact that he could not rid his stomach of the acid born there of bruised feelings and bleeding ego. He could imagine how stoic Don was doing in an atmosphere of such expensive wheeling and dealing; all that carefully cultivated disdain for worldly goods blown out the window. No wonder he was frantic. No wonder he needed his daughter—she would be the anchor in the storm that was probably threatening to capsize him.

Still . . . a full week and not a single word.

His stomach growled and he grinned. Carefully, he refolded the letter and placed it atop one of the book piles. Then he glanced at his watch, winced at the time, and made himself some lunch. Once it was done and eaten he rushed the Buick over to High Street and parked in front of the office. By the time he had slid out the passenger door, Felicity was waiting for him at the threshold.

Without thinking, he kissed her cheek lightly, and was startled when she grabbed his arm, threw her hands to the back of his neck, and yanked him down to her level. Kissed him. Hard. Pressing herself against him so violently he had to embrace her or lose his balance. When she released him her eyes were narrowed in a vicious glint of triumph.

"If you're going to kiss me, Miller," she said, "do it the hell right."

He eased her back until they were both leaning against the frame. "Fel," he said with a weak smile, "if I live to be a hundred . . ."

She was wearing a thin white blouse open to the middle of her chest, a wide gold belt that pinched her waist and flared her hips in a pair of shimmering dark trousers. She put her hands on her waist and did not shift her gaze from his eyes, lower her voice, indicate at all what her temper was doing.

"I am not one of the guys, Miller," she told him matter-of-factly. "I didn't play softball in high school, I never climbed a tree in my life, and the only time I wear a sweatshirt is when I do some jogging in the park. Am I getting through to you?"

He put a hand to his mouth, little finger curled under his chin. He nodded. And he wondered what

had ever given her the idea he thought her one of the
guys. A kid sister, yes; never one of the guys. But he
must have done something, or an accumulation of
things, and now was not the time to deny any of it. He
could see now the gentle flaring of her nostrils, the
effort she was making not to blink rapidly.

"You hungry?" he said finally.

She took a deep breath and let her hands drop to her
sides. "We've got work to do. It's after one o'clock."

"It may not have occurred to you," he said lightly,
thinking back to something Andrea had told him,
"but I'm the boss around here. If I want to squander
the firm's money taking my . . ." He hesitated. She
frowned. He couldn't resist. "If I want to take my
partner out to lunch, who's going to complain?"

He knew she hadn't heard him through her confusion and fight against her temper. She had been
expecting something else. And when it finally took
hold she scowled.

"That isn't funny, Miller."

"It wasn't meant to be, Lancaster."

The blinking began, and a speck of mascara dropped
to her cheek. "I don't get it."

He took her arm and pulled her out to the sidewalk,
closed and locked the door, and walked with her to
Centre Street. "It's simple," he told her, thinking he
should have done this a year ago. "You do as much
work for me as I do for myself. And I don't pay you
nearly enough as a secretary."

"Serf."

"Suit yourself." He smiled broadly, pleased she'd
fallen back on a familiar defense. "Still, it's official."

"As of when?"

They stopped in the center of the block, in front of a
jeweler's with a display of birthstones on black velvet.

"As of now," he said.

"What about . . . you know."

He cupped her hand around his elbow and moved

them onward, through patches of pedestrians jacketless and hatless, enjoying the warm weather before it grew unbearable. Across the street Iris Lennon was setting up a sidewalk table with remaindered books neatly arranged; there was a similar setup in front of the toy store, the corner tobacco shop, the music store. There was no special occasion to be marked. It was something spontaneous, and it would be gone the following day.

"Josh?"

He grinned down at Felicity. Though he knew it bordered on the cruel, he was enjoying her bewilderment, her momentary dislocation.

"We'll talk about money later, all right? Eat first, business after. I never mix the two if I can help it. It's bad for the ulcer."

She said little on the way to the Lounge, less during the meal. And while they dined he wondered if he had done the right thing. The reasons were solid, he knew that, but he was not at all positive about the timing. A reaction to Andrea's offhanded treatment? He shuddered once, buried it beneath an elaborate rolling of his shoulders as though he were fighting a stiff muscle. No, he thought. Then: maybe. And finally: it did not matter. He had not been lying when he said she did as much work as he; the only difference between them was the traveling he did. It was right, it was proper, and he knew that if he didn't stop smirking at his move he would be nominating himself for sainthood before the day was over.

They walked back slowly.

"Josh, is this one of those things that I'm supposed to be grateful for and refuse? Because if it is, I'm not going to do it." She spoke softly, but firmly. "I deserve it, you know. I'm not being conceited or anything, but I do deserve it." She stopped him in front of the Savings and Loan. "Thank you. I didn't say that before, and I should have. Thank you."

He felt like squirming. This wasn't the Fel Lancaster he knew too well. Or thought he had. "Don't thank me," he said, "until you've seen the books."

She slapped his arm. "I keep them, remember? I'm no fool."

He laughed and she hugged his arm, and he was just barely aware of the stares they received as they rounded the corner and she released him so he could pull out the key.

"Josh."

He looked at her.

"Josh, the door is open."

"Nope." He shook his head. "I locked it, remember?"

"I remember. But it's open."

She stepped to one side as he pushed open the door and hurried in, seeing nothing wrong this side of the partition. He was about to call out a gag, some remark to put her at ease (and ease his own nerves), when he saw the books, the files, the papers scattered in the aisle between their desks.

And the gleam of black paint that had been dumped over it all.

13

Josh sat numbly in one of the armchairs and stared out the window. Faces peered back, moving slowly, squinting, mouths working in silent speculation. A patrol car was parked behind the Buick, and several youngsters were lounging against the fenders, arms folded, heads together. Across the street and under the trees a small group of women chatted in subdued animation, every few moments one of them breaking off to continue on her way, replaced almost immediately by another walking in off Centre Street. Twice, Karl Tanner had ambled outside to move the spectators on, and now was seated opposite of Josh, his cap in his hand, twirling it slowly. His attitude was deferential, but definitely not subservient.

"That's about the best I can do now, Mr. Miller," he said. There was no apology in his voice—a simple statement of fact.

Josh hesitated before nodding. He did not look to Felicity, who had the chair beside him and was shaking her head glumly over a list she had made.

"Fingerprints," she suggested then, looking up at the patrolman without raising her head.

Tanner—whose face, Josh had decided, had been crudely hacked out of chipped marble—met her gaze solemnly. "From what we can see, yours and Mr.

Miller's, that's all. Either the door was picked by an expert, or he had a key. Nothing was damaged . . . there. The paint," he continued quickly, as though sensing interruption, "is simple black trim. You go over to Chase's Hardware, you'll find a zillion gallons of it have been sold since the middle of last month. It's the time of year. No way it can be traced." He looked back to Josh. "You sure nothing was taken?"

"Pretty much." He would not look to the back office again. His hands, clasped tightly in his lap, were already stained with streaks and blotches of black, as were his trousers from the knees to the cuffs. "Whoever it was yanked all those files from the cabinet and . . . damn! It just doesn't make any sense!"

Tanner rose, nodded to Felicity, and walked to the open door. The stench of paint was still in the air despite the crosscurrents, and he rubbed a finger hard under his nose. "I'll be in touch, Mr. Miller."

"Yeah, but don't hold my breath, right?"

Tanner shrugged and left, the patrol car slipping out of its space without benefit of siren or lights; and as if it were a signal, most of the onlookers vanished.

Josh slapped at his thighs then, moved stiffly to the partition, and stared at the piles of ruined papers he and Fel had shifted to her desk. Though nothing extremely valuable had been destroyed, it would take weeks before he could put the work together again, weeks more before they would be able to replace all the addresses and telephone numbers of occasional contacts, the routes he had taken for some of the most uncommon items he'd traced and retrieved. And though each town he had visited had not offered him a treasure, there were notes he had taken on things that he'd seen, from prints to handcraft, and they were all gone. A match and a flame could not have done the work more thoroughly.

Felicity rested a hand on his shoulder. "A mess," she said.

Absently, he rubbed a hand up and down her spine. "I suppose we might as well salvage what we can."

"I don't think I feel up to it."

"It'll be worse in the morning."

They stared for a few moments longer, then flanked the desk and began pulling the folders apart, peeling sheets, dropping those barely readable into one pile, those completely useless on the floor. At one point she noted they would have to replace the carpeting; at another he wondered aloud which gods he had offended.

"I mean," he said helplessly, "ever since I got back I've been going crazy. The lady at the station, Andrea, Don . . . it's like I've forgotten how to do anything right. No." He held up a blackened hand to Felicity's glare. "I didn't mean that. I mean . . . well, it's like that guy in *Li'l Abner*, the one who walks around with the cloud over his head all the time. Joe. Something. It's like I haven't shaken the storm that hit when I got here."

"You're weird, you know," she told him. "If you think about it without feeling sorry for yourself, you've had a perfectly good explanation for all of it."

"Except this."

"Except this. And there's probably something here, too, only you can't see it yet."

It was well after seven by the time they were done and had filled the trashcans behind the back door. Then, feeling a slow growing rage he could not control, Josh dragged the desks into the front and began to pull up the ruined carpet. Twice he jabbed himself with a stray tack, each time venting his frustrations so loudly Felicity was forced to close the front door. Afterward, the carpeting dumped unceremoniously out the back, he noted the time and announced he was hungry. Worse, he was starving.

"You look like hell."

He pointed at her own clothes derisively. "You think you'll make Miss America like that?"

They were too tired to laugh, too annoyed to smile.

"Fel . . ." He lifted a hand, lowered it slowly. "Fel, I'm really sorry about all this."

"It isn't your fault, you know."

"I know, I know, but . . ." He reached for a cigarette, changed his mind when he saw the smears on his fingertips. "This is hardly the way to start out a partnership."

"Listen," she told him, although her attempt to sound stern failed miserably. "I didn't expect it, and I don't think you expected it, either. To make the offer, I mean. Don't say anything, I know you too well, Miller. Besides, there was bound to be trouble sooner or later. This way we get it over with, right? And so far it's only going to cost my half umpteen thousand dollars. Hell, I'll be out of debt by the time I retire."

He smiled at her softly, glad of the effort she was making, distressed at the shimmering he could see in her eyes. But he refused to dwell on the possibility of error; it could very well be she wouldn't want to shoulder half the burden after a few months without her regular salary. It could very well be, and he hated himself for making it seem like an escape clause in a contract.

"Tell you what," he said abruptly, clapping his hands once and shoving away from his desk. "We'll get ourselves home, change into something disgustingly respectable, and I'll meet you at the inn in, say, an hour at most. For dinner. It's only Thursday, we won't need a reservation."

He didn't wait for her to offer an objection; instead, he hustled her outside and into his car. The early evening had taken a bronze cast through the leaves, had added a brush of dampness to the air that made him shiver in spite of the fact that the temperature remained unseasonably high. He glanced once back to the office before taking the wheel, buried a tight fist in his jacket pocket as he pulled away from the curb and took Felicity directly to her Steuben Avenue apartment. From there he drove two blocks west to Mainland Road, the two-lane stretch of highway that passed the village (and was the only road to do so) north to south. At the stop sign he waited, staring across the blacktop to the empty fields on the other side. There was no traffic.

Go home, he ordered silently when he realized what he was doing; go home before you kill yourself, idiot.

The response was automatic: narrowing his eyes against the sun directly ahead of him he floored the accelerator. The cumbersome Buick shuddered, almost stalled, then swept left onto Mainland with a deep-throated howl.

A moment, and the village was gone.

A minute, and the Cock's Crow blurred by him on the right.

There were no more buildings, there were no more farms, and the road curved right in gentle ascension.

Trees crowded the verges, their shadows snapping over the maroon hood to give his vision a stop-start distortion, a momentary feeling he was trapped in a nickelodeon.

Miller's Mysteries. A foolish name. A whim and a whimsy. But it was *his* whim and *his* whimsy, and he wondered if this was anything akin to a rape.

He slowed at a narrow wooden bridge, turning his head from the whitebright reflections of the sun's blind dying. And in slowing did not pick up his speeding again. Rather, he drove at the pace of a reluctant child heading home. Remembered for no reason that feeling he had had in April, that he was being watched, that he was being followed. But while the former was nothing but a sensation without foundation, this . . . this attack on his living (in both senses of the word) was equally without reason. Nothing valuable had been touched, nothing worthless had been stolen. Just files and papers and that miserable carpet.

At a cleared space centered by a chipped picnic table he turned around and headed back.

And the intrusion had accomplished little more than the creation of a nagging inconvenience. It certainly couldn't have been meant as a warning. Against what? Finding a handplow, a teaspoon, a piece of lousy sheet music?

Impatience nudged the speedometer.

Maybe one of Felicity's beaux was jealous and had struck back the only way he knew how.

He shook his head; that explanation made as much sense as the warning.

The Cock's Crow; Chancellor Avenue; he swung right and reentered Oxrun, in passing the police station tempted to stop to see if Karl Tanner had been successful. Shrugged it off and went home where he took a fast shower and changed into grey slacks, wine shirt, and a pale grey jacket whose lapels he didn't know were fashionable or not. Felicity, he had decided, would have all the answers.

They sat in the upstairs dining room.

The building had been a farmhouse two centuries before, was now divided into two primary sections for dining and dancing. Below it was noisy, catering to the younger couples with good wine and loud music; above, in a series of large, dark rooms, were scattered tall booths randomly across the polished pegged floors. Candles in amber globes were virtually the only lighting, aside from the fireplaces and the lanterns hidden deep in the exposed rafters. Here conversation was generally subdued, and even the waitresses moved as though they wore slippers. The prices were high and the food superb, and with the booths not confined to places along the walls there was a privacy not available except in one's home.

Felicity was wearing a high-necked cocktail dress unadorned save for a pendant the same violet as her eyes.

"I need to know something," she told him when their first drinks had been delivered.

"Sure." He cupped his glass with his palms, the dusk of the room giving a masque to her eyes.

"You did this thing, this partner stuff, on the spur of the moment, didn't you."

"You already asked me that already, sort of."

"And you sort of didn't answer."

There was no sense in lying, though the offer still made sense. He nodded. She nodded.

"As long as I know."

"I mean it, Fel."

"I know that."

"But I didn't tell you the condition."

An eyebrow arched.

"If we're going to do this, you've got to stop calling me Miller. It's bad for the image."

"Whose—yours or the firm's?"

Roast beef and Yorkshire pudding, thick gravy, fresh vegetables; it wasn't the fanciest meal he could have ordered, but it was his favorite for pulling himself out of the dumps.

Sherry afterward; Bristol Cream for him, Dry Sack for her.

"Who's after you, Miller?" she asked quietly. "I've been trying to figure it out. You do anyone dirt on a deal or something? You step on anybody's toes?"

He poked a burning cigarette around his ashtray, shifting matches and butts into a low pile as he tried to think. "No." He stared at a point just over her head. "I doubt it. I never gave anyone anything but a fair deal. I've never stolen anything to sell it, and I've never looked for anything that was stolen, just lost. I was innocuous in the Air Force, never worked for the CIA, and though not everyone likes me, as far as I can tell I don't have any enemies." He shrugged. "You tell me."

"Believe me, if I could I would."

"Great."

She smiled.

"What's so funny?"

She feigned umbrage. "I'm not laughing, just smiling."

"Inside, you're hysterical."

"Well . . ." She picked up her sherry and held it in front of her eyes. Lowered the glass and grinned. "Mrs. Thames."

"She wouldn't dare."

"That's not what I meant. Her file, I mean. It's the only one that was really wiped out."

"What's so funny about that?"

"All those maps, Miller. The ones you drew up to shade off the ground you covered looking for that dumb plow. One great big ink blotch now."

Josh crushed out his cigarette. "I thought of that already. It doesn't really make all that much difference. I can remember pretty well where I've been, and there aren't that many places left out there anyway. I would have sworn, you know, that the Station would have something like that. Now I guess I'll have to go out of state."

"So what else is new?"

"York, Jersey, Haven, London—"

"All right, all right." She emptied her glass and stifled a yawn with one finger to her lips. "So when are you leaving?"

"Beats me, Fel. Thames doesn't want me to rush it, so I have plenty of time. I'll take one more look through the woods up above the Murdoch place, then give up if I can't find anything. You might start making a few calls to Vermont, to that minister who found us the church a couple of years ago." He stopped. Said, "Damn," softly.

"It's okay," she told him, reaching over to cover his hand. "I remember his name."

He almost pulled back, not at her touch, but at the sympathy in her eyes. Then he scowled. "Nuts. Re-

mind me that Saturday is Mrs. Thames' birthday. I
forget that and I'm dead."

"Mine is the first."

"Huh?"

"Of July. July the first. Birthday. Can you make the
connection, Miller?"

He could, was fumbling for something to say to take
the awkwardness from the moment when, without
warning, she yawned again, broke into a laugh that set
her to choking. A waitress immediately came up
beside her, patting her back and offering her a glass of
water. Josh only stared helplessly, half out of his seat
with his hands pressed to the small table between
them. And when she was done, wiping her eyes and
sipping at the water, it was readily apparent the
evening was over.

He hovered about her solicitously, then, draping her
sweater over her shoulders and leading her down the
narrow staircase to the foyer below. She grumbled
over his concern but did not pull away, coughed into a
fist while he stood at the checkroom, chatting with
the woman there—Sandy McLeod's mother. As he
talked his gaze drifted, taking in the diningroom
immediately to his right. No booths here; captain's
tables and chairs, brighter lighting, more bustle and a
swifter turnover. From the larger back area he could
hear the small band playing contemporary music,
could hear laughter, and had turned around to Felicity
to ask her if she'd like a seat at the bar to listen for a
while when he saw a couple against the far wall.

A waitress blocked his vision for a moment, a
departing quintet swirling rudely around him until he
pushed through it to Felicity's side.

The man, though his back was to the entrance, was
Lloyd Stanworth. The woman, holding a silver compact to her face and dusting her cheeks, was Andrea.

"Miller, are you all right?"

He took Felicity's elbow and ushered her outside,

down the steps of the broad porch and into the parking lot. The flesh across his face was taut, his upper lip sucked between his teeth; an acid chill worked at his stomach, the aftertaste of the sherry bitter on his tongue.

"Miller?"

They were in the front seat before he turned to her, his breathing falling into a rhythm he could not feel. A hand cupped her chin, and she gasped softly. He would not permit himself the luxury of thought, could not rid himself of the image that made more lean Felicity's rounded face, darkened her eyes, lengthened her hair.

I love you, Joshua Miller.

"Miller, what's wrong?"

He leaned toward her, his left hand gripping the steering wheel. She tried to turn her head in his grasp, could not, frowned as he placed his lips to hers in a kiss not meant to be a gentle goodnight.

Keep your hands off Felicity.

He had never before believed himself capable of deliberate calculation, but when he started the engine and backed out of the lot he knew he had no intention of taking Felicity home. Not to hers. And she sensed it. She stared at his profile for several moments before shifting to face front, hands in her lap, twisting and scrubbing.

I love you.

So does Dad.

He pulled into the driveway and braked gently. Slid out and opened the passenger door. Felicity hesitated until he offered her his hand, eased her out, brought her to the porch where he released her to find his keys.

"Josh, I—"

With a hand at the small of her back he eased her inside, flicked on the foyer light and put his hands on her shoulders. Frowned when she refused to look at him.

"Fel."

She shook her head once, a tear skidding down her cheek untouched.

Bastard, he thought; there's no doubt about it, you're one hell of a bastard.

He slipped a hand down her arm, moving toward her waist. She slipped away and brushed a thumb under her eyes. Sniffed. Tried a smile and began crying silently again.

Bastard.

"Fel . . ."

There was nothing he could say that would take the hurt away, and he certainly couldn't tell her whom he had seen in the restaurant. Suddenly he felt gangly, awkward, clumsy, like a fool. He opened his mouth—a noise, any noise to cover the weeping—and she pointed behind him. He was groping for a wisecrack as he turned, the impulse dying, squashed like an ant beneath a sharp heel.

The study was a shambles. Most of his books had been dumped from their shelves, most of the cabinets opened and the files thrown about the room. Magazines had been leafed through and dropped along the floor randomly, his desk swept clear and pulled away from the window.

"It was locked," he said weakly. "Goddamnit, the door was locked!"

14

"Y ou've had enough, don't you think?"

He looked up from the couch with a frown that matched Felicity's, studiously ignored her then as he poured another glassful of bourbon.

"Miller, that isn't going to solve anything. And it sure as hell isn't going to get that room cleaned up."

"I"—he belched—"know that."

She threw up her hands in disgust, in frustration, and left the room. Moments later he could hear papers rustling angrily, books slamming back onto shelves. She doesn't know the system, he thought suddenly; she'll screw everything up. It'll be just as bad as it is now. But he didn't call her, didn't lift his head from the fringed throw pillow. It was too much of an effort, and as it was he could barely keep his eyes open. There was a buzzing behind them, and a throbbing at his temples, and when he emptied the glass in four great swallows he didn't taste a thing.

A scraping as the desk was shoved back into place.

Tanner, who had left not an hour ago, had stood by the window openmouthed and confused. The only thing he had said that Josh could remember was: "Boy, somebody doesn't like you very much, do they?" Big help. As if it were a revelation that con-

tained the clue they each needed to locate the culprit.
The neighbors sure as hell weren't any help. They
hadn't heard a thing, hadn't seen a car, hadn't noticed
anyone prowling around the house. They didn't talk
to him much anyway, not since his parents had left for
Colorado. They were their friends, not his. They
suspected he ran debaucheries and drug dens on
Saturday nights. No, they were no help at all. And
neither was Tanner.

"When you go through all this," he'd said, setting
his cap square on his head, "let me know if there's
anything missing. From the looks of it, though, I
doubt it. I think it's the same as the shop. Whoever it
was has been watching you, obviously waiting for you
to be gone." He'd waved a hand over the desolation.
"This didn't take long. Fifteen minutes tops, unless
they were looking for something. Like I said, I doubt
it. Nope. Just messing around, I think." His heavy
Maine accent grated on Josh's nerves. "You let me
know, hear? One way or the other. Maybe you ought
to change your locks, too." At the door he'd stopped
and looked back over his shoulder. "Small favors, Mr.
Miller. At least they didn't use paint this time."

He snorted, reached for the bottle on the floor
beside him, and scowled when he held it close to his
eyes and discovered it empty. He'd have to get into the
kitchen. He was thirsty. And his ears were picking up
sounds that he was sure didn't exist. He tried to lift
himself up and look back into the study to see what
Felicity was doing now, but a cramp lashed across the
back of his neck and he groaned, fell back, and closed
his eyes.

"Nice," he whispered. "That's nicc."

Who the hell . . . ?

Andrea sitting in the Chancellor Inn. Not supposed
to be back until tomorrow. *I love you*, she'd said.

"Miller?"

He had no idea what time it was. Somewhere close

either side of midnight. His eyes opened and Felicity was standing over him, slipping her arms into the sleeves of her cardigan.

"Miller?" The voice was soft. "I'm going home now. It's still bad in there, but at least you can walk around without breaking your neck." She leaned over and kissed his forehead, fire, and he flinched. "Don't bother to come in tomorrow, okay? You're going to wish you had a new head."

He managed a smile, and his hand fluttered over his stomach. She took it, held it, brought it to her cheek, and kissed the back.

"It isn't fair," he said hoarsely.

"I know."

"I ain't . . . what did I do?"

She shook her head and he couldn't watch it. Closed his eyes again and listened to the thunder of her leaving, the cruel snap of the lock, the silence of the house. He swallowed heavily and rolled onto his side. There was another bottle in the kitchen; he was sure of it. A few minutes' rest and he would search for it. He was thirsty. A drink would clear his throat and clear his head and he would be able to figure out quick as a bunny just why someone was out to make a shambles of his business. Shambles. He grinned sleepily. A curious word, that was. And a curious business. Miller's Mysteries. How was tossing papers on a floor, paint on papers, going to keep him from working? It didn't make sense. It simply did not make any sense.

He belched.

And what the hell was Andy trying to prove? That didn't make sense, either. Being seen out in public like that, only a week after Lloyd's wife had just about accused them of having an affair—it wasn't reasonable. But they were there, no question about it. It wasn't his eyes. He could see perfectly well. He opened them to prove it, groaned, and closed them a third time. They were there, sitting back by the wall with a drink in front of them. No plates, something told him, so they had probably just arrived. What in hell was she trying to prove?

It wasn't fair. He had rushed back from New York and had discovered that nothing was what it was when he'd left. Andy sure wasn't. She was lying to him and they weren't even planning on getting married.

Not yet, anyway. And definitely not now.

She must have a reason. She had to have a reason. She would call him and tell him and there would be a perfectly good reason. Of course there would be. There had to be. She couldn't have expected that no one would have seen them and not reported it to him one way or another. If nothing else, Pete Lee would have said something.

It wasn't fair, damnit. It just—he hiccoughed— wasn't fair.

Felicity had been right. When the sun glared around the edges of the shades he felt as though every straight pin he had ever lost had been rediscovered around the rims of his eyes. He lay quietly, breathing open-mouthed as slowly as he could, his right hand dangling over the side of the couch and gripping the fringe below. He tried, when he was able, to move as gently as he could, finally rousing himself upstairs and into the shower. There was no sense in admonition; he had done it, was paying, and claimed a small victory when he made his way through breakfast without gagging. Then he called the police station, but Tanner was not yet in, no news handy the desk sergeant could give him. A call to Felicity got him a mild scolding during which he gave his permission for her to hire a temporary to help put the files back in order. But he stopped dialing Andrea's number halfway through. That, he decided grimly, would be a personal confrontation.

She was waiting for him on the front porch.

White shirt and jeans, fringed high boots, her hair pulled back loosely and bunned at the nape. He

parked behind her car in the drive and sat for a
moment, tempted to play the outraged lover one
moment, thinking it best to feign ignorance the next.
Finally, he slid out and sat next to her on the steps. A
produce truck he judged at least thirty years old
jounced past from one of the orchards, dust lifting
behind it lazy and brown. They watched until it was
out of sight . . . close, but not touching.

"Well?" she said. "Aren't you going to say anything?"

"I saw you last night, at the inn." He did not look at
her; he didn't dare.

"I . . . I came back early."

"So I gathered."

"He called me, Josh." No apology, direct or im-
plied. "He wanted to talk to me before his wife did."

He nodded, slowly. "I think," he said, "I'm going to
feel stupid."

A pause. In the front yard a jay marched across the
newly mown grass, jabbing at the ground and hawking
to itself. Josh shifted his feet noisily and it bolted into
the nearest tree, shrieking. Sure, he thought at it; easy
for you to say.

"You were jealous."

He sidled along the step until he could turn and lean
back against a squared white post. His arms folded
over his chest. "Yes, I think so."

Furrows worked their way over her forehead, the
bridge of her nose; a faint blush highlighted her
cheeks. He wondered if she were angry or flattered,
and decided his head was still too delicately balanced
for him to give much to such a chancy contemplation.

"I understand you know Randy," she said, pushing
at wisps that feathered over her temple. "It seems she
told Lloyd he and I were seeing each other on the sly."
Her smile was sad. "I know she told you. Lloyd said
she had. He wanted to know . . . he wanted to make
sure I understood about Randy, how she is with him. I
guess . . . I guess he doesn't want me upset." She

glanced up at the trees, the hard blue of the sky. "You didn't say anything about it."

"I couldn't." His voice cracked and he cleared his throat impatiently. "It was the day I got back from the city. You were gone. I didn't know that. I didn't get your letter until the other day."

The silence this time was filled with the distant horn of a train. He waited until the valley had swallowed it before bringing up a leg and cupping his hands around it. "How did the deal work out?"

"Fine," she said, and looked at him suddenly. "Josh, are we going to have a fight?"

He almost told her no, realized that in fact he wasn't sure at all. Thus far they had spoken as though they were strangers, each of them sitting on a stranger's porch and waiting for someone to come along and chase them. It would have been better had it been raining; then there would have been an excuse for their company.

On the other hand . . . on the other hand he could not believe she was lying to him. In writing, in her actual handwriting she had told him she loved him; she couldn't be so stupid, then, as to flaunt Stanworth at him. Not like that. That, he thought bitterly, was something he himself would do (and winced when he remembered what he would have done to Fel).

She moved closer—still not touching though her touch was there—and examined his face until he had to smile.

"I had a bad night," he said, lifting an eyebrow in a shrug. "I'm better, but I still feel like I should be close to dying."

"You . . . you got drunk?"

"Don't look so surprised. It happens." When her eyes doubted, he explained the intrusions on his office and home as best he could, struggling with speculations and failing as badly as he had done before.

"Oh." She glanced back at the screened front door, to his face with a disappointed sigh. "And then you saw me and Lloyd and you decided it would be a good thing to . . . whatever."

"I told you it was stupid." He didn't, however, tell her about Felicity. Even now he wasn't sure he could look his new partner in the eyes.

"And you came out here . . . ?"

He shrugged, lowered his leg. "I don't know." He tried to smile. "Looking for a dumb plow."

He didn't think she would accept the unspoken apology, was inordinately grateful when she grinned back at him and stood, offering him her hands to help him to his feet. "Where do we begin?"

"The only place I haven't looked yet is up there," he said, pointing toward a hill to the left of the house. "I was saving it for last because as far as I can tell from town records there hasn't been a house there since Oxrun was founded."

"Well, there's only one way to find out, right?"

He started after her, feeling as if a concrete slab had been hoisted from his chest. Then, suddenly, he stopped. "Wait, Andy! I'd like to say hello to Don before we go."

She paused only a moment at the corner of the house. "Later. He's working."

"Counting his money?"

"He never counts anything until the contract is signed."

They hurried across the backyard to a split-rail fence. Andrea suddenly broke into a run and vaulted it; Josh didn't think his condition was stable enough to show off just yet so he strolled as casually as he could to one corner and used the post to lift him up and over.

Beyond was the small field that belonged to the farm, covered now with a haze of green weeds and stray grasses. He seemed to recall that the previous owners, like the others in the valley, raised small crops of vegetables that were trucked to the village, to Harley, as far east as Hartford. Nothing specific came to mind, however, and he spent the next fifteen minutes trying to decipher the remains he passed over. Lettuce, perhaps, or cabbage. Carrots, beets . . . he gave up as the sun made him shed his service jacket, and he hooked a finger at the collar and hung it over one shoulder.

He hadn't intended at all to hunt for Mrs. Thames' plow, but the words had escaped him unbidden, unthinkingly. Not that he minded, once Andrea had made up his mind; there was nothing else he could do except keep on looking, and reporting to the old woman that he would have to go out of state. He smiled to himself. That might not be so bad if Andrea would go with him.

The slope began, the walking more difficult. And once in the trees the temperature dropped under the mint haze of new green. He put the jacket on again and tried to keep up with Andrea, calling out once to tell her she was too quick.

"Nope," she said, turning around but still moving. "I walk in here all the time. I would have seen something, even if I didn't know what it was I was seeing. We'll have to go higher. Over there," and she pointed to the right.

He shook his head and angled in the opposite direction. He had already covered most of that ground, refused to change his mind when she tried to insist. "Hey," he told her, "who's the boss around here?"

"Fel's back in the office," she said laughing, and he snatched up a stone and winged it toward her legs.

An hour later he slumped to the hard comfort of a wide and flat boulder. He was perspiring freely, his shirt clinging soddenly to his chest, the slippage into his shoes uncomfortable and clammy. He draped the jacket over the top of the rock, put his hands on his hips, and bent over at the waist. Andrea scrambled to his side, one hand on his shoulder.

"You okay?"

"Hung over and paying for every damned moment."

"Maybe we should go back."

He straightened and surveyed the level ground they had reached. Below, the slope was packed with woodland, though he knew that in autumn the farmhouse would be visible without any trouble. Above, the slope steepened and the trees grew closer together, the few large gaps filled with boulders such as the one that supported him. He tried to imagine, then, how these hills had been when they had been young—jagged, rugged, much like the Rockies, trembling with latent volcanic activity. Vibrant. Alive. Growing old and wearing down like the teeth of a giant who had lived past his prime.

"Sometimes," he said quietly, because the forest demanded it, "sometimes when I'm up here I can hear the Indians still moving around. Before the Puritans and Separatists came along and gave them religion." He spat at the ground. "Not to mention guns and smallpox."

Andrea rubbed her arms as though chilled. "It's too far away from civilization to suit me."

Josh laughed. "What? All you have to do is roll back down the hill."

"It's spooky."

"It's the middle of the day, for god's sake."

She took the space next to him and leaned her head on his shoulder. "I still think we're going in the wrong direction."

"And I'm still the Natty Bumppo around here."

"Christ," she said to the air, "he's literary, too."

"Come on." He took her hand and pulled her around the boulder, moving left along the flatland. Stopping five minutes later to point at a hickory, and a smaller tree beside it. "That's a wolf tree," he said. "It takes up most of the sun, most of the water, and anything that grows next to it is stunted."

"Interesting." She sounded bored.

"You will also notice, O person who wanted to hunt plows with me only a few weeks ago, that the trees here are younger than the ones higher up and those down there. That could mean—"

"A fire," she said. "A lousy forest fire."

"Or a clearing that's grown over."

"How can you tell just by looking?"

"Practice." He grinned, then, as he started forward again. "And luck. Half the time, love, I don't know what I'm talking about." He had gone a dozen paces before he realized she wasn't following. "Hey."

"Damnit, Josh, I'm tired. And I'm hungry. I haven't had lunch yet."

He started back, stopped and shook his head. "You'll never make it in the big time, Andy. Wait here a moment. Give me a hundred yards or so and I'll know for sure what's going on."

She frowned, but nodded reluctantly, sank to the ground where she stood, and cupped her hands under her chin. He waved, blew her a kiss, and skirted a patch of briar. Almost immediately he could feel the solitude, the weight of the old hills, lifting his face to a stray breeze as though he were scenting.

The underbrush cleared slightly and walking was easier; and he wasn't aware of how long his stride had become until he glanced back over his shoulder and could no longer see Andy. He hesitated, thinking this was no time to tempt her anger, not now when he had managed to lose his own suspicion. Another ten yards; that would be it. And he was about to turn back when he came to a rough clearing spiked with dry and dead weeds that reached almost to his waist.

He had turned to call out when he saw the charred, grey stump half buried by a struggling, spindly shrub. Lightning. A bolt had struck here, a fire had started, the storm had doused it before it had gotten very far.

"Ah . . . damn!" More in disgust than anger, realizing how such a small thing had stirred hopes, and had crushed them. But he walked across the clearing just

to be sure, had started back when he saw another odd
shape woven over by weeds. He would not allow
himself a thought, a reaction; he knelt beside it and
tugged at the stringy stalks until he could see beneath
them.

"Andrea!"

It was a headstone, cracked across its base and
spilled back onto a rock beneath. Heedless of thorns,
Josh clawed the rest of the covering away and wiped at
the stone with his palm.

"Andrea!"

He peered at it closely, his nose almost touching,
but could find no grooves, no indications that anything had been carved into it, much less a name, a
date, one of the pious epitaphs that were part of the
markings. He pushed back to his heels. Thought.
Glanced around him and saw now there were others.
He had bent to clean another when he looked up and
spotted a double row of them at the back of the
clearing.

"Andrea, damnit!"

Unbelievable, he thought as he ran to them, forgetting his disappointment. Stopped and caught his
breath, less from the exertion than from the rush of
excitement. Nine. He counted nine. Low grey stones
he guessed were neither marble nor granite, but culled
from the hillside itself as the need arose. Brambles and
tangled grasses swept over the gravesites, wildflowers
holding close to the four in front. He reached out
cautiously, almost fearfully, and touched one, looked
back to the others toppled from their notches, and
frowned. Puzzled. Suddenly stepped back when he
realized he was standing directly on a grave.

"Josh?"

"Andrea," he said without turning around,
"damnit, come look at this! My god, it's fantastic!
There isn't a church in town that knows about these,
and there's not even anything in the Hall, either. I
can't believe it. It's incredible."

"It's only a little graveyard."

He smiled tolerantly. "Darlin', there's no such animal as 'only a graveyard' in New England. Every damned one of them is some sort of historical monument, and most of them—in places like this that have been around for centuries—can tell you more about a place than the existing records, sometimes."

"Josh?" Whispersoft, pleading.

He spun around and saw her at the clearing's far edge, hugging herself and wide-eyed. "Hey . . . hey . . . it's all right, Andy."

He crossed over to her and embraced her, felt a hard trembling nearly break her away. "Hey, it's all right," he said, his lips pressed to her hair.

A moment, a minute, five, and finally she shook herself vigorously and leaned away without breaking his hold. Her smile was embarrassed.

"You afraid of ghosts?"

"No. It just . . . I mean, all this time it was right out here and I never knew it."

"And you wanted to go the other way," he scoffed gently. "You must learn to listen to the Great White Hunter," and he brushed a hand slowly through his hair. Hesitated. Kissed her. Felt her teeth, her tongue, her lips working against his. Feverishly, then, and sagging until he had no choice but to drop with her to the ground. Wanting to protest and wanting to take her, staring up at her as she straddled his waist and tugged at his belt, pulled apart his shirt and began working on her own.

"Andy—"

"Shut up," she said, virtually hissing. She rose and stripped off her jeans, shadows of the foliage rippling over her gleaming breasts, her shoulders, masking her eyes narrowed and glaring. "Shut up," she repeated, softly this time. "Shut up, Miller, and do what you're told."

15

A centipede scurried from beneath the headstone and into a tangle of white-blond. It paused, drew in on itself, extended, moved on. Josh's scalp twitched, and the insect broke onto his forehead. Paused again. Moved slowly down toward one eye until a hand swept up and over and Josh jerked to a sitting position, shuddering, hugging himself against a sudden cool wind that set the trees to soughing, the weeds husking to themselves in soft straw laughter.

He looked down and saw the centipede vanish into the canopy of grass. It took him a moment to realize what it was, another before he felt as though his skin were covered with miniscule creatures searching for ways to burrow to his blood. Immediately, his hands began brushing across his arms, his chest, tugging hard through his hair while he prayed he would not feel something move beneath his palm. Slowly, then, he drew on his clothes. There was no sense in looking for Andrea; he knew she was gone. The clearing felt empty, and he seemed to remember a pair of lips against his ear, a whispering, a telling: *Dad will miss me I have to go.* Of course, it could have been a dream, just as the way she had forced him back onto the headstone had to have been a dream. He groaned, and rubbed at stiff muscles beside his neck. A dream was the only way to explain what the woman had done.

With legs spread to keep his balance he buttoned his shirt. The jacket, lying at his feet, seemed a long way down and he waited until he was sure he wouldn't lose his balance before reaching for it. Groaned again, and winced at the tracks of scratches that pulled on his back. Hell, he thought, not knowing if they were the result of the rough stones or her nails. Hell.

They had coupled swiftly and without speaking that first time, a second lovemaking that began immediately the first was done. Neither time did she give him endearments, and so taken was he by the ferocity of her strength and the intensity of her concentration that he gave her none, could not remember even thinking any. There had been moments when he'd thought himself engaged in wrestling bouts, others when he cried out almost savagely because it seemed the only way to force release of the pressures that welled within him like the approach of the tide.

Cried out. Struggled. Sank when it was done into a stupor that eventually sidled into sleep.

An owl questioned. Josh shook his head, vigorously and once, and glanced about him, closing his eyes tightly and snapping them open to clear his vision.

No. No dream.

The graves were still back there, and still curiously blank.

He took a hesitant step toward them before he realized he was squinting. An upward glance, and the foliage above had locked into a grey haze punctuated by black. He frowned, and stared at his watch. Slapped at his wrist when he saw the timepiece had stopped just after four. By the sky, then: it was near dark, and he must have been asleep (or unconscious) for nearly . . . "God . . . damn."

The graves would have to wait.

He swung around and made his way into the trees, one hand out to fend off twilight's traps. The other remained at his stomach, massaging it absently as he considered the episode he had somehow managed to survive.

Survive; he frowned again, this time at his mind's choice of words. It wasn't as if his life were in danger. And he had certainly not been exposed to any predators while he'd slept. Yet the word persisted: survive. Survive. But it wasn't, he insisted to himself (and whatever audience might be listening to his thoughts), he who had been the aggressor, not by a long shot. And it hadn't been his fears . . . he smiled. A fragment of a reading, or of a half-heard conversation: that fear can often be among the most powerful of aphrodisiacs. The smile to a laugh contained in his throat. If it had been theory before, he knew it now to be fact—Andrea, when she entered the clearing and saw what he had found, had been frightened. It wasn't unusual; there were lots of people who wanted nothing to do with death, not even in those places where death was memorialized. She had clung to him, had felt his comfort, and that had triggered her escape into a haven.

He was grinning now. And the discomfort he had been experiencing over performing the sex act in a cemetery was replaced by a sense of delicious absurdity. It was, he thought, something straight out of those murky Italian films of the nineteen-fifties— symbolism rampant, and a taste for the ludicrous that, by its very severity, was to him equally funny.

He stumbled into a bush, pushed himself out, and reminded his legs that he was no giant, reminded himself that in the half-dark of the forest he was increasingly vulnerable to a broken neck unless he got himself out and back down to the house.

The owl a second time, and the wind's soughing had grown to a keening goad.

In less than an hour, with only one mistaken turn, he broke from the treeline. Twilight had deepened to dusk, the sky black directly above and deep purple around the tops of the hills. A few lights broke the hazy curtain across the valley, but none in the farmhouse at the other end of the field. He forced himself to move slowly, mindful of ruts, of burrows, of tangled fallen branches; he jammed his hands into his jacket pockets, a feeble attempt to stave off the chill that had come with the dark.

Halfway to the fence, he stopped. Andrea's face shimmered before him, faded, but not before he saw the ferocity in her eyes as she lowered herself onto him. It made him nervous. Perhaps it would be better if he avoided her tonight. Though she'd used the excuse of her father to leave him alone in the clearing, it made more sense that she was suddenly embarrassed at what she . . . what they had done. To remind her so abruptly could be an error not as easily retrieved as others he had committed. Besides, he wasn't so sure he would be able to face her, either. Not without blurting out his love in front of her father. And that, he knew, was hardly what Don had intended to promote that day in his office.

He increased his pace, then, kicking as much as walking through the softly damp grass, angling away from the homestead until he had reached the road. Climbed over the bordering fence and walked the rough verge to the drive. And stopped.

The Buick had been taken from its place behind the MG and parked on the shoulder. A quick check through the open window, and he found the keys resting on the slightly lowered visor above the steering wheel. A melancholy grin. Andrea had indeed been thinking as he had, and putting the car by the road would allow him to drive off with disturbance at a minimum.

Mother, he thought as he slid in and fired the ignition, if you thought my life was sinful before . . .

He rolled up the window and released the shuddering that had been building since he'd wakened.

Slapped on the heater and let his teeth chatter. June it was, but it felt more like October, and he wondered when the warm weather would begin.

Slowly he pulled out onto the pitted blacktop. He did not dare speed now; despite the punch of the headlights before him, too many of the potholes gaped unexpectedly, jarring the springs (and his spine) to the point where he was moving no faster than he could walk during daylight. Muttering, then, to himself and the car, he eased along the spur, the window rolled up, the heater's fan ominously grinding.

He would call Andrea in the morning, he decided. He would return to the farm and see Don, see her, try to assure her he wasn't at all put off by what had happened. He would make her laugh, see the humor in it as he did, and she would, if he were lucky, love him even more than she had.

And he had just about relaxed when the left front tire dipped hard into a wide depression, and came out flat.

"Shit!" He slapped open the door and stood in the road, glaring at the hiss of air that joined the wind. His hair whipped into his eyes and he brushed it away angrily. Kicked at the hubcap and walked back to the trunk. Ten minutes later he was swearing again: the spare was flat, too.

"You," he said to the car, "are getting to be one pain in the ass."

He looked toward the village and shook his head. There was nothing for it but he would have to walk back to the house and beg either a lift into town or a telephone call. This was not the way things were supposed to happen; he had already constructed the scenario for tomorrow, and flat tires were not a part of it. With hands back in his pockets, then, the door locked and slammed shut, he trudged to the shoulder and began walking. Tripped several times over fallen rails, over sudden gouges in the earth, over rocks that had no business suddenly jumping in front of him.

The wind was giving him an earache. His stomach was telling him it was tired of going so long without food. The tiny cuts on his back were stinging. He zippered his jacket closed, and caught a fold of neckskin that made him yelp, made him stop for several seconds and take a deep breath to calm his bucking temper.

The night turned black.

Behind him a handful of streetlamps coldly marked the length of Cross Valley; ahead, however, there were only the winking sparks of windowlights which were little more than useless mirrors of the early evening stars.

He slowed even more. His right hand he kept slightly extended to brush against the fencing, to grip a railing when the sudden rush of a bat startled him into ducking. A nightbird whistled, another sighed. The wind through the grass, like a serpent in slow pursuit, took its confident time before it rose up and struck, and the flesh between his shoulders tightened in anticipation.

By the time he reached the Murdochs' drive he was as out of breath as if he had been running. The skittering crunch of his heels on the gravel was a welcome, grating noise—too often he had lowered a foot into the grass . . . and heard nothing, felt nothing, was sure he would fall.

As intent as he was on reaching the porch he didn't notice the MG until it was almost too late. A muffled curse and a sidestep, and he backed toward the steps with one fist brandished. Turned, still walking, with the unpleasant notion that perhaps his jittery nerves were trying to tell him something.

The screen door was unlocked. He pushed it inward, wincing at the quick shriek, closed it with both hands so it wouldn't protest again. Though the air here was no less chilled than it was outside, he felt a warm relief, and smiled. Rolling his shoulders to disperse the tension, rubbing his hands briskly to bring the blood back. Then he strode to the front door and raised his hand to knock, hesitated and cocked his head birdlike when he heard voices inside—high-pitched, arguing, a monotone of invective unintelligible through the thick wood.

This he didn't need. Bad enough he had probably given Andrea a frightful dose of shame; now he was walking in on what sounded like a major family battle.

Check, he cautioned; maybe it's only the television.

As quietly as he could, then, he walked to his right. The livingroom windows were shaded, no lights behind them. Around the side of the house to the kitchen, a rectangle of diffused yellow on the floorboards reminding him all too clearly of the graves he had found. He edged along the wall, feeling immensely foolish, and listened for a moment before easing into a crouch.

The kitchen was huge, haphazardly modernized as though the money invested there had finally run out. He was looking at a narrow slice that ran directly across the linoleum floor to a doorway opposite he knew led to the central hallway. On the immediate left was the bulk of a copper-and-gold refrigerator, on the right a corner hutch that held battered ironstone dishes and Don's supply of liquor. Against the far wall, by the doorway, was another cabinet, this one glass-fronted and holding delicately designed china and a few pieces of never-used crystal.

The woodframe screen had not yet been set in place here, and he leaned as close to the pane as he could, inching to his right to bring the battlers into view. But all he could see was the back end of the butcher-block table, and an overturned chair. He scowled and made to rise, froze when Don suddenly backed into the china closet, rebounded, and grabbed hold of the doorway jamb.

Josh ducked quickly, took a long steadying breath before returning to his place—and there was no thought at all of rapping on the glass.

Murdoch seemed to have lost a great deal of weight.

Jowls had worked their way out of the folds of his neck, and his cheeks were hollowed as though he'd been ill. His hair was unkempt, and though it might have been the light it seemed to Josh that grey had taken root through the mass of tumbled curls. He had not shaved for several days, and his white shirt was stained front and side with perspiration and spilled food. His trousers were baggy, beltless, the fastening button undone, and he kept one hand flat against his abdomen to keep them from falling. The other was held out, palm up, fingers crooked in pleading.

Josh watched his eyes, followed their tracking of someone else in the room.

Whoever it was seemed to advance, then retreat, was obviously pacing furiously across the floor.

Murdoch shook his head. Josh immediately rose and flattened against the wall, leaning forward to press his ear against the glass above the half-lowered shade.

"Don't say that!" Murdoch begged, his voice near to cracking. "You can't and you know it!"

A muffled response—the shrilling he had heard from beyond the front door.

"No," Murdoch said wearily. "No."

He heard one word: ". . . told . . ."

Murdoch seemed to be recovering. "That I did not. I won't deny the other, but that I did not. I'm not so big a fool as that."

Josh stiffened. A shadow blocked part of the light, grew, and someone stood directly in front of the window. The outline on the shade was vague, unformed, but below he could see a white gown, and sleeves that ended at the elbow. An arm. An arm so old, so veined, so pocked with brown it could be either a man's or a woman's. The hand that now pressed against the lower pane was thin, fingers like talons, knuckles large as though swollen with arthritis. He had no time to ask himself the question; the hand spasmed and swept from his sight.

"You're headstrong is what your problem is." It was a woman's voice. Not cracked with age, but solemn and breathless with years. A strong voice nonetheless, and one not accustomed to brooking disobedience. The shrill was gone. Josh sensed a kind of weary peace descending. "You could have ruined it. If you had gone out there, you would have ruined it."

"I'm a writer." Not bragging. A tentative statement of fact. "I could have thought of something."

"No, you couldn't."

"I was concerned."

A single explosive laugh. "I'll bet you were. Now you understand this, Donald, and you had better learn it well because I have no more patience with you. Not any longer."

Sullenly: "I'm listening."

"And you will be respectful! If nothing else around here, you *will* be respectful."

Josh slipped a foot along the floorboard, away from the window. He kept his eyes straight ahead, staring at the dimly grey patch of screen that held back the night. A moth had landed there and was fluttering weakly, several other insects winged and crawling swarming about it without coming near. He swallowed, while his hands gripped his jeans at his thighs. The effort to keep his mind from being overwhelmed with questions raising cords at his neck, breaking perspiration across his forehead.

Three, he finally thought; there were three in the farmhouse, not Andrea and Don only. And if there were three, were there more?

He shook his head violently, cracked it against the wall, and froze, eyes closed, waiting for the rage of discovery. When it did not come he released the breath he hadn't realized he was holding, and swallowed again.

The woman's shadow shortened slightly.

"I will impress upon you again the need to keep hold," she said, her voice lifting toward a shout. "I

don't know how many times I have to do this, you
should know it by now."

"Damnit, woman, I do!" Murdoch bellowed.

"Then damnit, why do you insist on making mistakes? My god, you've almost got it, right there in the
palm of your hand you've almost got it." She quieted.
". . . time left, Donald . . . insist on care . . . will
happen to Andrea, huh? What will happen to
Andrea?"

Josh stepped away from the wall, gaping at the
window.

And sneezed.

16

Josh felt the sneeze coming and clamped his hands over his nose, spun around in a crouch just as the explosion surfaced. Once done, he wasted no time waiting to see if he had been discovered. As silently as he could he hurried around the corner to the front door, pulled the iron ring away from the sculpted lion's head and released it. Inside, a series of chimes sounded melodiously, and within seconds he heard the rattle of the knob.

"Josh, my god it's good to see you!"

Don took hold of his arm and guided him swiftly over the threshold.

"I am honest to god sorry we didn't connect in New York. If I'd known you were there we could have gotten together for a drink." Into the livingroom, cramped as always with furniture Spanish, bulky, and completely out of place in the century-old building. "But that's Andrea for you, isn't it. She's worse than a mother sometimes, I swear to Christ. Sometimes I think she wants me to wear diapers because she doesn't think I can even go to the john myself." Into a couch and drink pressed into his hand. "Jesus, man, it's after eight already. What are you doing out here this late? Hey. Hey, don't tell me you're going to pop the question to my little girl." A pose by the fireplace:

elbow on the mantelpiece, tall glass in his free hand. He was as rumpled as Josh had seen him through the window, but all trace of his fear, and of his sullen rebellion, were gone. Only the eyes betrayed a nervousness Josh was in no way inclined to pacify. "I was only kidding about the proposal, Josh, you don't have to be so dumbstruck. I know about you bachelors, you know. You like the free life. No strings. Few responsibilities. Get a little when you feel like it, live like a goddamned monk when you don't. Well, for god's sake, drink up, drink up. You'll make me feel like a lush."

Josh listened patiently while, at the same time, he let his gaze rove from the doorway into the kitchen to the dark shadows of the entryhall and the first three steps he could see through the banister. He wasn't sure if he'd been lucky enough to have gone unheard out on the porch, had decided as soon as he entered the house that he would say nothing about the old woman. If Don was going to lie to him—or at least present him with the absence of truth—it would serve his case better . . . though he was still uncertain exactly what his case was. After all, despite the degrees of intimacy he'd had with both father and daughter, he still did not know very much about them. Don was always too busy posturing to let the past escape, and Andrea . . . just never brought it up, and he had never asked.

He sipped the scotch and smiled, hoped that new contract and the implication of greater monies would bring a better brand into the house.

"Well," Don said, shifting a brass andiron with his foot, "you still haven't told me why you're here. You want Andrea?" Without waiting for an answer he called his daughter's name twice. "She said she was going to take a shower. What the hell. So?"

"So," Josh said, "my car had a flat, the spare's flat, and I need to call for a tow."

"I'll be damned."

He shrugged. "Lousy luck, that's all."

Murdoch took a long drink, the ice cubes clicking against his teeth. When he'd swallowed, and choked, he wiped his eyes with the back of a hand. "You were out there, then."

"Yep. Looking for that plow."

"You didn't find it."

"Andy didn't tell you?"

Murdoch shook his head, but not before he glanced toward the staircase.

"Didn't find a thing." Josh waited, but there was no reaction.

"Right, not a thing, and don't get up."

Andrea stood on the bottom step, dressed as he had seen her in the woods. She was pulling a brush through glistening damp hair, wincing at a snag as she stepped to the floor and entered the room. Josh stared at her impassively, saw Murdoch turn away. And immediately he did, Andrea shook her head quickly and mouthed *superstitious*, breaking into a grin when her father turned back.

"Hell of a quick shower."

"Not much hot water left," she said, dropping onto the couch beside Josh and taking his hand.

"You take so damned many of them you're going to turn into a goddamned prune."

"Dad, please . . ."

"Josh, here," Murdoch said—and paused to empty his glass—"Josh had a flat out on the road. Two flats," he added, and Josh nodded confirmation. "He needs a tow."

Andrea was on her feet immediately. "I'll call," she said, and was into the kitchen before either of them could object.

Josh shrugged and grinned; Murdoch moved away from the hearth and stood in the middle of the room, absently booting aside a low stack of magazines.

"Josh, how good are you at keeping secrets?"

Suddenly wary, he waited a moment before nodding. "Good as most, I suppose. No." He smiled. "Better. In my business you have to be, or you lose customers, not to mention friends."

"I imagine." Murdoch walked quickly to the kitchen doorway and listened, nodded to himself, and returned to the hearth. This time he abandoned his posing to lean against the brick that covered most of the wall. "It's about Andrea."

Josh kept his mind a blank.

"Her birthday," Murdoch said. "You know it's next month?"

"She never said anything to me."

"Well, it is. On the dumbest day of the year."

Josh frowned. "Jesus . . . the Fourth of July?"

Murdoch pointed at him. "You got it, Josh. An Independence baby is what she's been called all her life. I guess that's what makes her so bloody independent." He laughed shortly, pushed a hand through his hair, hard over his face. "I don't know what to get her."

"That's a secret?"

"No." He reached behind him and switched on the lights, and the glow from the kitchen fell back over its threshold. His face was pale, made sickly by the contrasting black of his hair and straggly growth of beard. "The secret . . . you want to marry Andrea, don't you."

Josh lowered his glass to the coffee table and clasped his hands over his knees. "It's crossed my mind, Don, I have to admit it. But I've not made it up completely, if that's what you want to know."

"I never thought it," Murdoch said softly.

He felt a rush of warmth at his cheeks. "It was your idea, if you remember. You're the one who came into my office and practically begged me to take her out."

"I know, I know." He lifted his glass and saw it was empty, scowled, and reached to the sideboard for the bottle he left there. He didn't bother to measure; he poured until the scotch reached the rim and sloshed over. "I like you, Josh, you know."

"Thanks, Don. I think."

"No, no, I mean it. That's why I don't want you to marry her."

Josh felt as if someone had stirred a gel into the air, thickened it, made it more difficult to breathe. And to think he had once accused Felicity of living in a soap opera. "Obviously, I don't get it," he said, his voice neutral. "Why not? Does she have some sort of strange disease?" He had meant it as a joke; he did not expect Murdoch to stumble, though he hadn't even moved, his hands out to catch the spilling glass before it shattered on the hearth. "Don?"

"She's very much like her mother, you know. The two of them—like peas in a pod."

"You told me her mother was dead."

The man looked at him as if he didn't comprehend; then he nodded, slowly. "I did, didn't I." He turned and walked to the kitchen. "Andy, you dead in there?"

"Fixing some snacks," she called back. "Just don't get him drunk before I get back."

His laugh was strained, but he seemed inordinately relieved. "I did say that, didn't I."

"Well, either she is or she isn't." He waited a moment. "I take it she isn't."

Murdoch looked pointedly at the side window. Josh knew what he was indicating and, after a moment's thought—in for a penny, in for a pound—he nodded. "Hell."

Josh did not need to ask if that was the secret. Whether it was or not was now beside the point, apparently. He had stumbled onto something he would have learned sooner or later, and he could not decide how outraged, how righteously furious, how hurt he should feel. Curiously, he felt nothing at all. Not now. Not even pity for the life the man had been leading, or sympathy for his plight, or protection toward Andrea for the bizarre situation she was in. He felt nothing. He only waited. He needed more facts before he could get up and walk out.

Andrea returned, smiling brightly and chattering, setting down a tray laden with sliced cheese and crackers. Murdoch smiled at her, Josh tried to grin, and realized abruptly he was living a movie: the isolated New England house, the eccentric family, the parries and thrusts of ordinary conversation that the hero or heroine discovers has several layers of meaning. And most importantly—the relative kept locked away in the attic: batty old aunt, murderer brother, mother, sister . . . straight out of Lovecraft by way of the Misses Brontë. One day . . . one night . . . the prisoner escapes and terrorizes the countryside, the peasants band together and burn the house down. The father dies bravely, and the daughter cleaves to the hero and lives happily ever after. No mention of nightmares. No mention of dying.

He held his glass against his cheek to stop his imagination, saw that Murdoch had been watching him and had guessed what he was thinking. He nodded solemnly, with a tilt of his head sadly toward his daughter.

Anything else, Josh thought then; had the man done anything else but that, he might have believed him.

And since that was the case, who was—

"—said he would be out in thirty minutes, Josh."

"Huh?"

Andrea poked his arm playfully. "Where were you? Still hunting for that plow?" With her face away from her father's gaze she winked at him broadly, and he couldn't help but smile. "I said, the truck will be out in . . ." She checked her watch. "About fifteen minutes, now. When I called he said thirty. That was fifteen minutes ago so—"

He took hold of her hand and squeezed it. Then he

looked to Murdoch, who was staring at the charred logs. "Look," he said, "it seems like I've come at a bad time."

They protested, but he overrode them. "Come on, I'm not blind. And I'm not deaf. When I came up to the door I could hear your . . . discussion. Now you're both as jumpy as cats, and I'm not helping by sitting here and staring." He rose, though he did not release her hand. "And if that guy's going to be here soon, I'd better start walking so I'll be there to watch him."

Murdoch said nothing, only lifted his glass as Josh pulled Andrea with him onto the porch.

"Josh, what did you hear, for crying out loud?"

"Nothing," he said. "But it was sure loud enough that I knew you weren't telling each other how much you loved each other."

"I see."

And he wondered if she knew the depth of his lying.

"Josh?"

That tone again. He braced himself.

"I told him I wanted to marry you." She flung open the screen door and hurried down the steps. He followed a moment later and caught up with her by her car. Took her shoulders and turned her around. She was crying. "I . . . I didn't want to leave you out there, but I didn't want him to come looking. It was bad enough . . ." She managed a smile he returned earnestly, quickly. "I mean, if he'd found us . . . that way, he would have had the shotgun out in a minute. And in a graveyard, yet. God, Josh, you don't know what it's like, living with a man who tosses salt over his shoulder, won't cross a shadow, hates black cats and dark moons, and counts all the glasses every time he breaks one just to be sure there aren't thirteen left in the cupboard. Crazy. I love him. If he knew there were those things out there he'd pack up and leave and I'd never see you again and god Joshua why the hell is this so damned crazy?"

She collapsed into his arms, sobbing against his

chest until there were no tears left to shed. And when she was done, drying her face against his jacket, she looked up again.

"I . . . he knows we were out there, of course. I had to tell him that much. Then I said . . . well, it took me a long time to get up the nerve and I don't want you to be mad at me, but I said to him that I wanted to marry you and I thought you would probably feel the same way. You do, don't you? Feel that way, I mean? Jesus, I'm so goddamned stupid . . ."

"That's what you were fighting about?"

She hesitated, touched his cheek, and nodded.

Her head rested against his shoulder, his head against her hair. "When you were in the kitchen," he said softly, as though the night were eavesdropping, "he told me your mother was still alive, was still living in the house. He said he didn't want me to marry you because, I gather, he figures that whatever she has you have. Something like that."

"God, Josh," she said, "do you believe it?"

"Not for a minute."

Headlights bobbed erratically, far down the road. Slowly, the backs of his fingers wiping her cheeks, he pulled away and kissed her. "I'll call you tomorrow morning, first thing. Please don't disappear on me. We have a lot to talk about." He took a deep breath, then, and waited for her to say something, anything that would let him know she wasn't hiding from him. The air came out in a slow whistle when he understood at last she would not help him.

"Are you mad at me, Josh?" A little girl, now, toying with the points of his collar, peering up at him from beneath her eyebrows. "Are you?"

"No," he answered truthfully. "No, I'm not mad."

"Then why so quiet? Oh. That story, what my father told you."

He tried not to hit her, tried not to weep. "Yes."

"The strain," she said, trailing one hand over the MG's fender. "There are times when I don't think he

even knows me. He gets so . . . so damned wrapped
up in his work I might as well not even be here."

The old woman, he thought, praying she could hear
him. For Christ's sake, Andy, who is the old woman?

"Darling, are you all right?"

He couldn't restrain a short, bitter laugh. "A lot of
people have been asking me that lately. And the truth
is—I don't know. I honest to god don't know. Right
now I am so confused I could scream."

"Maybe it's because you've never been raped before."

"Is that what that was?"

"Close enough for a cigar."

She didn't know, he thought suddenly, blinking at
the revelation. Damnit, she didn't know the old
woman was there.

He looked back at the house, at its size, decided
there was no place within where someone could hide
all this time without being discovered. And if that was
the case, she was from somewhere else, another place
along the spur. Andrea had been taking a shower; it
was conceivable she hadn't known. God damn, she
hadn't known!

He grabbed her again and kissed her hard, released
her before his arm took root. "Remember, I'm going
to call tomorrow. Please don't go away on me."

She looked at him sideways, puzzled. "I won't."

"Okay." But he didn't want to leave. He felt no
premonition of danger, but he did not want to leave
her alone with her father. "Andy . . ."

A finger brushed over his lips, tickling, stirring.
"Hush, hero. I can't go with you."

"What is this, you can read my mind?"

"Your eyes," she told him. "Lustful. Filthy. Ob-
scene."

"Yes, but will you go anyway?"

"No, love, and you know it. Dad is in trouble, and
he needs me. A good night's sleep, and he'll be all

right. Now git before the tow trucks leaves you walking."

He wanted to stay and protest, knew she was right and kissed her again. Tasted her. Took the scent of her freshly washed hair and savored it before giving a blind wave to the house and hurrying down the drive. Heedless of the traps the road set for him, he broke into a loping trot as he watched the garage truck illuminate the crippled Buick, heard the gears grinding into a whine as it turned around and backed to the front fender. By the time he reached it, the driver was already slapping the winch into operation, and there was little he could do but stand by and watch helplessly.

He was given a lift back to the house, the Buick promised for first thing in the morning.

He waited on the stoop until the truck was gone, dragging the car behind it. Then he closed his eyes and pictured the old woman on the other side of the Murdochs' window. She was there. He had not imagined her; she was definitely there.

And what the hell did Don have that, if he lost it, would harm Andrea?

Andrea. Andy. My *god*, he loved her.

17

"No, I am not crazy, Fel. I know what I saw. I was there, wasn't I? Look, just take my word for it. There were eight or nine of them, I don't remember exactly how many. Soon as you get ready tomorrow . . . hell, I forgot it was Saturday. How about as a favor? Never mind. But first thing Monday morning I want you to open up, then go over to St. Mary's, St. Andrew's, all the others and see if they have any records at all of a church back there. I didn't find anything myself when I looked through the records before, but I could have missed something, no cracks please. Then I want you to get some dimes and get to Town Hall. Copy those maps again for me. While you're doing that, I may get over to Hawksted tomorrow and talk to Grange Williams. He's a nut on Oxrun, claims he knows everything there is to know about it. Maybe he can help."

"Josh, do you have any idea in your crooked brain what time it is now?"

"Fel, I said I was sorry for calling so late."

"And before I waste my time, *partner*, running all over creation trying to track down a stupid graveyard in the middle of the hills . . . what, if anything—god forbid—does this have to do with Mrs. Thames'

plow? Or anything else we have going, for that matter."

"Nothing."

"I didn't think so. Just so I know, Miller."

"Felicity . . . Felicity, don't you have any curiosity
at all? I mean, doesn't it bother the hell out of you that
there are nine graves, give or take, out there in the
middle of nowhere that aren't marked, that have been
there for at least a century, and nobody knew it before
now?"

"Nobody we know about, you mean. The whole
town may know it, for god's sake. It's not exactly
something that comes up in everyday conversation,
you know."

"All right, point taken—nobody we know about.
But that doesn't change anything. At least not for me.
Lord, Fel, doesn't that—"

"No. Absolutely not. Listen, Miller, one of us has
got to keep an eye on the till, if you know what I
mean. I honestly don't know how you managed to get
along before I came around, but as long as I have
something to say about things now, I'm going to keep
reminding you until it sinks in that my income is now
dependent . . . is more dependent on you than it was
before."

"I understand that, Fel, believe me. But listen—"

"Don't interrupt, Miller. I'll do this thing, don't
worry about it. I'll do it, okay? But Monday only, and
it's the last time. If we come up empty when we
compare notes, you're not going to waste another day
on it. Let Reverend Harris or Father Hill get all
excited. You, dear, have work to do. You promise? No
hunting graves on company time after Monday?"

"Yes. All right. Fel, I promise."

"Good. Jesus, I should have listened to my mother.
And Miller?"

"Yeah?"

"When you talk to Professor Williams tomorrow,

give me a call, okay? It's the least you can do for waking me up."

Josh listened to the dial tone for a moment before replacing the receiver and letting himself slip back into the hot, clear water. She was right, of course, and there was no question about it. He did have to stop letting his insatiable curiosity run away with his checkbook. On the other hand, this particular puzzle was right here in town and wouldn't cost him more than one day's work, if that. She would be doing most of the running around anyway.

And he needed to know.

First, because it was there, and he sensed it did not belong. He wished now he had taken the time to examine the clearing more carefully, to sweep through the underbrush for signs of a church, or a caretaker's cottage . . . anything that would indicate the history, and the setting. That he could do tomorrow. And he would, since the second reason was far more important—the work, and the day it would take, was something he had to have, something that did not relate in any fashion to the way he made his living. Something that would keep him from thinking of anything else. By rummaging through Williams' mind, then, and stalking the graveyard again, he would be clearing his own; and in clearing his own he might, just might be able to understand more clearly what was going on at the Murdoch house.

He sank lower, the water lapping at the underside of his chin. He had already washed, had drained the soapy water and refilled the lions'-claw tub with water as hot as he could stand it.

His sigh was loud, and it made him grin mirthlessly.

It wasn't the nameless old woman so much; he suspected it wouldn't be all that difficult to find out which neighbor she was. What nettled him were the lies that had sprung up around her. Murdoch's lies. And so blatantly transparent he could not fathom their purpose. The man certainly couldn't believe Josh was so blind as to miss them. Why, then? A stalling, perhaps.

"Yes," he whispered, a slow smile breaking. "Yes."

For reasons still unclear, Murdoch did not want him to marry his daughter. Therefore the argument before Josh had had a chance to solidify the commitment; Andrea had jumped the gun, and Murdoch had been taken so unprepared that he'd had no opportunity to formulate a better device.

The smile to a grin.

That commitment, nebulous before, was approachable now without his wondering what it entailed.

"Yes. Lord, yes."

He laid his head back against the rim of the tub and stared at the tiled ceiling. The air in the bathroom was slightly hazed, but he could see through the slow-moving mist Andrea's bright smile.

"Hell, yes."

It was done. Backpedaling over, fears faced and vanquished, a very definite future charted and approved. Damnit, he *would* ask Andrea to marry him; he *would* invite her into his business and his life; and he felt pleasantly giddy because he knew she would accept. She had said it already; she had told her father where her heart lay and what her desires were. He disapproved.

"Tough shit, old man. You can't stop progress."

He laughed and slapped at the water, ran his hands lovingly along the outward curved rim. Of all the items in this oddly furnished house, the freestanding tub was unrivaled in his affection. He thought of the countless times, child and man, he had dropped soap bars between the porcelain and the wall, had groped for them giggling while his mother yelled from the hall to keep the floor dry; of the invisible oars and paddles he had used to propel the white oval creature through rough seas and across Loch Ness; of the winter afternoons when he had come up here to lie on the floor and stare at the heavy feet, touching the arched claws with one finger and imagining them gripping the tub in place.

Andrea too would love it.

The shower stall was for washing, quickly and efficiently. The bathtub was for cleansing, whether he used soap or not.

Andrea. Mrs. Joshua Miller. Mrs. Andrea Miller. He smiled lazily and let the weight of his eyelids blot out the light, felt his arms dizzyingly buoyant, the water pushing up the backs of his knees. Andrea. He supposed he should feel more concerned, more alarmed, at leaving her alone with her father and, possibly, that strange old woman. He supposed he should be more the white knight champing to leap astride his impatient Arabian stallion and ride to the rescue. But though he did not see yet the connections between the writer and the woman, neither did he doubt her competence in handling what was, it was now obvious, not a physically dangerous situation. If she did not know about the woman, he would tell her tomorrow and they could track her down together; if necessary, they would pin Murdoch in place and demand explanations.

No sense, he thought, in following the dictum of that old country saying and throw himself on his horse, only to ride off in all directions.

No sense at all. As it was, after an afternoon that had both unnerved and bewildered him he was feeling remarkably fine. And he congratulated himself for not diving off the deep end, for taking the time (for a change, he reminded himself) to think things through and examine what he had, instead of what he thought he had.

It was indisputably a hell of a better way to get things done.

He felt the water cooling, then, and considered getting out and into bed. He pushed himself awkwardly to a sitting position and reached for the towel

he had folded nearby, on the floor. Thought about
leaving the warmth of the tub for the cold of the
house, and pulled the hard-rubber plug. Waited. Replaced it. Ran the hot water again and squinted
against the steam that billowed into his face.

Lovely. Anybody who didn't know how to take a
proper bath was missing out on the greatest and most
indolent luxury ever devised.

He had almost fallen asleep where he sat when the
telephone rang. He started, the water swirling into
wavelets as he pushed himself toward the back and
grabbed for the receiver. His hand was too slippery; it
dropped to the floor. Muttering to himself, he leaned
over the rim and fumbled for it, finally snatched it up
and jammed it unthinkingly hard against his ear.

There was no one on the line.

"Beautiful," he said. "The hell with you."

The water level rose, and he turned off the faucet,
delighting in the paradoxically cold feel of the anach-
ronistic plastic-and-metal handle. But before he could
resume his nearly submerged lounging the phone rang
again.

"Goddamnit, who is it?" he demanded before the
receiver had reached his mouth.

"Hey, is that any way to talk to a slave?"

"Sorry, Fel," he said. "You forget something?"

There was a pause. "Miller, are you in that stupid
tub?"

He grinned at the far wall. "Sure. Naked as an
innocent babe."

"I'll let that pass. I am too far above cheapshots,
especially near midnight."

"God, is it that late?"

"You started it."

"So I started it. So . . . what?"

"Manuscripts."

He wiped a drop of water from his eye. "What,
more?"

"No. Those you picked up in the city, remember? I

mailed them out, just like you told me, with invoices and everything."

"Yeah, so?"

"So they came back today, Josh, in the afternoon mail. All four of them. Weird."

"What's so weird about putting on the wrong postage?"

"That's not the problem," she said. "The addresses were wrong. I double-checked the ledger, and they're the same. Josh, I didn't make a mistake. I called around. The addresses were phony."

He half rose out of the tub, staring blindly at the floor. "I don't get it."

"Neither do I. I didn't blow it, Josh. I took down the addresses just like they were given to me. False. No such places in any of those towns."

"Then—"

"It was for nothing, right. All that time for nothing."

He considered, then shook his head. "Well, it's done. A hell of a note, but it's done. We'll check it out again on Monday, okay?"

"You're the boss. Sort of."

He did nothing more than grunt, rang off, and slid back into the water, frowning. With a warm hand wiped the frown from his brow and closed his eyes; pranks he would deal with later, much later. Right now he had some Andrea-inspired daydreaming to do.

Again he slipped down until the water lapped at his chin, let his hands slide down the glass-smooth inner wall until they were caught and held, knuckles breaking the surface. His left leg drifted to one side, his right to the other, while his feet pressed lightly against the tub's far side to keep himself from dropping under.

But the mood was broken. He could not recapture the grand feeling he'd had earlier. Scowling at Fel's poor timing, he reached for the rim to haul himself up, snapping his eyes open when his fingers would not grip. He tried again, and the movement ducked his head beneath the surface. Sputtering, slapping, he rolled onto his side and tried again. This time, however, he could not reach the top . . . and his feet drifted down, far below where the bottom should have been. He felt himself sinking, the water growing warmer, hotter, and he flailed wildly, kicked viciously, saw the rippling ceiling above him as he climbed to the surface.

The rim was at least four feet above him.

And there was a roaring, a thundering, while the water grew hotter and his skin began to redden.

The faucet was on, and the water flowing was black.

He opened his mouth to cry out, and swallowed heat, and gagged. Had the presence of mind to swim in place until he could stop his lungs from working like frantic bellows. Then he reached out for the side again, and his hand slid off, all friction gone.

Impossible, he thought. This is my tub, this is my bathroom, what the hell . . .?

The water shaded to grey, and he could feel his skin puckering, the soles of his feet beginning to burn.

A squealing of metal against metal. He spun around and saw the faucet turning. Slowly. Grinding. Until its mouth was aimed up, and there was a rain of liquid fire. Clouds of steam. Flames at his groin as he ignored what should have been truth and stroked for the back, pressing his palms against the porcelain in an effort to gain traction to keep himself from sinking.

His hands slid again.

The water turned black.

He felt blisters on his heels, at his knees, at his elbows, felt the flesh across his buttocks split as though razored. He screamed and lunged upward, his eyes open wide as he almost caught the rim. Slipped down . . . and under . . . and felt the skin at his nostrils slit into flaps and his tongue begin to harden and his eyes begin to dry. Panic over reason as the pain slithered deeper, as his chest began to throb, as he *felt* his skin separate from his frame in tattered red. A desperate scissors kick and downward thrust of his arms, and the surface boiled with his passing, and he screamed as his fingers caught the rim . . . and held.

Black water running down the deep crimson of his arms.

Blood dripping from his nails, vaporizing and spitting.

Andrea; he thought of Andrea and hauled himself upward, keeping his eyes tightly closed against the numbness below his waist. Keeping his eyes closed as he reached the top, sobbing, threw himself to the floor and rolled over to his back.

Waiting to die . . . and feeling the cold of the tiles.

Hearing the silence.

And the weeping beneath it.

An hour later, at the kitchen table, he finally shoved away the bourbon and wiped a towel over his mouth. Gingerly at first, until he remembered. The light was on. All the lights in the house. The trembling was over, and the racking coughs had subsided, coughs he kept telling himself were not part of sobbing. Twice he had started to return upstairs—to check, to remind himself he had only drifted off to sleep after talking with Felicity; and twice he had stopped at the foot of the staircase, peering up at the landing and feeling the heat, seeing the black, smelling the stench of his flesh boiling off him. He had thought to get himself drunk in an effort to bring sleep, but he could drink only in sips, each taste separated by more than a few minutes. He stared at the bottle, finally rose and capped it and shoved it back in the cabinet.

And nearly laughed with joy when he broke into a yawn.

Tomorrow, he decided; tomorrow he would try to examine the dream, see what similarities it might have with the fear he had of wasps. He was sure, now that he could think about it without feeling a chill, there had to be one. He had never feared water before, had on more than one occasion dozed off in the tub for a couple of seconds. This time was different. This time his subconscious was telling him something and, like the graveyard, he would learn its secret sooner or later.

If nothing else, it would be a hell of a story to tell Andrea in the morning.

He smiled and scratched at his scalp. One by one the lights were switched off and he made his way to the bedroom, not realizing the apprehension had gone until he'd slipped between the sheets.

He woke only once, shortly before dawn.

He could have sworn the faucet in the bathroom was dripping.

18

Admonitions about dreams and foolishness and overreactions were useless; Josh grabbed his shaving gear and soap from the upstairs bathroom and washed in the kitchen sink, crouching down and using the polished side of the toaster when he was ready to take razor to lather. Tonight, he thought, he would be over the jitters. This morning, however, the faint sound of water plopping into the tub through the darkness was enough to reconstruct the dream more vividly than he wished.

There was also the heat.

He had felt it shortly before rising; a humid, lethargic heat that had insinuated itself into the village as the sun broke over the hills. A July heat. By noon it would be enough to wilt hedges and soften blacktop, make walking on the pavement like walking over a skillet, add a hunch to pedestrians' shoulders and lead to their shins. He grinned sardonically as he poured milk into a bowl of cereal, remembering the complaining he had done about the previous evening's chill. But at least he had the air conditioning, one of the few additions his father had made to the house that no one bothered to object to, not even when the electric bill scolded them for overuse. It hummed now, just below hearing, and made the glare of the sun

more intense by comparison. And the idea of leaving
the house to see Andrea seemed somewhat callously
less appealing than it had the night before.

He finished eating and lit a cigarette, using the plate
beneath the bowl for an ashtray. He had already tried
calling the Murdoch farm once and the line had been
busy. He would give them another ten minutes and
try again. He knew Andrea would be waiting for his
call, knew too he would not ask to see her this
morning as he'd planned, as he'd told her. He needed
a clearer head than he had right now, one not bothered
by remnants of his dream. And the first thing he
would do, he'd decided, would be to tell her about the
old woman. Somehow, he suspected, she was involved
with Don's sudden physical decline, and whether it
was blackmail of a sort or dependence on something
exotic like drugs, Andrea would have to know about
it. She would have to know about it today, before her
father was forced into doing something stupid.

He stared at the telephone affixed to the wall by the
doorway leading into the study. Someday, he thought
(as he did nearly every morning), he was going to have
to knock a hole through the wall at the side of the
staircase, so he wouldn't have to fight his way through
the books and papers just to get to the refrigerator.
There had been an entrance into the living room his
father had plastered over, for reasons he now forgot
. . . if, in fact, he had ever known in the first place.

The cigarette smoldered brown on the plate. He
glanced at it with distaste and stubbed it out, rose,
and dialed Andrea's number. Busy, and he hung up
quickly. Sighed and scratched at his throat. Moved to
carry his dishes to the sink when the doorbell rang.

The car. He had forgotten all about the car, and he
apologized to it silently as he hurried to the front,
slowing when he saw through the study window no
truck at the curb, no Buick at the end of the drive. He
pulled open the door, startled simultaneously by the
slap of the day's heat and the sight of Lloyd Stanworth

coolly suit-and-tied on the stoop. They stared at each other for a moment before Josh smiled and waved the doctor in.

Stanworth headed immediately for the kitchen, a "you look like hell, Josh" floating back over his shoulder. Josh paused in the study to catch his reflection in a small mirror beside the rear window, grimly noting that his friend was right. Despite the shave and the wash, he looked as though he had been going for forty-eight hours in a bar whose name no one ever remembered. His hair was tousled, his cheeks and eyes still slightly puffed, and there was a pinched look to his nostrils, indication of a stench nobody else sensed.

Stanworth was refilling the kettle when he joined him, the two of them grunting nonsense while cups and saucers, sugar, and a jar of instant coffee were set out on the table. When it was done, the room redolent, Stanworth took a chair and loosened his tie. "I figured," he said, "it was about time I saw you."

It took Josh a second to identify the thread. "I just hope you and Randy have worked it out, that's all."

Stanworth passed a forefinger lightly over his scars. "It's been miserable, Joshua, I can tell you that. But yes, I think we understand each other better. Now, that is."

Josh sipped at the coffee, wincing at the light burn at his tongue. "I have to admit, Lloyd, I was rather . . ." He grinned. "Pissed when I saw you two together at the inn that night. I thought for a minute Randy was right." He ignored the pain in the doctor's eyes. "Andrea, however, managed to set me straight."

Stanworth nodded, and glanced around the room. "I assume it's over, then. All the misunderstandings, that is."

"As far as I know, Randy had the misunderstanding."

"Yes."

Josh could feel the warmth from the back-door

window spread over his back. He shifted. He said nothing; Stanworth, he was sure, had not come here to talk about something that was clearly well buried. But his puzzlement grew when the man would not meet his gaze. Instead, he continued to examine the room as if he had never been here before, the lines about his eyes tightening and relaxing, a corner of his mouth pulling back in what would have been a smile if the rest of his face had accommodated itself accordingly.

"Hot day, isn't it," Josh said at last, pushing the sugar bowl toward Stanworth's hand.

"Rotten. You'd think it was the middle of the summer."

"Know what you mean. Been a damned crazy spring."

"Good for the grass, though. The crops. I spend more time on that fool lawn of mine than I do in the office. Sometimes I think I ought to be a gardener."

The warmth reached the back of his neck, and he rubbed at it impatiently, trying to erase it. The refrigerator snapped on, a beetle cracked against the windowpane, Stanworth's spoon clicked unnervingly against the inside of his cup. Josh glanced toward the telephone, wondering if Andrea had stopped talking, returned his gaze to the doctor with a smile he hoped was friendly and inviting. When it produced no visible result, he cleared his throat loudly.

"Didn't see your car," Stanworth said then. "I thought maybe you were out. Working."

Josh explained what had happened to the Buick, his voice trailing into a puzzled silence when it was evident the doctor was not at all interested. The coffee in both their cups cooled. Stanworth sipped at his anyway; Josh pushed it to one side with a slow shake of his head. He would have to change his seat; the sun was boiling through the doorpane, tightening the flesh at his nape in an uncomfortable reminder. Again he smiled; again he cleared his throat; and he frowned suddenly when he heard a muted angry sound like

that of a lawn mower on the far side of the block. It
sputtered, grew louder, stopped abruptly for several
seconds before resuming.

A chill surged from his stomach to his throat.
Moisture fled his mouth. He saw Stanworth's mouth
open and close, a fish gulping air, and a sheen slithered over his vision. Suddenly, he jumped from his
seat and put the table between himself and the door.
Stanworth gaped at him, stretched a hand for his wrist
but Josh snatched it away.

The single pane in the door was uncurtained, un-
shaded, clear to invisibility as it framed the grass and
the screen of trees beyond. In the upper lefthand
corner a wasp walked across the glass. Dropped away
and batted itself harshly against the obstruction before settling again. Its frustration filled the room. Its
abdomen coiled to strike, its antennae searched
vainly.

Josh knew it had seen him, knew it was only a
matter of time before it tired of its game and launched
the assault. But he could not move. The backs of his
hands were drenched in perspiration, his neck taut
and trembling. *The jungle the tree the bolts of fired
lightning.* He licked at his lips and blinked rapidly,
tried to swallow and found a barrier there that also
caught his breath. His lower lip quivered; he wanted
to speak, to tell Lloyd not to just sit there but do
something damnit before it was all over and the wasp
escaped. *Attacking flying ripping through flesh to the
blood beneath.* The room was so hot. It shouldn't have
been this hot. He knew, then, it was the wasp that was
raising the temperature. The voice it had, the rasping
drone that worked to deafen him, that's what was
doing it, that's what was turning the the whole house
into an oven. The air conditioning had failed, and
there was nothing he could do but wait until it moved.

The wasp crawled to the center of the pane, momentarily blending into the dark of the trees, breaking out
again as it moved toward the bottom and the lighter

green of the grass bleached by the sun. A black spot
black water that shimmered at the edges.

A magazine, he thought; and without moving his
head he tried to locate a weapon within reach. It
would have to be within reach; at his first move the
wasp would know that he finally knew and it would
flee to the thousands of corners, of dark places, that
existed in the house. Would bide its time. Would wait
until he wasn't looking before sweeping toward his
neck . . . or his arms . . . or his unguarded eyes.

Calmer, now. There was no question he would have
to approach it because anything thrown would act as a
warning. That ruled out the sugar bowl, the saucers,
the cups, the jar of coffee. The hand towel draped over
the rim of the sink—he nodded. He would have to
inch his way over there and draw it up, fold it in half
and be prepared to snap it at exactly the right angle,
with exactly the right speed. A miss, and he was dead;
too soft, and he was dead, unless he were lucky
enough to stun it to the floor. If he erred, however, the
wasp would forget about hiding, and waiting, and
stalking—it would come straight for him, and he
would be defenseless.

The towel. It was the easiest thing, the handiest.

He blinked again, and felt a drop of perspiration fall
to his cheek. Slowly, he pulled his hands from the
edge of the table and dried them against his shirt. A
deep breath, calming, filling him with the confidence
he needed to make his first move.

And he almost cried out when a sudden, large black
shape filled the room. Hands up to cover his face. A
grunt, the crack of glass near to breaking, and hands
soon after took hold of his arms and lowered him into
a chair.

"Christ, Joshua!"

"Is it dead?" It was all he could think of to say.

Stanworth rummaged through the cabinets until he
located the bourbon, filled a shot glass, and pressed it
into his hand. He looked at it stupidly, nodded to

himself, and drank. The liquor was like the slow sting of a wasp, and he shuddered, forcing himself not to vomit. Another sip, and he wiped his mouth with the back of a hand, noting the professional in Stanworth taking over, from the smothering of a sense of urgency to the quick, precise works of his hands as they mopped his face and neck with a cool cloth, monitored his pulse, pinched at his cheeks and temples for signs of blood loss that might prelude a fainting. When the man was satisfied Josh was comfortable and would not pass out on him, he sat again and faced him, his hands clasped together on the table, elbows at the edge, back straight, and gaze competently steady.

"Do you always react so violently when you see a wasp?"

Josh shook his head. Then he began a rambling, and he knew not always coherent narrative of the childhood afternoon when he'd been poking around in his backyard jungle and discovered the wasp-nest instead of the treasure. Whenever he felt himself dropping while he spoke, he locked onto Stanworth's gaze and used it for an anchor. By the time he was finished—adding a quick précis of the dream he'd had—he could hear his voice settling, could feel the saliva return to his mouth.

Stanworth nodded when it was over, a thumb thoughtfully at the point of his chin. "I see."

Josh laughed, not bothering or wanting to stifle the sound, and the feeling it produced as the specter of the wasp faded. Tears filled his eyes, an aching blossomed in his chest, and he allowed it all to drive the last of the demons from him as Stanworth rose and dumped the magazine he'd used to kill the wasp into the trashcan by the door. The laughter subsided, broke every few seconds into a bubble of giggling. His sleeve dried his cheeks.

"I'm sorry, Lloyd," he said, biting his lips to keep from grinning. "God, I'm sorry."

Stanworth gestured it away: *don't worry about it, it's not important.*

"Lord!" He gulped, asked for a glass of water, and drained it slowly. "God, and you still haven't told me why you came."

"That's all right," Stanworth said. "What's important is that you're okay now. I trust . . ."

"Yeah," he said. "Yeah, I'm fine."

"The dream was the main thing, you see. That wasp was only a catalyst, the trigger. I imagine you've killed wasps before without such extreme reactions."

"Sure. Every one I can. Brother, I must have looked like some kind of nut."

A smile now, shadowbrief. "Hardly a nut, Joshua, hardly a nut. Phobias aren't always signs of impending nuthood."

"Nuthood?" He laughed again, this time cleanly. "You amaze me, Lloyd, you really do. Nuthood." He shook his head and fetched himself another glass of water. The room was cool again, the sunlight back to its bleaching of the outside. Before he returned to the table he tore off a strip of paper towel and washed the doorpane of the smear the wasp had left behind. When he took his seat, however, he was disturbed by the expression that settled over Stanworth's face.

"What."

"You," the doctor said. "This isn't like you, you know. We all have nightmares now and again, but this . . . this type of response isn't like you at all." He paused. "Joshua, this isn't Randy talking, it's me—is there anything wrong that I can help you with? I mean, I might as well be frank. The few times I've seen you over the past couple of months you haven't exactly been yourself."

"I haven't?" Josh frowned, unsure himself of how he should respond.

"I don't mean you go around muttering to yourself," Stanworth said quickly. "You just seem . . .

preoccupied." He sniffed, and smiled halfheartedly.
"At first I thought it was because of Andrea. Young
love and all that. Maybe it is, but I get the feeling
there's more. The business all right? Your health?"

"Sure," he said, though not emphatically. Lloyd was
not his closest friend, nor was he a confidant—he had
none of those, or none he could think of—but the
man's manner was tempting, the concern he'd shown
an invitation to an opening. He decided to take it one
step at a time. "I . . . I can't deny that there've been
times lately when I've wished for a miracle or two,
though."

"Your family all right? They live where, Nevada?"

"Colorado, and they're fine the last I heard from
them. None of us are great letter writers. No, it's not
that, Lloyd. And it may not be anything at all. I guess
you could say that I've just had my share of confusion
this spring. Nothing big. Nothing to air out the
rubber room for, if you know what I mean."
Stanworth did not smile. Josh shrugged. "I just can't
seem to stick to one thing for more than a little while.
Except for Melissa's—Mrs. Thames'—handplow.
And even that's a lost cause. Hell, I didn't even know
it showed."

"It doesn't, really. I just noticed something bothering you around the edges, so to speak, and wondered
if it were serious. I can see it's not, though. You're not
any more confused than most of us are these days."

"Thanks," he said sarcastically.

Stanworth accepted the lefthanded gratitude with a
wink. "Now, look, this isn't—"

The telephone rang. Josh immediately scrambled to
his feet and snatched up the receiver, waving
Stanworth back to his chair when the doctor half rose
as if to leave. "Hello?"

There was a few moments' harsh static, a buzzing.
"Hello? Can you hear me?"

The static cleared. "Joshua?"

"Mrs. Thames, good morning!" He grinned as he

looked over Stanworth's head to the outside. A leaf swept by, another. With the air conditioning keeping all the windows down, he hadn't noticed the rise of the wind.

"Nothing good about it. You should see it from where I'm standing."

The maid's cottage, he thought, devastated again by dust that dared creep in through the chimney. Then he snapped his fingers and grimaced.

"Damn, I forgot! Hey. Melissa, happy birthday. Many happy returns. Whatever you want to hear."

"I want to hear what you found out from Dr. Stanworth, Joshua. You were going to ask him about . . ."

The static returned, a faint and sweeping howling somewhere beneath it.

"Melissa? Hey, Melissa, we've got a lousy connection, at least from my end. Can you hear me?"

" . . . Joshua . . ."

"Look, I've got Lloyd trapped here in my kitchen even as we speak. Why don't I—"

He frowned, as much at Stanworth leaving his chair as at the renewal of the interference, and at the reduction of Mrs. Thames' voice to a hollow, drifting whisper.

"Melissa, listen, this isn't going to do any good. Can you hear me? I'm not getting anything at all. Tell you what—"

" . . . Joshua . . ."

"—I'll do, I'll hop in the car and . . . damn! I forgot. The tank is in the repair shop. They were supposed to deliver it—"

" . . . help . . . no . . ."

He stopped, his frown deepening, his free hand darting toward Stanworth to keep him from leaving. "Mrs. Thames, what's the matter?" Silence. "Melissa?" The static crackled, the howling increased. "Melissa, are you all right?" He half turned to the wall and slapped a finger at the receiver's rocker, once, twice, not ridding the line of its disturbance until, suddenly, he was listening to the dial tone. He stared, then rang off sharply and headed for the study.

"Joshua, what's—"

"Come on, Lloyd, I need your help. There's something the matter with Mrs. Thames. I need you to get me out there."

Stanworth followed slowly. "From what I heard it's only a bad connection, Josh."

Josh waited at the front door, holding it open, and beckoning impatiently while he squinted at the street. "Where the hell's your car? Jesus, Lloyd, did you walk over?"

"No, it's at the corner. I—"

Josh grabbed his arm and pulled him down the steps to the walk. He cursed at the man's reluctance, cursed at the heat that had his shirt plastered to his back and chest before they reached the curb. If Lloyd had balked more forcefully, if he'd demanded an explanation, Josh knew he would only be able to give him stutterings and vague sensations; as it was, however, he was able to strong-arm the man behind the wheel and slip into the Jaguar's passenger seat without having to do much more than scowl.

"Joshua, really," Stanworth said, one last attempt to make him see reason. "You know her as well as I do. One little—"

"Damnit, Lloyd, will you please drive this goddamned thing?"

Stanworth gave him one look of exasperation before pulling away; and Josh punched at his leg, listening to the old woman's voice like a worn tape in his mind.

And then he remembered how afraid she had been.

19

Despite the size of the automobile and Stanworth's insistence on keeping well within the speed limit, the wind buffeted the vehicle unmercifully, swerving it jarringly from side to side in its lane. Josh gritted his teeth against the assault, swearing his impatience silently as the Jaguar took the two blocks to Park Street and made its turn. The street's namesake was on the right, the trees above the fencing lashing at the air while a number of Saturday strollers huddled at the ineffectual protection of the gates as though they were being whipped.

Another right turn and they were on Williamston Pike, caught now behind a station wagon that drifted over the center white line whenever the wind shattered down from the leaves.

"I don't believe it," Josh muttered, biting at the words and flinging them to one side. He tried to find a way around the wagon, but the verge was too narrow, the traffic coming in the opposite direction timed just wrong. Stanworth, he noted with increasing frustration, was acting as though they were in no hurry at all, his hands just so on the steering wheel, his lips pursed in a quiet, tuneless whistling.

"For god's sake, Lloyd!"

"Relax, relax, we're almost there."

Three quarters of a mile past the reconstructed Toal mansion they turned into a drive that began between two ten-foot concrete posts topped by rearing stone lions. Josh leaned forward, trying to see through the debris that rained across the windshield, his hands hard on his knees when the white-and-brown of the Tudor finally split through the trees. He didn't wait for Stanworth to set the handbrake; as soon as the car slowed almost to a halt he was out the door and racing up the flagstone walk to the porch. The steps were taken two at a time. He faltered only for a stride before lunging through the open front door.

"Melissa!"

Leaves scuttled in behind him, joining a swirling pile that bunched against the foot of the staircase. The wind took to the ceiling and rattled chandeliers, dropped dust from rafters in a greywhite shower. Lampshades trembled, skirted beds rippled, a magazine left in the master bathroom flapped its pages weakly as he raced in and out with only a glance at the empty tub.

As he took the stairs down again, one hand burning along the banister to keep him from falling, he shouted to Lloyd in the doorway to get to a phone and call the police. Then he was around the newel post and into the corridor that took him to the back.

The kitchen was empty, utensils on their wallhooks swaying and clanking; the library door was closed, deathly silence inside. He was on the back porch, hands on his hips while he tried for easy breathing and stared over the immaculate back lawn to the maid's cottage in the rear. There was no phone in the small building, but he ran to it anyway, thinking she might have gone there for protection; he didn't dare ask himself against what.

Halfway back he slowed to a walk, realizing the wind had died and the heat had returned. He kicked at a tangle of twigs blown from the trees and punched a fist into a palm, kicked the back door open, and punched at the wall as he hurried back to Stanworth.

"Gone," he said as he turned into the livingroom. "Goddamnit, I knew I should have come out here today. You didn't see her, the way she was last week. She was really frightened of today, Lloyd, really scared out of her wits. Jesus, I should have . . . Lloyd?"

He turned in a tight circle. Stanworth was gone.

"Lloyd? Damnit, Lloyd!"

Into the diningroom, where he moved to the front windows and pulled aside the curtains.

The driveway was deserted; the Jaguar and Stanworth had left him alone.

He wasted no time chasing shadows to the pike; instead, he picked up the telephone and dialed the police. Within seconds he had snapped to Fred Borg and received a puzzled promise he would have company in a few minutes. Then he walked through the house again, slowly this time, not stopping until he found himself in the library, in front of a rolltop desk obviously Melissa's. He had just started to leaf through a packet of correspondence placed neatly in the center of a leather-rimmed folder when he heard the patrol car pull up outside. He was at the door before Borg had climbed the porch steps, trailed after him talking, explaining the call he had received and his haste to get out here before anything happened. When he'd arrived, however, the old woman was gone, and no, there was no sign of a break-in.

"The front door was unlocked, that's all."

Borg nodded, took Josh's tour of the house and the building in the yard, then returned inside where he sat in the livingroom, somewhat discomforted. "You say the door was unlocked?"

"Opened, actually," Josh said, pacing on the hearth. "Just a little. But now that I think about it, she didn't lock it anyway."

Borg glanced around at the quietly elegant,

understatedly expensive furnishings and grunted disbelief.

"No, really," Josh told him. "The only things she really valued around here were the portraits." He followed the policeman's gaze. "I don't know who did them, but you can see it'd take a damned truck to get them out. Those frames alone must weigh a hundred pounds apiece. The rest . . ." He shrugged. "She always said she had enough money to refurnish the house a hundred times over. And as far as I know all her jewelry, what there is of it, is still there."

"No kidding."

Josh felt uncomfortable. "I looked around. I couldn't sit still."

Borg snapped his notebook shut and stuffed it into his breast pocket. Crossed his legs at the ankles and folded his arms over his chest. "To tell you the truth, Josh, I don't know what we got here. No sign of forced entry, no . . . no body, no blood, nothing like that. All we got is a call to your house, a bunch of static, and you come charging out here like you were the cavalry or something." He jerked his head to keep Josh silent. "It ever occur to you she didn't even call from here?"

"No," he said flatly. "It was her birthday. She has no family left. Where would she go? Especially in the morning?"

"Beats me. Just asking, is all." Borg hesitated. "What about your friend?"

"Lloyd?" Josh shook his head; not a denial of the man's guilt, but a confession of bewilderment.

"Maybe he went out looking."

"Yeah. Maybe."

Borg hauled himself out of the chair and walked to the door. "I'll look around, Josh, send out the word. She drive?"

"A Lincoln. Grey. About ten years old."

"Christ, a goddamned battleship. That won't be hard to find. Unless you already looked in the garage."

"No, I didn't think of it."

Borg smiled without malice. "I'll take a gander myself, then."

They walked around the side of the house to the converted stables that housed Mrs. Thames' car. The upward swinging door was closed; one look through the window in its center and Josh felt the first stirrings of doubt.

"She could be halfway to Hartford by now," Borg said, heading back to the patrol car. "Well, I'll put out the word anyway. You know, you shouldn't stay here, Josh. I mean, I can't order you away since we don't know if we got a crime, but . . . don't stay too long."

"Fred . . ."

Borg turned as he slid in behind the wheel. "Josh, I can't tell you anything right now because I don't know anything. You seen for yourself all we got is an open door that don't prove anything. And look, Mrs. Thames wasn't one of your average little old ladies, either. If she was in trouble, she wouldn't have gone out without a fight. Tough old bird, that one is. I think maybe this is all pretty innocent, but I'll scout around anyway. What the hell. The car's got air conditioning. The ones at the station all broke down." He shook his head and started the engine, waiting to see if Josh had something to add. When there was no reply, no comment, he nodded and drove away, and Josh walked slowly back into the house, closing the door softly behind him.

. . . Josh . . . no . . .

It could have been a misunderstanding. The connection they'd had was certainly poor enough, certainly broken up enough. In the state he was in with the wasp and the dream it was a wonder he didn't imagine the old woman shrieking about murder and rape. Nevertheless, he could not shrug off the feeling that he was right this time, that something had happened here not only to Melissa, but also to start a series of switches working in his mind, switches that would soon begin to form connections.

Without thinking about it, he found himself back in the library and sitting at the desk. The letters he handled carefully, shoving each off the pile with the tip of a finger against its edge. Bills, circulars, correspondence from as far away as Liverpool; all of them were as yet unopened, none of them carried any names he recognized. He felt no guilt at all, then, when he pulled open a drawer and poked through it, did the same to another, finally gave in to the temptation and made his way methodically through them all, and through the warren of cubbyholes that pocked the desk's back.

An hour later he pushed the chair back and swiveled to face the rest of the room. Scowling without knowing it. Gnawing on his lower lip, the inside of his cheek, one foot tapping on the thick carpet to a rhythm he did not feel.

Here, he thought; if it isn't in here, it isn't anywhere.

He allowed his gaze to drift aimlessly, focusing, blurring, taking in but not seeing the books in their shelves, the hunting lithographs, the freestanding globe slightly yellowed with age, framed photographs on the various endtables flanking armchairs and a love seat. He rose and walked around, touching and brushing, wishing he had his pipe to chew on when his left hand tapped his hip pocket and came up empty.

Where are you, he asked a picture of her in summer whites, a tennis court behind her, a sprawling mansion behind that.

Come on, Melissa, he goaded a picture of Melissa and her late husband, seated at a round, white table under a striped umbrella with a pool behind them and an ocean behind that.

Melissa, damnit—to a group picture in front of the Tudor, ten women, all smiling broadly, not a shadow of self-consciousness among them as they stretched their arms around each other's shoulders and looked directly at the camera.

He moved on and decided to check the maid's cottage again. Maybe there was something out there he had missed the first time. After all, he had been in a hell of a panic earlier, and she might have dropped something behind a chair or a table he had overlooked, something innocuous and . . .

He stopped at the threshold and turned slowly, as if not daring to believe the corner his mind had just turned. A full minute he stood there, waiting for something to tell him he was wrong. Then he returned to the picture of Melissa's gossip society. Names had been scratched on the negative, were sprawled white beneath the shoes of each woman. He picked it up, holding it gingerly by the silver frame, looking for and hoping he wouldn't find Thelma Saporral's name.

But it was there. In the center. Right beside Melissa.

I recalled it was her birthday—seventy if she was a day . . .

On the other side was Agatha West: *certainly gave herself a hell of a birthday, I'll say that for the old bat.*

Esther Braum on the far left end; Mabel Cushing on the far right.

Melissa was in the center, a full head above the others. She was wearing a loose, ruffled blouse and loose-fitting tartan slacks that made it seem as if her hips were much larger than they were. She was grinning. She was happy.

It's my birthday next week. And I'm being watched. I know it.

When he felt himself swaying he realized he'd been standing in place too long. He closed his eyes tightly, opened them, and walked over to the desk, the picture still in his hand. The frame trembled in his grip, and a ball of remorse settled in his stomach like a pellet of hot lead—he had promised her to check, and he had forgotten. If he had done as he'd said, if he had kept his word he might have noticed the connection before; as it was, too much had been happening, too many divergent circumstances had roiled his thoughts until it was all he could do to keep Andrea in mind.

He looked at the picture.

He dialed Stanworth's home number, thinking that if Lloyd had not returned there, at least Randy would be home. But there was no answer. When he called the Murdoch farm, however, the phone was picked up on the second ring.

"Andrea, it's Josh."

"Josh?"

He laid the picture flat on the blotter. "Josh Miller, or have you forgotten already. I tried to call earlier but the line was busy."

"Oh, Josh, I'm sorry!" Worry, and relief; he watched one finger snake around the coil. "Josh, I hope you don't want to come out now, because I don't think you can."

"I wasn't going to," he said stiffly. "In fact, I was going to find out if you wouldn't mind seeing me later. I've got things . . . it's Melissa Thames." He explained briefly what had happened, though he made no mention of the convergent birthdays; that, he had decided, he would have to think about further, to be sure he wasn't creating conspiracy of coincidence. "I'm going to stick around for a while, to see if she comes back. If not . . ." and he left the rest dangling.

"God, Josh, this is one of those days, isn't it. You've got Mrs. Thames and I've got Dad."

"What's up? Is he all right?" He recalled her concern and felt a prickling along his spine. "He hasn't . . . done anything, has he?"

Her laugh was forced. "Of course not. It's . . . well, I think we hit him pretty hard last night, love. I couldn't stop him drinking, and now he's ill."

"Hung over, you mean."

"No, I mean sick. Really sick. I'm almost ready to call a doctor."

"You'll want company, then."

"No," she said, though her gratitude for the offer

was wrenchingly clear. "No, Josh, you have your own worries right now. Maybe . . . maybe you could drop out later on. You know, to hold my hand and pray for Dad?"

"Sure thing," he said. "I'll try to let you know how it goes here. If not, expect me when you see me."

"Mrs. Thames," she said quickly, before he rang off, "is she . . . I mean, you don't think she's . . ."

"Dead?" His gaze touched the picture. "I don't know, Andy. I don't know what the hell is going on. But something is. Something Lloyd is involved with somehow."

"Lloyd?" She said it quietly, so quietly he almost missed it. "What does Lloyd have to do with Mrs. Thames?"

"That's one thing I have to find out, love. He's gone, too, and if I don't get in touch with him soon I'm . . . shit, I don't know what I'll do yet. I'm just talking. Look, you see to your father, try the hair of the dog or something, and I'll talk to you later. And Andy . . . remember I love you."

"I do," she told him tenderly. "God, it's the only thing that keeps me from screaming."

He smiled, disconnected, and tried the hospital. Stanworth had not been in all day and was not expected; nor was there any answer at his home again. He could not think of any place else to call, did not know the name of the private clinic to which Stanworth had sent Mrs. Thames' friend.

The grins in the photograph slowly grew strained.

He called the police station and was surprised to discover Fred Borg was already there. "I thought you were going to look around?"

"Look around," the sergeant said, "not start a manhunt."

"Yeah."

"Listen, Josh, I know how you feel, but without evidence there's nothing I can do. I told you that already. It's like your place, your office? I mean, we can't pull nothing out of our hats, right? We work on it, something comes up and we go with it. Hell, you know I can't promise anything more than that."

"I know, I know. It's just so frustrating."

He could hear men laughing in the background, the sound of a door slamming. Normal, all perfectly normal.

And all perfectly in order, except . . . Melissa was gone, on the anniversary of her birth.

"Fred, listen, remember you told me about that guy, the tourist who was killed out on Cross Valley last April?"

"Remember? How the hell can I forget, for god's sake."

"You told me you found out it was his birthday, right?"

"Jesus." Paper shuffling, a pencil tapping against something hard. Borg inhaling slowly, a muffled whistle. "Yeah, that's right. Christ, you got a memory, Josh."

"Comes with the territory. Listen, do you have a name for him? Or can you tell me when the body was released to the family?"

"What? You know I can't tell you anything like that, Josh. You're not one of us, if you know what I mean. Chief Stockton'd skin me alive if he found out."

"So who's going to tell him, you?"

He could see the stocky patrolman shaking his head, wanted to reach through the receiver and take hold of his throat. But he knew the man would not change his mind. Favors against a favor for his wife was one thing; circumventing police regulations was another matter entirely.

"But I can tell you they didn't take the body nowhere, if that's any help."

Josh took his hand from the photograph, held it poised over the dial. "I don't understand."

"You can't give back what you don't find. We ain't

magicians, Josh. Fancy uniforms, but we ain't magicians."

"Hold it." He closed his mind, trying to recall a conversation that had happened too long ago. There were bits and fragments, but he wasn't positive what he actually remembered and what he thought he remembered. "You told me, when you told me about the birthday business, that you found the body about a mile away, back in the woods off the pike."

"Never said any such thing, Josh. The body wasn't found at all."

He almost blurted out what he knew about the missing corpse—or thought he knew, if he knew anything at all—and about Melissa and her vanishing coterie of gossipers. But he held his tongue and mumbled his thanks, waited for the dial tone before trying Stanworth again. Waited fifteen minutes and tried one last time before he slammed the receiver onto the cradle and pushed violently away from the desk. Walk. He had to walk. He had to keep moving so he would stop thinking about Lloyd. Lloyd and a missing body, Lloyd and some missing old women, Lloyd and Randy . . . into what? What the hell could the man be doing that would involve him in something as outlandish, as impossible, as . . . god almighty, was he crazy?

Through the doorway and into the corridor. The kitchen. The livingroom where he stood in front of Mrs. Thames' portrait and stared at it as if her pose and her blind gaze would furnish him a clue. To what? he asked himself then; a clue to what? The vanished and mangled corpse was one thing; but it was quite another to link it with several old women who had decided at various times over the past year to up and leave. All of them, if Melissa had been any judge, of reasonably sound mind, and certainly of adequate means. What was so wrong about wanting to go away? Just because they were old didn't mean they couldn't emulate a past generation and drop out of sight, for whatever reasons that convinced them it was right.

But it always happened on a birthday.

And Melissa was positive she was being watched.

He turned away from the fireplace. At his foot a crumpled leaf already turning brown at its serrations. He knelt and picked it up, turned it around by its stem, and stared at it.

"The wind," he whispered, and remembered the scream he had heard at the depot. The scream on the day that Agatha West had vanished.

20

Josh wondered why the chair he sat in, the chair that was Mrs. Thames' favorite, was called a Queen Anne; he wondered why anyone would want to build a Tudor mansion so obviously impossible to heat and to cool; he wondered if Felicity were really going to wait until Monday to do the checking he had asked of her or if she would work true to form and waste a Saturday rushing around the Station so she could once again silently mock him with a superiority neither of them felt; he wondered when the Red Sox were going to play ball for one entire season, when the Whalers were going to learn how to skate, when his parents were going to stop trying to lure him to Colorado; he wondered anything at all to keep from wondering about the wind.

He crossed his legs and stared at the tips of his shoes, at the cuffs of his jeans worn to a pale white, at the fading knees that reminded him he would soon need a new pair. He listened to the house. He felt the afternoon's heat insinuating itself through the curtained windows, driving back the chill of the shadows and driving the shadows up to the rafters, the beams, the nooks and niches of the crawlspace that passed for an attic. He glanced up at the portraits of Granville and Melissa Thames, at the hunting outfits they wore, and could not imagine Melissa shouting "Tallyho!" He shook his head and took a deep breath, sighing as he exhaled until his lungs emptied and he was ready to think again.

Then he allowed his mind the freedom of wandering, picking its way through whatever popped up and grinned, studying various images that stayed for a while and drifted. He paid no attention to his watch. His sense of urgency had been sated by his call to Fred Borg; whatever had happened to Melissa was done and there was nothing he could do but attempt to figure out what and try to prevent it from happening to someone else. And it would. He had no clear reason for it, but he was positive of that much. The whys and the wherefores would have to come with the looking —the birthdays, he suspected, being only a small part of a whole—and if six people were missing he feared there would be more. How many, however, eluded him; aside from the birthdays he could find no connection between the one-armed tourist and the five old women. Assuming, of course, that there weren't others he wasn't aware of. And he knew there was no real reason why he should make that assumption at all. He wasn't even sure he could assume they were still alive.

He thought of the wind when he could think of nothing else. But there, too, he was blocked. The wind and Melissa, the wind and Agatha West, and he finally admitted to himself that the wind that had killed the bird on his car had risen about the same time as the accident on Cross Valley. Fierce and of short duration; he didn't think it worth checking the *Herald* for mention of earlier bursts. Fierce and of short duration; if he let himself go, if he let his mind tip over the edge of extremes, he would have himself believing the storms were deliberate, were used for covering up the kidnapping of victims. That was too much. The birthdays he could understand, though the significance still escaped him, but there was no question but that the wind had to be an unnerving coincidence.

"You really should tell Fred, you know," he muttered to the hearth. "If you uncover something, he'll have you paying tickets from now until doomsday for not informing him sooner." Fred was a nice guy, but he tended to hold grudges. "On the other hand, he did tell you, pal, that you weren't part of the fraternity. He really did." And if that was a warning not to work on his own in a field not his profession, he knew (with a slight grin he was glad no one saw) he was just obstinate enough to go ahead anyway. To prove . . . something or other. Or to alleviate the guilt he felt for not keeping his promise to Melissa about the clinic.

Which led him to Lloyd Stanworth.

There was an ornate, French telephone on an ebony cocktail table just behind him. Groaning aloud to give himself some noise, he reached around the wing of the chair and snagged it with two fingers, lifted it, dropped it into his lap, and examined the dial as if it held all the answers in its white-framed numerals. Then he called Lloyd's office and Lloyd's home, barely holding the receiver to his ear because he knew there'd be no answer; a call to King's Garage on Chancellor Avenue, being hypocritically magnanimous at an apology for not having the car ready and asking the owner to bring it out to the Thames'; a call to Information that told him there were six private nursing clinics in West Hartford—and calls to all six that told him what Melissa had already offered: no one by the name of Stanworth had entered a patient by the name of Saporral at any time, ever, but thank you for calling.

"Jesus Christ, Lloyd." Wearily, fearfully, pressing the receiver to his forehead and closing his eyes. "Jesus Christ, what in hell are you doing?"

He remembered his father telling him, just before he entered the Air Force, to always cover his ass when trying something new. Or even something old. Give yourself more outs than you can use, a dozen or so excuses, and a way to fix the blame so widely that you'll never get caught when it all goes up in smoke.

He called Fred Borg and told him what he knew.

"Well . . ." A hand scraped over the receiver at the other end and he could hear mumbling, sense shrugging. "Josh, you there? Listen, I appreciate your telling me this. But we ain't got any other complaints on these people, you see. Sounds weird, but what do you want me to do about it?"

"You might try looking for them."

"You say some have been missing for six months or so?"

"Give or take. There might be more. You could check, you know, in your Missing Person files, see if anyone else has turned up gone in the Station. On their birthday that is."

"Josh, you got to give us some credit, you know. I . . . we all go through those folders once a week, just to keep our minds fresh on them, if you know what I mean. None of us here ever seen anything like that. And when you consider how many people take a walk during the year . . . hell, during any six-month period, it ain't surprising some of them got to go on their birthdays. You think about that, Josh. And if you come up with anything else, something we can really use, you let us know."

"Fred, I called because I don't think it's going to end. And don't ask me how I know, because I don't. It's a feeling, that's all. A hunch. You do know what a hunch is, don't you?"

"Don't be a wiseass, Josh."

He stuck his tongue out at the voice. "No, sir, I wouldn't think of it. But don't forget what I told you, Fred. Maybe mention it to Abe when you see him."

"He's on vacation. I'm in charge for the next two weeks."

"I feel real safe."

He wasn't hurt, neither was he angered when Borg

hung up on him. He had thrown a sop to his conscience by alerting the authorities to whatever it was
he had gotten himself into. They had noted it. They
had told him what he'd been telling himself since he'd
first taken hold—that signs of foul play were distress-
ingly absent, and all they could do was thank him for
his interest.

He wished, then, he had told Fred about Lloyd
Stanworth's lies.

Once upon a time, he told himself while he walked
through the house without really looking at what his
gaze touched, there was a young man who had an
occasional feeling that someone, somewhere, was
keeping an eye on him. During this time he was the
victim of two break-ins, one at his office and one at his
house, though nothing at all was found to be missing
in either place and the insurance more than adequate-
ly covered what little damage there was. The young
man, whom we will call Joshua just for the sake of
convenience, was also in the process of acquiring
himself a partner (one Felicity Lancaster, she of the
violet eyes and violently touchy temper) and a lover,
who eventually came to admit that she loved him too,
but neither of them did anything more than that in
regard to taking out mundane things like marriage
certificates. This was because (he explained as he
walked into the library and picked up the photograph
in the delicate silver frame) she had this father, see,
who was an author who had just been negotiating for
what was apparently a very large contract, and the idea
of all that money apparently knocked him a little off
balance since he then began to make funny noises
about Joshua not wanting to marry his daughter even
though the two men got along just fine, in spite of the
fact that the author served godawful cheap scotch,
and no bourbon at all. Not to mention (because no one
else did, in spite of the opportunities Joshua gave
them) a very strange old woman who was in the
Murdoch (that's Andrea and Donald Murdoch—she

of the incredible sexual technique, and he the writer aforementioned) house on the night that the two lovers managed to break their intentions to the father. There's also all the old women who keep upping and vanishing under circumstances that might be curious if one (like Joshua) tended to look at them that way instead of taking them for what they most likely were, and that was . . . perfectly innocent disappearances. An obvious contradiction, if not in terms then in intent.

Let us also not forget the wind. And the scream. And the telephone call from Melissa. And the missing body of the young tourist who left his arm behind. And the doctor who lied. And the lover who may have lied. And the father/author who damned well did lie. And the partner with the beautiful violet eyes and the Burmese cat who thinks her partner is crazy but sticks with him anyway because she's either stupid or in love with him or doesn't know any better . . .

"And whose birthday is on the first of July."

He dropped into the Queen Anne and picked the telephone off the floor. Dialed Felicity's number, and swore without apology at the blind faces of the portraits. Then he called the office, and rolled his eyes upward when Felicity answered on the fifth insistent ring.

"How did you know I was here?" she asked. She sounded tired. The heat weighted her words like a damp cloth over her lips.

"Lucky guess. Fel, I have to talk to you."

"So talk. By the way, I have something to tell you, too."

"I'd rather do it to your face, Fel."

"So come over then." She was puzzled, clearly, but would not ask.

"I can't. I'm at Mrs. Thames' place and I'm waiting for my car. It'll take too long to explain. Just do me a favor and stay there. Don't go away, all right? Wait until I get there."

"Miller . . . what's going on?"

"If I knew that, my dear, I'd be talking to the police. Or jumping out a window."

"Miller—"

"Don't," he said sharply. "I definitely do not need you asking me if I'm all right. Not again. Because I am not all right and I don't know why and if I found out I may not want to know. Just stay there and do whatever it is you're doing and I'll be there as soon as I can."

He broke the connection without giving her a chance to reply, replaced the phone on the cocktail table, and walked to the front door. The urgency was back. He did not understand what had rekindled it, but he sensed more than logically accepted that all the incidents and emotions and infuriating sidetracking he had dredged up in his fairy tale were connected. Tenuously, powerfully . . . he didn't know. But he was beginning to feel as if he had come into the middle of a film without knowing anything about it—not the title, nor the stars, nor the scriptwriter's intent. Time had been what was needed, and a galvanizing disappearance. His worry, once scattered among a dozen or more matters, had concentrated, and in concentrating had begun to brush aside the inconsequential, leaving the clear impression of a plot, a story line, a common denominator that was, finally, beginning to bring together all the diverse elements he had been watching into something cohesive.

The problem was, he also had the feeling the film was almost over, barely enough time to sort out heroes and villains before the climax thundered from the speakers and made the audience gasp.

Better yet, he thought as he walked down the drive to meet his car on the pike, it was like waiting for condensation on a bathroom mirror to clear after a hot shower. Impressions first, then clarity; but again . . . if there was someone standing behind him with a knife, the recognition of the murderer might come too late to save the flesh of his back, the back of his heart, the blood of his living.

Morbid. Too damned morbid. Calm yourself, boy, before you see ghosts in the trees and monsters in the gutters.

The Buick almost ran him down at the gateposts. He thanked the attendant, drove him back to the garage, and gave him ten dollars more than the bill. Less than five minutes later he was seated at his office desk and waiting for Felicity to pour him lemonade she had made to keep the heat from wilting her. It was laced with Southern Comfort, was virtually too sweet to abide without puckering and spitting.

When she was done, artfully adjusting a blouse tied at her midriff and exposing a tanned stomach, she flopped into her chair and cupped her hands behind her head. Grinning when she saw him staring at her breasts, shaking her head slowly as if he were an incorrigible adolescent. "So?"

"You first," he said. He knew, then, he was stalling, but he needed to hear her, to listen to sanity before he tried to tell her what he had told himself before.

"All right." She glanced at a note-covered pad by her phone. "I called around instead of walking, if you don't mind. This heat would kill a camel. Anyway, I found out that neither the Episcopal church on the pike nor St. Mary's knows anything about a graveyard out in the valley. Since they're the oldest churches going around here, I figured those people would know. They don't. I also figured you wouldn't get around to talking to Professor Williams, so I tracked him down in New Haven—some conference or other at Yale, the snob—and he says no such place exists. If it did, he would know it. And I believe him. That means you're crazy."

He grunted and nodded for her to continue.

"A few contacts at Town Hall brings us exactly zilch. Nada. Empty-handed. Matthew Grueger, who lives over on Kind Street, is one hundred and one years old and a dirty old man." She grinned softly at a memory. "My father used to take me over there to listen to the old guy talk. What Professor Williams doesn't know, Grueger does. And Grueger says the same as Williams." She spread her hands and shrugged. "Miller, it's a bust."

"Impossible," he insisted. "The headstones I saw were at least a century old."

"How close did you look at them?"

He held back a wince, remembering the afternoon. "Not very," he admitted. "But I've seen enough of them to know at least that much, Fel."

"Oh, hey, I'm not doubting you saw what you saw. But . . ." She squinted at something on the wall behind his head. "Did it ever occur to you that those things aren't native to the place you found? Maybe they came from somewhere else."

He opened his mouth to protest, changed his mind, and lapsed into a silence Felicity knew better than to disturb. Five minutes later, quietly and giving her clear evidence of his doubts, he began to tell her what had happened to him that morning. She stirred but said nothing; she sat up when he mentioned the collection of birthdays; she grabbed a pencil and began scribbling when he mentioned the dead tourist; but she was unable to help him when he asked for the thread that would bind them together.

"Something . . ." she said, her gaze darting about the office.

"Yeah, I know. A title on the tip of my tongue, so to speak."

"A clear head," she told him, then. She rose and headed for the door. "I'll go over to the luncheonette and get us something to eat. We'll talk about baseball or something and just let it come."

But nothing did but mutual headaches that had them both laughing because there was little else they

could do. And when they parted he kissed her quickly
in thanks for her work, and she kissed him back
before he could pull away.

Damn, he thought as she hurried away, this is
getting too complicated by half.

But Andrea would set it all right. He would drive
out to the farm and talk with her, sit on the porch and
let the warm night close its black around them and
they would talk. She might be able to see what he and
Fel could not, or convince him that he was making too
much of events that were not connected at all. She
might. He half hoped she would, since he was certain
he wouldn't be able to sleep until he knew.

He drove slowly, all the windows down, the temperature under the interlocked foliage over the pike
considerably below that of his office and that on the
streets in the center of town. A number of automobiles passed him in the opposite direction, and a few
of the drivers waved or honked their greetings. Saturday night in Oxrun Station: a trip to Harley to the
movies and a late supper, to the inn or the Cock's
Crow to listen to the music or plan assignations, to
the park and the protection the shrubbery offered.
Quiet walks. Sitting on porches. A play at the college,
or a film festival, or a lecture. Not exactly the most
exciting place in the world, he thought without ran-
cor, nor a place so firmly locked in the past that it had
forgotten when and where it was; but even the young,
unlike the young elsewhere, understood the value of
nights such as this, though that value might be apparent only in memory.

He squirmed against the seatcover, brushed a languid hand over the dashboard. He could not imagine
what attractions there were in far-off Colorado that
would lure his parents away from dreamstates like
this.

The estates drifted behind him. The stretch of
woodland was now broken only by a few scattered
houses set well back from the road, their lights on

even though the sun had not set, made bright by the twilight already growing beneath the trees. He wondered what it was like to live out here, essentially alone though the village was within reach of a brisk walk or a quick drive. It was something to consider, though not to plan on, and as he slowed to take the thump of the tracks he decided that no matter how ill Don was or what mood Andrea was in, tonight he would propose. What the hell, why not. Tonight he would take haven from the winds that dogged him.

The Buick stalled.

At first he didn't realize it, so entrenched in his fantasies that he thought himself still moving. Then the stench of gasoline told him he had flooded the carburetor. Marvelous, he thought, and turned off the ignition, switched it on again and listened to the battery working its magic. Working, and not producing. He scowled, sniffed, thumped a palm against the steering wheel, and realized he hadn't even cleared the tracks. Looking to his right he could see through the open window the tunnel of foliage that stretched south toward the station.

And a light.

Small, glaring, and unquestionably moving toward him.

His first reaction was to smile, his second to try the engine again. When it still refused to kick over, he shifted the gears into neutral and pushed at the door. When it didn't open at his try he pushed again, harder. Glanced over his shoulder at the light still approaching. He put his hands together, palms flat, fingers stretched, and held them on edge against his lips and closed his eyes. A slow inhalation, and he jammed the ignition over, the battery grinding swiftly, slower, sputtering and dying. He pumped the accelerator and smelled the gasoline, reached over to the passenger door and found it was locked. Nervously, then, he decided to climb through the window and push the Buick clear. There was plenty of time; the light was still tiny, wavering slightly and beginning to flare at the edges.

He reached for the outside, and his hand stopped, stinging, as if slapped against glass.

"No."

Reached over the back seat; the windows were the same.

"No."

The ignition again, but the battery was dead. He kicked at the doors, and only numbed his legs. Fumbled in the glove compartment and grabbed out the heavy flashlight. He had no idea what was blocking the open windows, but he tried to shatter the obstruction with blows that grew increasingly desperate, increasingly frantic as he watched the light expanding whitely, touching at the leaves on either side and above. The tracks rumbled beneath the car, the heavy wheels of the train cracking over the gaps in the rails.

Closer, and he began to whimper. He knew he wasn't asleep, felt as if he were back in the bathtub and the water was boiling him while it turned black and swamped him.

"No. For god's sake . . ."

He could do nothing but stare. His arms were too tired to wield the flashlight anymore, and his legs jerked in spasms without touching the doors. He looked, and saw himself gripping the steering wheel, waiting for a miracle to restart the engine and hurtle the Buick away from collision. He licked at his lips and felt his bowels loosening, wrinkled his nostrils at the stench of his own soiling. His left hand touched at the unyielding air at the door, brushed over his face as the compartment grew brighter. Shadows of trees sweeping over his lap. The hood ornament gleaming at one side like the moon. The road ahead black, the road behind the same.

A scream for a whistle, and he spun around to stare, his eyes narrowing for clarity, widening in fear: the engine was a locomotive, coal-bearing, not diesel. The cowcatcher was painted bright red, the bulging sides of the engine sleek, black, and spouting brilliant white steam. Pistons churning, the rails talking back, the light like a comet whose tail was in darkness. A locomotive, not a diesel. And the Buick so old.

He swallowed, wondered if it were really the engineer he saw leaning out of the cab and staring in horror at the car stalled on the tracks. Wondered if he really heard the sudden shrieking protest of the brakes as they were applied, steam and smoke reaching to the stars, to the trees, to the roadbed . . . to the car. Wondered how it would feel when the locomotive stopped barely an inch from the door and saved him the embarrassment of explaining why he was there.

Then he stopped wondering.

And the locomotive didn't stop.

21

He knew he must have dreamt something, down in the dark, but none of the images (if images there were) returned to him when he bid them, nor did any of the sensations of fear or relief or terror or death. He knew he wasn't dead. He also knew he could not prove it. For all his rationalizations he might very well be in some actual limbo where souls waited for judgment, assuming judgment was to be had and there was someplace else to go. But he didn't believe it. He *couldn't* believe it. Not when there was all this pain—spirals and lances of it, tides of it, throbs of it. Not when he could feel without moving each portion of his body on some bed and reclining.

Not when he could still see the locomotive bearing down on him.

Alive, then. Somehow he had managed to escape the collision with at least his brain intact, and somehow somebody had found him and dragged him out of the wreck . . . he tried to move, to shift, to see if he still had both of his arms. He thought he did. He wasn't sure, but he thought so. And suddenly he did not feel quite as safe as he had. Suppose he wasn't in the hospital on King Street. Suppose whoever . . . whatever . . . he shook his head violently though he didn't feel it move . . . suppose *whoever* had found him was the same who had taken the tourist and the women. Suppose he was entrapped in someone else's nightmare.

Alive; but there was no way to tell how long that would last.

The spirals, the lances, the throbbing increased. He heard himself groaning as though standing at the lip of an immense and deep well. There might have been an added pain then, though he could not be sure, and the throbs and the lances and the spirals receded. He was alone. He was drifting. And he was glad he was alive.

The jungle had changed. Where there had been trees so high they obliterated the sky, now there were monoliths of black iron and white steel; where there had been colonies of wasps that thrummed through the air, now there were robins whose necks were all broken and flew nevertheless with wings tipped with blood; where there had been grass and shrubs and cooling deep shade, now there was sand and spikegrass and no shade at all. He was astonished he was not afraid, eventually chalked it up to a fascination with the strange that had dogged him all his life. The problem was, he could not remember living that life at all. As hard as he strained and as much as he delved, he could recall nothing of what had happened before the jungle had changed. There were only the black iron and the white steel, and after a century or so a series of ventings that blew steam at the robins, fogging them, drenching them, weighting them until they dropped to the ground and were speared by the spikegrass while he watched in fascination. Always in fascination. Always without thinking. He watched only, and observed, and could not help but wonder at how the jungle had changed. With only the black iron and the white steel until all the birds were dead and the steam had become fog and there were women in the fog who strolled briskly past him, eyes straight

ahead, arms rigid at their sides, soft smiles on their
faces that had been softened with age. He made no
attempt to speak to them. He did try, once, to reach
out and touch one, but a sudden shriek of metal
crawling against metal stayed the hand in midair, and
all he could do safely was watch the odd parade and
wonder with a bemused smile at how the jungle had
changed.

But at least, he thought, all the wasps were gone.

The locomotive stopped a handsbreadth from the
Buick. The engineer clambered down from the cab
and ran over to the hood, slamming a huge fist onto
the maroon metal and shaking his head in shocked
disbelief. Josh yelled at him, demanding the oil-
stained man find a way to let him out. There was a
spell, he screamed without making a sound, a spell on
the Buick and he could not get out. But the engineer
evidently couldn't hear him, couldn't see him; he only
pounded on the hood until his hand turned red. Then
he stopped and mopped his face with a huge red
handkerchief, pulled at his soiled cap, and walked
around the car as though, in his whole life, he had
never seen such a thing in front of his train before. He
touched at it and stroked it and whistled his admiration. Shrugged and beckoned to his companions in the
cab. There were four of them, and they hunkered
down in front of the Buick and pushed it back off the
tracks. Josh refused to stop shouting, leaping around
the inside of the car like an ape demented by torment,
like a man attempting to escape a glass prison. But
none of them heard him; or if they did, they ignored
him. All they wanted to do was remove the obstruction and carry on to Hartford where the next crew
would take over so the train could go to Boston. Josh
sagged, and shrugged, and once the car was off the
rails and the locomotive gone by—with no coaches
behind it—he reached out and touched the ignition
key. Turned it. The engine started. He laughed,

rocked, threw the car into gear, and headed out to
Andrea's. Or tried to, at least, until the tracks stopped
him and the locomotive reappeared and the engineer
screamed and the engine didn't stop.

Though he could see no texture, he could have
sworn he was looking at a solid black curtain. It *felt*
right, the curtain; there was no sensation of depth to
the blackness he saw. And he grinned in vindication
when he realized a glow had begun on the other side.
Faint. Somewhat distant. A glow unmistakable. Increasing slowly, and he was in no hurry to goad it. He
thought—quite naturally, he thought—of the light
on the locomotive, and he did not want a repeat of the
incident that had landed him . . . wherever.

Eventually he could see folds in the black, folds like
thick draperies. And the black itself began to fade into
a deep velvet green, a deep velvet green that rippled as
though a giant were breathing somewhere to one side.

He was fascinated. He watched it. He saw the glow
diffuse and he knew it wasn't the train; he saw the
green begin to separate and he knew it wasn't a
drapery or a curtain or a wall; he saw the green vanish,
saw a series of pale green squares each pocked with
holes that were shadows in themselves.

He blinked, and heard someone in the room gasp.

The spirals and the lances were gone now, no traces,
but the throbbing remained and he tightened his jaw
against it. Shadows in white drifted in and out of his
vision, limbs were moved gently, the snug sheet across
his chest drawn back and something done to something below his waist. He tried to speak, but his throat
was too dry. A hand cupped his chin, and he felt
moisture at his lips. When he tried to swallow too
quickly a gag reflex took over and the hand snapped
away. Waited. Returned. He smile his gratitude, and
the hand tapped his neck *you're welcome*.

He drank until the water was taken reluctantly
away. Smiled again. Saw a face he didn't recognize

break out of the blur and stare down at him, thoughtful and solemn, while hands did other things to other
places around him. He licked at his lips. The face
nodded expectantly. He let his head roll slowly on the
pillow, and saw through the dim haze a dimmer room
and bright light. Someone was with him, but whoever
it was did not approach whatever bed he was on. He
wanted to ask where he was, what was wrong, but he
recalled—dimly, fearfully—what his choices were,
and he was afraid.

A voice; it was the face: "Mr. Miller, can you hear
me?"

He nodded, though he kept his expression wary.

The face looked away, grew onto narrow shoulders
encased in white. A person. Josh sighed.

The doctor looked back. "Mr. Miller." He spoke
softly, but not quietly. A normal tone for conversation with a man who should have been dead. "Mr.
Miller, how clear is your thinking?" The doctor
grinned suddenly, laid a mocking slap to his own
cheek. "Stupid question. I apologize. Is the pain bad?
It has been, you know, but I don't want to give you
any more medication of that strength if I can help it.
Can you talk, Mr. Miller? Can you tell me how you
feel?"

Josh licked his lips again. He felt himself drifting,
but it was suddenly important that contact be estab-
lished. "Yes," he said, and felt utterly exhausted.

"Yes what?"

"Yes. There's pain. I can't tell you where. Hard to
feel. I'm not dead."

The doctor grinned again. "A long way from it, Mr.
Miller. You weren't even close." He sat on the edge of
the mattress and laid a hand on Josh's arm. Lightly.
Very lightly. "No casts, as you may be able to tell.
You're very lucky. You only broke a few ribs, which is
why you may feel a certain constriction around your
chest. Bruised worse than a rugby player everywhere
else."

With the injuries vocalized he began to feel the throbbing return to his system. His smile was strained.

"I know," the doctor told him. "But I expect you'd rather know it all before you fall asleep again. It'll help with the nightmares."

Maybe, he thought; then again, maybe not.

"You were also cut up pretty badly. A fair number of stitches on your face, legs, and arms. Not a record, by any means, but for a while you're going to look like Frankenstein, I guess."

He licked at his lips. "The monster."

The doctor looked puzzled.

"The monster," Josh said. "Frankenstein was the scientist. It was the monster who was stitched up."

A voice muttered something beyond his hearing, and the doctor turned around. "Yes, you're right. He does seem better. If, that is, this is what you call normal." The second voice again. The doctor clapped once and stood carefully, adjusting the replaced sheet as though filling time to the next stage. Then he fingered the pens jammed into his breast pocket. "There are a number of people who have been trying to get to see you, Mr. Miller. We've kept them out, because of your condition." Pensive again. "Perhaps tomorrow. Right now, though, you're going to sleep."

Josh shook his head. He didn't want to sleep now. He wanted to know what miracle had saved him.

Instead: "How . . . long?"

The man seemed surprised. "Oh, a few more days. All the pictures are clear, no internal injuries or concussions. Your system just had a nasty shock, Mr. Miller, and we want to be sure you don't jar loose those stitches. You were quite active while you were out. You must do a lot of jogging."

Josh had an immediate image of himself trying to run while he was flat on his back. He laughed, heard himself croaking, and laughed even harder. There were tears in his eyes. He choked, and water was given

to him again. As he lifted his head to take it he noticed
the IV stand, and the clear tubes, and the bandages.
He grimaced, and the doctor misunderstood.

"They do tend to pull when they're healing, don't
they. Don't worry, though. As long as you promise
not to get back into your sweatsuit for a couple of
weeks there should be no problem." He patted Josh's
shoulder. "You take it easy, now, all right? I'll be back
before I leave, just to see how you're resting." His
smile became less professional, almost envious. "You
have a lot of friends, Mr. Miller. Every one of them
has been demanding I take care of you and forget the
rest of my patients. You're very lucky. I'd be proud
just to have one of them."

Josh could think of nothing to say, nor could he
imagine who had been so insistent. He was a loner.
He . . . He swallowed and lifted a hand weakly. "The
Buick."

The second voice again, and this time the doctor
shook his head in gentle exasperation. Shrugged, and
stepped to one side. Josh waited, holding his breath,
closed his eyes slowly when Felicity grinned into
view. Pale, her face lined, an umbrella in one hand.

"Miller?"

"Hey."

"Fool."

He shrugged as best he could. "The Buick?"

"I told you he was all right," she said to the doctor.
She turned back. "King's already working on it. He
says he'll have it good as new by the time you hit the
streets again."

"Impossible."

Felicity frowned. "What are you talking about?
He's good! You keep telling me he's the only one
around here who understands that car as well as you.
It was the first place I thought of to take it, for god's
sake."

"Miss Lancaster." The doctor touched her arm.

"A minute," Josh said. Looked to Felicity, bewildered. "It . . . the damage . . ."

"The grille, the hood, the fenders. A few lousy scratches."

"All right, Miss Lancaster," the doctor said, taking hold now. "You can see him tomorrow. Mr. Miller, please get some sleep."

"Fel," Josh said as they reached the door, "the train—"

"Huh?" She frowned at the doctor, at him, at the bed. "What train, Miller? You plowed into a tree."

He slept without wanting to. Woke again when it was dark and suffered the humiliation of having his bedpan changed. Was bathed with a sponge and warm water. Slept again. It was light. Dozed off and on, aware that at one point during the day there were people in the room waiting to talk to him. But he could not find the energy, could not find the will. He could do nothing but see the astonishment and concern on Felicity's face, could hear nothing but her saying something impossible about a tree. He may have been banged all to hell, but he knew what he saw—there had been a locomotive, and it had struck the Buick broadside, and there was no possible way the grille and the fender and the hood could have been the only things damaged by the collision he'd suffered. No way at all.

So he decided there was something seriously wrong. Something so terrible that whoever was in authority, with the complicity of his friends, had decided not to tell him about it. His first thought had been that they'd licd about his limbs, and he spent hours making sure that arms and legs were still there; then he considered the possibility of brain damage, something done to his reasoning processes that would drive him out of business forever, perhaps even into a home where he would be "taken care of," like a child. But once he had swept through the multiplication tables, to ninety-times-ninety, he dismissed that avenue, too. During the second or third evening after his awakening he sat up groaning, wondering if someone had been killed through his negligence. That, too, would be hidden until he was emotionally stable enough to handle the guilt. And that, too, was discarded because there had been no one else but him, and the Buick, and the train.

On the fourth day he was sitting up with his lunch when Felicity walked in, kissing his forehead lightly before saying a word. He grinned, felt himself blushing, and finished the meal while he told her how Dr. Anderson had been slowly but surely prying loose the stitches. Seeing them scattered over his lower body had been only mildly disconcerting; what had bothered him the most, though he would not admit it, were those laced over his cheeks. There would be scars, he was told, because the depth of the glass' penetration; scars, however, that could easily be taken care of with cosmetic operations once all the flesh had healed and had grown as sturdy as the rest of him. He remembered, or thought he remembered, talking to the man about Frankenstein. He couldn't recall the context, but the name was enough. Dark lines, angry pink and healing skin—enough, he thought, to scare off the bogeyman.

"It'll give you character," Fel told him then, pulling up a ladder-back chair and sitting close to his hip. "I take it you're feeling better?"

"Still stiff," he said. "But they have me walking around so I don't get rigid." He pushed the tray away and folded his hands at his waist. "Fel, about the accident—"

"I know," she interrupted quickly, with a cautious glance toward the closed door. Then she touched nervously at her hair, at the collar of her flower-print blouse. Looked at him with a slight cast of suspicion. "How are you?" she asked, and held up a hand. "I mean, you look okay, but how's your head? Can you think straight?"

"I guess so." He did not push her. The barely perceptible narrowing of her eyes, the attitude of her seating kept him from exploding with the questions his mind demanded.

"I hope so," she told him flatly. "You know, you raved a hell of a lot while you were damned near in coma all that time. I was here. I . . . I heard all about the train and what you thought was happening."

"I didn't think the accident, Fel."

"I can see that," she said, no humor in her tone. "I can see that, Miller. That cop, Tanner, he says you fell asleep while you were driving and ended up in the tree. That's what it says on the report. I told him you weren't all that tired when I saw you last, but he . . . it doesn't matter. He's got his report, and he's happy."

Josh plucked at the sheeting. "You're not?"

"Andrea's been here a couple of times, too."

He didn't remember, but his smile told her he was glad she'd let him know. Somehow, even long after the fact, it was a comfort. "Did, uh, she hear me babbling?"

"Sure. We all did. We had a long talk a couple of days ago—her father's still pretty bad. I understand—and . . ." A pause for reluctant admiration. "She thinks a lot of you, Miller, god knows why. But she doesn't understand where you got the idea about that train."

He eased himself back onto his pillow, the bed cranked almost ninety degrees up. He did not want to say anything now because the tone of her voice told him more than her words—that Andrea may not understand, but she certainly had a damned good idea. And if that were true, it was more than he knew right now. Bad enough he had lost two weeks in this place, most of it slipping in and out of consciousness and nightmares; the whole world could have gone up in smoke and he never would have known about it.

Finally, when he could no longer allow the silence to continue, he nodded to her. "Okay. Okay, Fel, tell me what you think."

"You're in no position to laugh, you know."

He held up a hand and turned its back toward her. Exposing, displaying the healing scars of his wounds. "I have nothing to laugh about, nothing at all."

She nodded. "And I want you to promise to hear me out before you strangle me."

"Don't push it, Fel. Don't push it."

Immediately he said it, he regretted the threat and the effect it produced on the color of her cheeks. But he could not take it back, and he would not. Blown back and forth like a balloon on the wind, he was tired of turning around and every time finding someone had reorganized his world. If Fel had any clue, any clue at all, he wanted to know it because someone was going to pay for his fear.

"I've said this once before, Miller," she whispered. "I'll say it again—who's after you? No. Wait. Don't say anything. It's more than that now. Miller . . . who's trying to kill you?"

22

A trembling dizziness drifted over him, and he closed his eyes against it. It was not so much the question itself that bothered him as it was the assurance that both of them understood she had asked the right one. Nothing about the train, nothing about the accident and how it might have been caused, but the acceptance in spirit (if not yet in fact) that no matter what Tanner's report said, it wasn't an accident at all. It was an attempt. A clear and deliberate attempt to take his life. And worse: for no reason that he could understand. If he were an important banker, stockbroker, any one of the hundreds of financially and politically powerful men in the village, he would be able to take hold and comprehend it. But he wasn't. He ran a small specialty business on a sidestreet, known to only a handful of people; he had no enemies except those in similar pursuits, and they would hardly lease locomotives to run him down; he had wronged no husbands and had impregnated no women, never cheated at cards or baseball, didn't owe loan sharks, and never bet on the horses. He was dull. He was ordinary. And someone, it seemed, didn't think of him that way.

"I don't know," he said, appeal in his voice.

"Neither do I," she told him.

"But you have a suspicion, don't you. And I don't have to guess who, do I."

She shook her head.

"Fel, the obvious thing would be for me to accuse you of being spiteful, jealous, all those cute little explanations that fill up bad movies." He looked down at his hands, flat on the sheet over his thighs. "The trouble is, too, I know you too well to dismiss them out of hand while, at the same time, I know you've probably fought like hell to neutralize them." He looked up; she was staring, her lips pale in indignation. "I know. A hell of an assumption."

"I'm trying to save your life, you bastard."

"Convince me," he said. "I mean, convince me there's someone out there who wants it."

They didn't speak for several minutes. A nurse interrupted to take blood pressure and temperature, an attendant to take away the remains of his lunch and fluff his pillow and caution Felicity not to stay too long. Then Dr. Anderson came in, too cheerful by half, and told Josh he could leave anytime after tomorrow, left him with an appointment to come back for the stitches' removal.

Alone, they watched the sunlight white through the venetian blinds, the oak that barely reached here to the top, fourth floor. When a summons chimed faintly in the corridor, Felicity shook herself as though out of a dream and pulled the chair closer, using the bed to punch out her emphasis.

"While you were in dreamland, partner, I did some more checking, this and that, and thought a lot about what you told me the day you hit the tree."

"I didn't—"

She hushed him with a scowl. "We can argue that later, okay? Right now, we've got too much to get straight. You going to listen, or am I going to walk?"

She grinned, and he grinned back, lifted a hand imperiously toward her. She snapped at it and he snatched it back. The tension was still there, but the animosity was gone.

"What I did was," she said, "I put to the test all the lessons I thought I learned from the guy who's trying to teach me this silly business of pop archaeology. What I did was, I made lists—of all the things I could remember about your having trouble. Not just with the office, but with your personal life, too. I don't know what you haven't told me, but I could make some pretty good guesses, I think. Anyway, I did anyway . . . and I have a theory."

"You found the handplow."

She grimaced at him. "Funny."

"You found Mrs. Thames."

"Maybe."

He stared.

"Listen. Just listen. You promised not to interrupt, remember?" She waited. He couldn't stop staring. "You know, when you told me what Dr. Stanworth said to you the morning Mrs. Thames took off, it rang a bell. I thought about that first, and I realized he was right. You haven't been yourself lately, Josh, you really haven't. There are days when you're the same sweet old son of a bitch I used to know, and days when you act like someone dropped a fog over your head. So I made the list.

"Josh, please don't think I'm crazy, but I think everything that's happened to you over the past couple months has been deliberate."

He looked up to the ceiling, but kept his expression as blank as he could. There were any number of sarcastic replies he could have offered, but all of them suddenly seemed petty and untoward. Instead, he waited, already traveling along the lines she had suggested.

"It's like someone out there doesn't want you to do the things you do best, Josh."

He heard her, felt the moisture break on his palms as he believed her.

"I mean, you get going on the handplow and something comes along to distract you. Then something else comes along to distract you from that. And then something else. And something else. Like you were being herded around in a corral or a circle, and you never have time to stop and really think. Your head gets filled, Josh. You know that. You get a bug and you don't let it go, you worry the damned thing to death, and more if you're not satisfied with the corpse.

"So every time you get close to one thing, you get turned around to something else. And it was the handplow, Josh. It was the handplow that started it."

He nodded. She continued to speculate, to apologize for the speculations, and he nodded through it all because she was right. He had felt it once before, and the feeling now returned: one of quiet, unobtrusive, long-range manipulation. Events orchestrated to keep him in line, but events spaced out over days and weeks so that discovering the connection was virtually impossible. Until Melissa had given him the clue, the clue he hadn't known until it was too late.

Felicity had gone to the Thames house, had searched through the old woman's desk until she'd found an address book. She called some of the numbers and learned that none of the other women in the group had left town unexpectedly. Then she reminded him of the four manuscripts he had unearthed in New York, searches that had come in after he had left the Station to look for Dale's sheet music. It was obvious now, she told him, that the idea was to keep him away as long as possible, away from the village so his curiosity wouldn't inadvertently lead him to someplace where he didn't belong. At least not yet.

"The office, your place . . . it was all what they call a plant. Something like that. Smokescreen. Keep you off balance. Keep you from thinking, Josh. Keep you from *thinking!*"

The greatest invention man had yet devised was not the wheel, he thought, or the printing press or the

automobile or spacecraft or television; it was hind-
sight. A hell of a thing that made experts of fools . . .
especially fools like him.

No. He frowned at himself. No, not a fool. Only if
he had known from the beginning what was happening and had ignored it. Dupe. Not much more elegant,
but better than fool. He had been a dupe.

"Thinking about what?" he asked, refusing to meet
her gaze.

"About . . ."

He looked at her, hard, reached out, and took her
wrist. "Felicity, it's Andrea, right? It's all right, I'm
way ahead of you."

"I don't think so," she said. "I think it's her
father." She rushed on. "Look, he's not there when
you want him, he can't be found when he's supposed
to be in the city, he's got Andrea prancing around like
a goddamned trained horse, and when I talked to her
it was clear she's scared to death of him. I don't know
what he's doing, but he has something to do with all
the people who aren't around anymore. They leave,
not officially missing because there's no sign of trouble, and it's all on their birthdays. Significant, Sher-
lock, significant. Don't ask me why, but it is. You
already know that. What you don't know is that
King—the garage guy?—he had a guy working for
him last fall, just walked off the job. A drifter. Lived
on Devon Street, one of the boardinghouses like mine.
Never took his stuff. Gone. Poof. A waitress at the
inn, young and sexy—poof. A young guy who used to
work in the park, cleaning up after the kids—poof.

"Poof, Miller. Nine of them. Poof."

He chuckled, covered his mouth with an apologetic
hand . . . and let it drop slowly into his lap. "Nine."

She nodded.

"Felicity, there were . . ."

"Right," she said. "I didn't have the nerve to go out
there myself, but I remembered what you told me.
Nine people nobody would miss, nine graves that

aren't supposed to be where they are. I thought of that. I made some calls."

"I'll bet." But his admiration increased a hundred-fold as he smiled.

"Vandalism in almost a dozen cemeteries across the state. Graves marked up, torn up, monuments toppled, stuff like that. Also, headstones stolen. Old ones. Ones nobody really cares about because they're too damned old and the names on them have been practically worn off."

The nurse returned, gently adamant that visiting hours were over and no dispensation would be given. They both protested so loudly a small crowd gathered at the door, but the head nurse would not be budged. She glowered, and gestured, and Felicity picked up her purse.

"Think some more, Miller," she said as she left. "I'll see you tomorrow. Rain or shine it'll be a nice day."

He waved dispiritedly, fell into a silence that not even the doctor could shatter.

Sunset, and he stared at the opposite wall. Everything Fel had told him made a foul kind of sense, though neither of them had yet ventured to clear up the *why*. Off balance; that much he could accept, but he didn't know why. Felicity said the handplow was behind it, and he thought she meant because his searching would have eventually led him to the new/old graveyard. As it had when he had gone out there with Andrea.

His hands gripped the sheets, ready to toss them aside. His clothes, if he had any left from the accident, must still be in the closet. He would have to get out to the farm somehow, tell her he knew what her father was doing. Her father obviously in league with Lloyd Stanworth. A conspiracy of killing. A collection of murder.

Off balance. Why him?

Supper came and was eaten, was taken away. Shortly

after nine the night nurse came in and stood by his
head, her hands behind her back. "I guess you're not
going to sleep, are you."

"Can't," he said, a disingenuous shrug. "A lot on
my mind."

"There's no medication prescribed for you."

"Don't want any, thank you."

She wasn't young, but she carried middle age well.
She exposed her hands, and in them a telephone. "I
talked with my friend before I came on. She's in
charge of days. She told me about your heavy meeting
with your . . . friend." Her eyes crinkled into a smile.
She plugged in the phone. "I'm going to come back in
fifteen minutes and I'm going to discover that you
have an unauthorized phone. Naughty." And she left.

Josh wasted no time. He tried first for Andrea, but
there was no answer and he pounded at the mattress
until his arm tired. Then a futile attempt at the
Stanworth's residence before he called Felicity.

"I don't have much time," he said, "but don't ask
me why. Is there anything else you have to tell me?"

"The dreams," she said. "The wind."

"What about them?"

"They were caused."

"Felicity, you're crazy. I'm sorry, love, but you've
been great until this. What the hell do you mean, they
were caused?"

"Somebody is doing something to you, Miller. I
don't know what, I don't know how. Think about it.
You feel watched, you have these dreams, you think
you've been hit by a train when there wasn't any train
on that track that night . . . all of it. Damnit, Josh, it
was caused!"

He could hear the fear in her voice, draping her
words, catching her breath until she sounded ragged.
"How?" he whispered harshly, with one eye at the
door, an ear picking up footsteps heading for his door.
"How, Fel, how?"

"I don't know!" Hysteria, then, unbidden, uncorked. "Hypnosis, the supernatural . . . how the hell should I know? Drugs, maybe, in your food. I can't answer that, Josh. I wish I could, but I can't."

"Fel," he said urgently, "you've got to try to get hold of Andy. Make her leave that house if you can. I've tried once and no one answered. If you have to stay up all night, for god's sake try to get her."

"Josh . . . I'm scared. If her father finds out . . ."

"Yeah. Damnit, yes, you're right." He put a fist to his teeth and chewed hard on his knuckles. He couldn't think. Nothing made sense, and everything did. And he almost screamed when the nurse returned with an orderly to take out the phone.

Feigning sleep wasn't difficult; he was exhausted without having to move a muscle. Twice, three times, he went over their conversation and attempted to find out where the new clue lay. There had to be one. He couldn't miss it as he had the others—telling himself he hadn't known there was a mystery, so don't blame yourself, idiot—but the attempt was futile. And probably would be until he discovered what Murdoch and Stanworth were up to. And how they had managed to invade his mind to produce those hallucinations, how they had timed them so precisely, how they had learned where he would be and when so they could exploit him when he was vulnerable. Like in the bathtub, and in the car.

Felicity knew. Felicity had called him while he was bathing. He almost accepted it until he remembered the call prior to hers, the call he had cursed because there was no one at the other end.

Some *thing*, then, that stalked him? That watched him? That knew him? He wanted to dismiss it as patently idiotic, but he could not deny that the windstorms had been real.

He trembled and held tightly to the edges of the mattress. He trembled and shut his eyes against the helplessness he was feeling. First there was fear that he could almost believe there was something in the Station that was supernatural and real: *I've seen things here; you can't live in the Station all your life without knowing the place isn't what you call your normal town;* then there was the molten-white rage that his life could be so altered, be tampered with, with such arrogant impunity. He could almost follow the reasoning, almost admire its planning: let him get his teeth into something, then shake him off. Use dreams, use friends, use Andrea and her sex. Use anything we can, but let's keep him hopping. Tired. Until he doesn't *want* to think anymore, until he just goes where we take him.

What they hadn't counted on, obviously, was his love for Melissa Thames. He hadn't known what it was before, but he recognized it now—a love of respect and of revering, a love that breeds loyalty no matter how late it's known.

He saw the graveyard; that made him dangerous. He saw the old woman; that made him risky. He fell in love with Andrea, and she fell for him, and that made them both most likely expendable.

Feigning sleep, then, was easy. He waited until the nurse had made her rounds, checked his pulse, fussed with his covers, then slipped painfully, stiffly out of bed and stumbled over to the closet. A clean shirt and pressed jeans hung on a hook, his boots stuffed with a pair of socks were set on the floor, underwear and a belt on the narrow shelf above. He closed his eyes and blew a kiss to his partner, shed the hospital gown as quickly as his ill-used muscles and tender skin would allow, and dressed. Slumped on the bed to catch his breath. Listened to the sounds of the hospital sleeping.

Five minutes later he was at the door, peering through a crack at the station near the elevators. The night nurse was there, reading a magazine. An intern

wandered by, leaned on the counter, and began bla
tant flirting. The round-faced clock on the wall behind
them told him it was eleven.

It was ten past midnight when they both wandered
off.

He waited, slowly rolling his shoulders in an at
tempt to loosen them, shaking each leg in turn to get
them to work. Then, with a deep breath and a whis
pered prayer he pushed into the corridor, did not
bother to look around but headed directly for the fire
stairs and made his way down.

Once outside and encased in the shadows of well-
tended shrubs, he leaned heavily against the wall and
gulped at the night air. It was cool, the heatwave
passed, and insects slammed suicidally against the
globes of the lampposts. A car hushed by, an ambulance with red lights flaring. He expected an alarm to
be raised, but he needed to rest, needed to think of
how he could get a car. His own was out of the
question, and Felicity didn't drive. But when his mind
cleared of the throbbing that cloaked him as he'd
descended, he recalled one place he would have to see
sooner or later, one place where they wouldn't dare
refuse him admittance.

When he was ready, then, he pushed off the wall and
hurried across King Street, keeping to the shadows
until he reached Fox Road. He turned right and
counted four houses down, stood in a short driveway
and nodded at the Jaguar parked out of the garage.

Stanworth was a coward. He would tell him everything he wanted to know. Josh knew he would. Josh
knew, too, he would strangle the bastard if he tried
anything funny.

A breeze chilled him, reminding him of the wind, as
he walked around the ranch house to the back door.
Knocked. Knocked louder. Stared at the windows
where he knew the bedroom to be. Dared not make
too much noise and tried the knob. It turned and he

eld his breath, pushed the door open, and sidled nside.

The stench was overpowering. He whirled around and collapsed against the kitchen wall, gagging, clamping a hand to his mouth and nostrils as he fought to keep his stomach from churning more bile. His free hand rested on the wall switch, but he didn't move it. He didn't have to. There was moonlight. It was grey. It sifted across the fake brick floor and highlighted the table, the freestanding oven, the chairs, the utensils in their copper racks on the wall.

A darker patch of shadow lay huddled in the doorway that led to the front. The moonlight touched its fringe, crept over it, and moved on. The fringe was made of two pairs of shoulders . . . two pairs of shoulders that no longer supported heads.

23

Oxrun Station was quiet, not silent. Leaves rasped in dark conversation, hedges shied at the passage of cats; trucks on Mainland Road lumbered toward Hartford, most of the drivers not noticing the village hidden behind the thick towering pines; the few neon signs on Centre Street crackled softly, buzzed off and on, while the converted gaslight lampposts popped softly to the explosions of moths. It was too late for walking and too early for trains, and only the Jaguar moved through the shadows.

Josh had no idea how he had managed to fish the keys from Randy's pocketbook. No memory of staggering out of the house to fall on his back to gasp for fresh air.

All he could remember were the flies that rose sluggishly from the bodies on the threshold. Rose and circled and settled again.

He had thought they were wasps.

And in driving—more slowly than a walk—did not understand why he had not stopped at the police station to report the murders. He had passed it, had glanced at it, and had kept on moving, up Centre Street to the pike and out toward the valley. His clothes were soaked, clinging to his skin like clammy, sometimes prickling fingers; his hair felt like a steel cap, and his tongue refused to stay away from his lips. He swallowed convulsively until his throat ached. The sedan swerved erratically, several times thumping alarmingly against the low curbing.

He began to choke, the onset of weeping. Not for the loss of the Stanworth's, but for the utter and complete weariness that finally overtook him. No matter how hard he tried he could not drive straight, no matter how often he ordered his mind to go blank he could not ignore the dull pain that banded his chest and his legs, blurred his vision with dim sparks. He used Andrea sweet Andrea for the carrot to tempt him, danger of losing his life the stick to thrash him; none of it worked. He was human, nothing more, and his body was screaming for a time to rebuild.

The posts with the lions blind and enlarged. He swerved into the drive and winced when the right fender scraped the concrete. Sighed as he jounced over the driver's border and drove over the grass to the back of the mansion. It was better than nothing. So he thought as his hand fumbled with the door's handle, failed to hold a grip, and fluttered to his lap. He sat there, staring, and did not feel himself tipping, felt only the cool of the leather against his cheek and the protests fade under the blanket of black.

Hypnosis. Supernatural. Drugs.

Not a normal town.

. . . Josh . . .

Stiffly he slid out of the car, shading his eyes against the light glaring through the trees. His bladder was aching, his stomach filled with acid, and the right side of his face was creased with leather markings. The back door was still open. He dragged himself inside and used the bathroom, made himself a meal from the tinned goods in the cupboard and forced himself to eat it in spite of the efforts of his system to reject it. Slowly. So slowly it pained him. But he would do

Andrea no good if he was still a cripple when he saw her—assuming, he thought sourly, that she was still alive when he got there. And immediately he thought it he pushed away from the table and rushed into the library, grabbed up the phone, and dialed the Murdochs.

Someone picked up the receiver on the fifth ring.

He listened, heard breathing, put the knuckle of his thumb between his teeth to keep from speaking.

"Hello?"

He sagged to the floor, head lowered, free hand gripping the back of his neck. "Andy," he said, "it's me, Josh."

"My god, where are you? I've had people calling me all day. Josh, where are you? Are you all right? What's—"

"Andrea, I know it. I know it all. Are you . . . has he done anything to you?"

A pause. Breathing. "No." A whisper.

"I'm coming out. He killed Lloyd and Randy. I don't know how but he did it. I found them . . ." He stopped, feeling the weakness slip over him again.

"Josh, tell me where you are and I'll come for you."

He was surprised. "You can get away?"

"If I hurry."

"Andy, don't stand there then. Get . . ." He listened hard, heard a door closing and Andrea catch her breath. "I'm coming," he said harshly. "Don't be afraid, I'm coming!" He slammed down the receiver and struggled to stand, changed his mind and called the police to tell them what they would find if they sent a car over to Fox Road. He rang off on a demand to identify himself, was out of the house and into the Jaguar, speeding across the lawn to the drive, before he realized with a sardonic grin that he was still holding a piece of toast in his hand. He shoved it into his mouth, squealed onto the pike, and jammed the accelerator as far down as it would go.

At the tracks he almost faltered, could not help a glance along the line and a slumping relief when he saw the tracks were clear.

It was adrenaline, he knew, that was dulling the aches that had sprouted over his body, and he only hoped it would last long enough for him to get Andrea out of the house and back to the police. It should be simple enough: Andrea, if she was still thinking clearly, was right now working on a way to leave, maybe only going out to the porch for a breath of fresh air. Murdoch would be watching her. She'd said there'd been calls, and there was nothing to guarantee that Murdoch hadn't taken any of them. Josh had to assume the man knew he was out of the hospital, had figured most of the plot out and was . . .

The Jaguar sped onto Cross Valley, skidded as it took the turn onto the spur road. The steering wheel wrenched side to side as the potholes jarred the tires. He thought of the Buick. He blessed Felicity for taking care of it while he had been working his way back from darkness. He swerved to the left side, back to the right, had the farmhouse in sight when he felt the first buffeting of a swiftly rising wind. The grass in the fields flattened, and the hills were in turmoil. He threw up one arm instinctively when a gout of twigs and leaves swarmed around the windshield. The sedan skewed, and careened off a sturdy fencepost, the crunch of metal like artificial thunder.

The engine stalled.

He was facing diagonally across the road, the nose of the car aiming toward the northern hills, the orchards and crops sweeping toward him in banshee agitation. Forcing himself to remain calm, and unable to keep himself from glancing repeatedly at the rear-view mirror, he turned the key over. Waited. Released it and tried again.

The wind increased and the automobile shuddered. Something . . .

With one hand on the steering wheel to support him he leaned suddenly across the seat and stared out the passenger window. It had struck him that the distant woodland he'd been staring at was still. So were the hills that lowered toward the village from the south. But behind the farmhouse there was manic turmoil, branches stretching upward, straining, as though the wind were born of the earth itself.

Medication, he thought; it was residue of medication.

The air turned a deep spiraling grey over the trees. A faint cloud without definition, a tornado reversed, rearing above the foliage without casting a shadow, without blocking the moon, without dimming at all the sky's heat-soft blue. Rearing, twisting, riding above him in the belly of the wind.

He whirled to grab the back of the seat, saw the cloud-not-a-cloud writhe toward the Station. Bunching, narrowing, dropping out of sight.

Not me, he thought in congratulatory relief; my god, it wasn't me; and he buried his face in the crook of his elbow, shaking his head slowly and listening to the wind calm.

He turned around when the silence was too much to bear. Thumbed stinging from his eyes, swallowed, and reached for the key.

Not me.

And as abruptly as it had stopped the wind returned, settling a chill in his blood that kept his hand from moving. Not me, he told himself and the wind; it isn't me, it isn't me. He felt a grin at his lips, the rictus of a corpse.

Dervishes of pebbles spattered against the door. Dust rose and fell. He stared at the dashboard and tried the key a third time. The engine caught, and he laughed, was about to straighten the car and rush on when, quite without warning, he remembered a soft voice:

Rain or shine, it'll be a nice day.

"Oh my god," he whispered, his elation and relief dying, the hasty meal he'd prepared churning into acid.

He hadn't bothered to check on the date while he'd been in the hospital, hadn't seen a newspaper, hadn't listened to the radio. The medication he'd been administered had pacified and dulled him, had not been fully shocked from his system until he had begun fearing for Andy.

Andy; it was always Andy.

Blinding him, herding him, and only the wind—a ghostwind, he thought—told him in silence it was the first of July.

It was Felicity's birthday, and it was too late to save her.

He paid no heed to the road's condition; he gripped the steering wheel and stiffened his arms, bracing himself against the assault he would suffer as he plummeted through the windstorm, his head striking the roof, his teeth aching, his eyes no longer turning away from the debris that pelted and pitted the sedan.

It wasn't hypnosis; he understood that now.

It hadn't been drugs.

And despite the logic that supposedly governed him, despite the laws he had been taught in school and in the service, he was ready to believe there were other laws working; and he wondered if his father had known of them, too.

Oddly, so much so that he smiled mirthlessly to himself as he approached the farmhouse, the thought of the supernatural didn't fill him with terror. It may have been because there were still too many questions that had to be answered, or because of the condition of his body, or the single focus on Andrea and the danger she was in. It was, simply, another field to be explored, another mystery to be unraveled, another obstacle to be overcome. At the same time, he knew the feeling would not last; as soon as emotion caught up with reason there was every possibility he would drive himself mad.

But not now. Not now. He had failed too many people since this horror began, and he wasn't about to fail the one who counted most.

The drive way was empty. The MG gone and the porch door swinging wildly in the last battering of the wind. He was out and running before the engine stopped turning over, tripping once on the walk and catching himself on the flats of his hands. He groaned, rolled, and was on his feet again. Running. Swallowing hard the call that he was here, Andrea, and everything was all right.

Stopped at the foot of the steps as though he'd run into a glass wall.

The screens along the front of the porch were rippling, shimmering, hiding the bulk of the house beyond.

There was no sense in counting; the wasps numbered in the thousands.

They sensed him; he knew it. They had been waiting for him, and he knew that, too. And they lifted from their post in a single black cloud, hovering and swirling and driving him back.

"Andrea!"

Their buzzing covered her name, covered his sobbing, and he whirled to flee to the safety of the car, veered madly away when the Jaguar rippled and shimmered and the wasps lifted to the air.

He ran.

They followed.

When he made for the road a contingent clouded ahead of him, keeping several yards distant but their intent abundantly clear. Again he swerved, and ran, and sobbed, his arms pumping as his mouth gasped as the wasps in their droning shepherded him onward, away from the house and across the backyard, over the back fence and toward the first line of trees. And immediately he realized what they were doing he calmed; he could not keep his flesh from tightening nor his nightmares from intruding, but he knew they would not attack him until he was where he should be. So he slowed to an ungainly trotting until he was in the woodland, not looking at the massive escort as he headed for the graveyard. Tripping once and striking the ground hard with his shoulder, cringing when he heard the angry volume of the waspcloud increase as though it had settled above his ear. "Don't fight it," he muttered as he scrambled back to his feet. "Don't fight it, don't fight it." He didn't need the telling, but he needed the voice; he didn't need the urging, but he needed an excuse not to look around him. At the wasps crawling on the leaves, on the bark, over the grass and the rocks—a fragmented shadow of himself gone to terror. "Don't fight it, don't fight it." A twig jabbed his arm and he screamed, grabbed his elbow, and saw what had been done. His eyes closed, but still he ran. Another twig, another scream: "Don't fight it, don't fight it."

He fell into the clearing before he knew he was there.

He crawled on hands and knees into the center, sat cross-legged and began to whimper, his head low and covered by his shuddering encircling arms.

The wasps lifted to the foliage, and suddenly it was silent.

Without wind the heat increased; without wind the shadows stilled. He could hear nothing but the ragged and moist breathing that broke from his lips erratic and harsh. Could feel nothing but the ground beneath his buttocks, and the weight of the wasps as they waited for the killing. The train should have killed me, he thought; the train should have killed me. It isn't fair. It isn't goddamned fair! The train should have killed me.

"Well, well, well."

His arms were cramped from holding position so long; it was several seconds before he was able to take

them from about his head and let them fall limply into
his lap. His vision was blurred; there was salt caked on
his cheeks and his eyelids; the sour odor of urine at his
groin, and perspiration on his chest. If that was what
fear was, he thought while he waited; if that is what
fear does . . .

"Are you dead?"

A sleeve over his eyes, under his nose, across his
lips.

Murdoch stood ten yards from him, arms folded
loosely over his chest. His hair was gleaming with
incredible youth, the jowls gone and the sagging
stomach reduced. He seemed taller, more confident,
and the working of his lips supplied the clearing with
an unspoken arrogance born of an enemy long since
defeated.

"I understand you know what's going on," the man
said. And he shrugged.

"I thought I did," Josh said weakly, slowly straight-
ening his legs. "I know it isn't natural." There was no
sense in leaping to his feet; he could still feel the
presence of the wasps waiting above him. And he had
no doubt that a cabalistic word or a simple nod from
Murdoch would be all that was needed to return Josh
to that backyard jungle and let the wasps finish what
they'd started. "But I don't know it all."

Murdoch laughed soundlessly.

Josh wiped his face again and looked around the
clearing. Stopped when he saw the headstones and
counted them quickly. Counted them again. As far as
he could tell, now there were eleven. One of them
marking a pair of closed violet eyes.

Then he looked at Murdoch, realized the man was
standing at the mouth of an open grave, its headstone
lying in place, a huge uneven block of freshly quarried
granite.

"I hope that's for you," he said.

Murdoch laughed again. "It would be easier,
wouldn't it, Joshua."

"I don't know. You tell me." Then he thought of the date again, and his hands snapped into fists. "Andrea."

Murdoch shrugged.

Josh used the ground to help him, used his rage for a crutch to haul him to his feet. Murdoch backed off a pace but did not drop his hands. "Well? Are you going to tell me why you brought me here?" He tried not to wince at the whining tone to his voice. This was when he was supposed to be a hero, not a child.

"You said something about this not being natural," Murdoch reminded him. "You couldn't be further from the truth. It is, in fact, the most natural thing in the world." He smiled; his teeth were yellowed, dark around the edges. "It's about life, Joshua, and continuing to live. It's about yearly cycles, miracles, freezing."

Josh listened carefully, but he could not understand. "Freezing?"

"Freezing."

"But it's . . ." He paused, frowning, caught in spite of himself in the slow answering of all his whys. "Oh." He looked more closely at the man, at the grey still shot through the fresh black of his hair. He turned toward the graves, looked at Murdoch sideways. "You mean frozen in time, something like that."

Murdoch applauded mockingly, his hands not making a sound. "You *are* a bright little fellow, aren't you?"

"And I suppose there's some sort of a god, is that it?" He gestured toward the graves. "And these are sacrifices or something. Am I getting closer?" The train. The wind. The man with one arm. Josh grunted. Birthdays. "There's something special about a birthday, I take it." He couldn't help himself. "Bastard! You mean to tell me Felicity is the only one in this whole place with a birthday on the first?"

Murdoch shrugged. "It doesn't make any differ

ence, Joshua. She knew, you see."

He glanced again at the open hole, the black earth that lined it, looked away to Murdoch. "Not for me," he said. "For Andrea. In three days."

"I admire you," Murdoch said. "I like the way you think. And you're right. About the birthdays, that is. It's silly, isn't it, how we try to forget them the older we get, try to pretend they're just one more day in the year and they don't matter. But we always remember, don't we, Joshua. Something when we first wake up in the morning tells us this day is special. This day is the one that culminates a lifetime and embarks on another. There's energy there, you know. Energy few of us realize. The old ones know about it, but they learn about it too late and they don't know how to harness it." He lifted a finger as Josh took a step toward him. "Don't, my friend. I may have found out about it at the age at which you see me now, but it doesn't mean I'm decrepit." He grinned. "I could break you in half."

"So . . ." Josh swallowed. "They die on their birthdays."

"Only every cycle," Murdoch said, as though it didn't matter. "Twelve years. Give or take."

"Depending on the victims you can get," Josh said bitterly.

Murdoch grinned again. "You really are a bright one, you really are." He nodded. "They die on their birthdays. But they don't really, you see."

"No, I don't see." And he wasn't sure he wanted to, wasn't sure his acceptance of this bizarre explanation would take once he had a chance to think about it further. Assuming, he cautioned a burgeoning hope, he would have time left to do any thinking at all.

"Oh, they live again," Murdoch said, stepping around the grave. "Not in fact. You'll never see that little bitch again, Joshua. But she will live. What made her birth date special will be transferred to another, will be used, will be . . ." He smiled. A death's head smile. "Will be used."

"To keep you alive."

Murdoch frowned. "You try for too many answers at once, my friend. "You'll be confused again if you don't watch out."

"I am," Josh admitted. "But what you forget is that people out there"—he gestured toward the village—"know I'm gone from the hospital, know about the Stanworths. They'll be looking for me, you know. Sooner or later they'll find this."

"Tell me something, Joshua," Murdoch said, "how stupid do you think I am?"

It was then that Joshua realized Murdoch had been closing on him, was less than ten feet away and moving swiftly. He turned to run, to hunt for a weapon, heard Murdoch shout a warning, and could not help a look toward the trees.

The wasps were gone.

But in that moment of hesitation Murdoch threw himself at his legs, and Josh barely thrust his hands out to keep the ground from breaking his jaw. They rolled, Josh kicking and Murdoch clinging, the quiet in the clearing broken only by their grunts. Clots of earth rose, weeds snapped, Murdoch slowly climbed Josh's legs until he had a grip on his belt. A fist, then, into the man's face, pummeling to draw blood that splashed from his nostrils. Murdoch yelled and released him, and Josh stumbled to his feet. There was no thinking, no plan; his rage had supplanted the wiser course of escape—he was in the air before he knew what he was doing, covering Murdoch and grabbing his hair, pounding his head against the ground while he wept. Saliva flew from his mouth, tears from his eyes, and he didn't care about the wasps or the police or the fact that Don was Andy's father. He wanted to kill him. He wanted to split the man's skull and gouge out his brains, scatter his blood to whatever force the man had harnessed.

He screamed out his fury.

Screamed until he felt a sharp weight crash across his shoulders.

24

This is getting monotonous, he thought. The pillow was soft, the mattress soft, the sheets beneath his naked chest cool and stiff from a recent washing. A desultory breeze spiderwalked across his spine, and he could feel the hairs stirring at the back of his neck. And a scent he was unable to place— pungent, aromatic, not labeled at all with a hospital's mark. The house, then; someone had carried him back to the house after someone else—the old woman?— had clubbed him unconscious. But instantly the memory of the blow returned he realized he had been given no added pain. There was no pain at all, anywhere it should have been. The scent once again, and the giving, sliding feel of an oily balm spread thin across his shoulders. He tested them without lifting his head from the pillow—there was no stiffness.

A moment to test the room for company. He heard nothing, no one, sensed only an open window and the light streaming unchecked. He opened one eye, the other, eased himself gingerly onto his back.

It was a bedroom. Small, the walls uneven, the floors bare. A window directly opposite the foot of the bed, another to his left. A chest of drawers, vanity table and stool, wall-hung mirror on the right. No curtains. No

frills. The plaster was aged, cracked, and going yellow.
The whole room smelled of decades and disuse,
though as far as he could tell it was extraordinarily
clean.

He closed his eyes briefly, took several deep breaths
in preparation to move. He had no doubt that the door
sharing the wall with the headboard was locked, but
he wanted to see what was outside, to see if the world
as he thought he'd known it was still there to be seen.
He wouldn't have been surprised if it wasn't.

The bedframe creaked when finally he swung his
legs over the side and sat up. With hands splayed by
his buttocks he stared out the near window. At trees,
at tantalizing glimpses of distant hills and fields, a
single huge orchard losing its flowers to a dark fresh
green. He stood. Waited. Felt no dizziness and made
his way to the second window. The front porch roof, a
slice of the driveway, a segment of the road. There
were no cars that he could see; the MG and the Jaguar
had been moved. By the sun glaring at him he knew it
was late afternoon; he had no idea, however, what the
day was.

His arms stretched toward the ceiling and he
twisted from side to side without moving his feet. He
felt surprisingly strong, so much so that he frowned.
Deeper when he heard the touch of footsteps on the
floor outside the door. Quickly, he hurried to the bed
and lay down, staring at the ceiling and waiting. His
right hand was a fist, hidden by his hip.

The door opened slowly, an entrance to a sickroom.
Closed just as silently, with a sharp intake of breath.

Her hair was hidden beneath a red towel turban, the
rest of her swathed in a thin white robe imprinted
with oriental trees and birds on the wing. She wore no
makeup, her face gleaming with a blush that marks
the newly washed. When she sat on the edge of the
mattress he did not move, though he was tempted to
move away. Instead, he rolled his gaze toward her,

sorting through the questions, the demands, to say only: "Why?"

Her smile was resigned, her gaze lowered to her lap. "He's afraid of you."

"Don't!" he said sharply. "Don't cover for him, Andy, for god's sake. I saw the grave. I know it's for me. I must be the . . . I don't know, the final killing he needs." He laughed, once, explosively and without humor. "Listen to me, will you? Jesus, I'm talking like he wants to fix my car, not my wagon." He laughed again, then reached out for her hand. It was cold. Fearcold. "Andy, why the hell . . . all this time, why the hell didn't you get away? Why didn't you say anything to me?"

"Would you have believed me?"

He nodded. Considered. Shook his head. "Of course not. I would have thought you were crazy."

"Do you now?"

"For not getting away, yes. You could have at least tried to warn me. To warn . . . oh god, poor Fel."

"You saw the wind," she said. "You've seen what he can do. How far do you think I would have gotten, huh? He would have brought me back anyway. Josh . . ." She covered his hand tightly. "Josh, do you have any idea what this last year has been like? Christ, do you have any idea at all?"

"No. No, I suppose I don't." He followed a tormented crack in the ceiling. "I guess the train . . . he didn't want me dead, did he. To frighten me."

She shifted and he moved, and she was sitting crosslegged beside him, the robe drifting away from her thighs. "You were watched because you might cause trouble if you caught on . . . and believed it when you did. The office thing, the other at your house, it was to bother you, to keep you off balance. The bathtub, too. You were never in any danger. Not then." She began to toy with his fingers, stroking them one by one, scratching them idly. "The train. He wanted to kill you, then. I wouldn't let him. I'd been passive until then, thinking he would let you go. Then he would let me go and we could be together. But he wanted to kill you. I stopped him." She sighed loudly. "Your car was always moving, you know. Most of it was an illusion. I just stopped the train, and you hit the tree, just like the police said."

His eyelids fluttered, lowered, while his hand climbed to reach over her wrist. "Fel. She had it all, or most of it, anyway." He paused. "Lloyd? Do you know about Lloyd and Randy?"

He heard her hold her breath, heard it sift through her nostrils almost as a whimper. "Dr. Stanworth gave him the information he needed. Randy helped him. Then you started getting nosy, and he panicked. He told Don he wouldn't have anything more to do with it. He said you could make real trouble if you wanted to, and ruin it all."

"But why?" Josh whispered, then held up his free hand. "Never mind, never mind. That freezing in time business. Don proved it to Lloyd, and Lloyd jumped at the chance. Randy, too. Yeah. Randy would, you know. She started coloring her hair long before it would have started greying. I think she would have slit her throat at the first hair."

He sat up suddenly and took hold of her shoulders. "Christ, and all the time you were forced to cover for him you were trying to cover for me as well. Jesus, Andy, you're a hell of a woman!" He kissed her, stroked her back, smelled the shampoo she had used and the lingering touch of her soap. "And that old woman? She's real, isn't she. Yeah, sure she is. Don was telling me the truth about that much; she's your mother, and she's after this freezing thing too. They're in it together, and you're the one who has to . . . shit." He slapped at the mattress as he released her and slid back to rest against the headboard. The agony that paled her face made him wince, made him caress her arm with one finger.

"Josh, it's been . . ."

"Don't," he said. He glanced at the door. "Where is he?"

"In the graveyard." She swallowed. "Josh, he's drugged you. You've been out for three days."

He wanted to protest. Checked himself when he saw the tears working their way onto her cheeks. Looked toward the front window blindly, remembering without reason all the Fourth of Julys he had spent here as a child—the fireworks in the park just after dark, the band concert in the gazebo, the parade down Centre Street, the picnic tables spread over the ballfield, the wading in the spring-cold pond. His father carrying him home on his shoulders, his mother, walking silently beside.

"All right," he said decisively. "At least I know one thing."

"What?"

"He's not immortal, Andy. I mean, he can live forever as long as he has his victims, but he can be killed in the meantime, right? I could see it in his face when we were fighting. He was afraid to die. He was afraid to die!"

"We all are," she said softly, a forefinger marking a trail down the center of his chest.

"I know," he answered quietly. "But this time we're going to beat him." His grin was bravado. "What have we got to lose, Andy? Either we kill him, or he kills us and keeps on killing. Him and your mother. We either stop it all now, or we get stopped."

"I'm afraid."

"So am I."

Her hand reached his belt buckle, in one smooth motion unfastened it and unsnapped the top of his jeans. But she did not look at him. She only moistened her lips.

"When?" he asked.

"After dark," she told him. "It doesn't have to be then. There's no special time, as long as it's before midnight, before the day is over. But he usually waits until after dark so there's no one around. And out here . . ."

He nodded, then reached out to still her hand. He needed to think. Somehow he had to get into the woods and to Murdoch with a weapon before whatever ceremonies, whatever rites there were to be performed had started. Before Murdoch could summon the wasps, the train, god only knew what else to stop him. And once the man had been taken care of, he and Andy could concoct a story to tell the police. They would have to be told, if only because the families of the dead would have to know where the bodies of their loved ones were.

"Joshua?"

He hadn't realized how dim the room had become. Twilight had taken most of the sun's glare. Shadows were slipping down off the sills. The breeze had quickened, had sent a chill to the air, and he felt his skin raise in gooseflesh as Andrea uncrossed her legs and crawled over to straddle him. He wanted to stop her, but his hand cupped a breast instead, slid down the front of her robe and he watched as the white material hissed off her shoulders and pooled on his legs. Backlighted, she was dark, made taller by the towel still wrapped around her hair. His mouth opened. She traced his lips with a finger. Rose and slipped his jeans down off his hips, grabbed him and inserted him and settled herself again. Moving so slightly he could barely feel her aside from the warmth. Moving so tenderly he wondered if he were dreaming. She touched his eyes with her thumbs. She touched his nipples with her tongue. Moving. Twisting. Lifting her chin, arching her back, her hands braced on his knees and her knees pressed to his ribs.

He almost laughed aloud when the fireworks in the park began filling the sky.

But despite her languid motion, despite the perspiration that encased both of them in thin glass, he could not free himself to disown his fear. At night, she had told him; he would begin it all at night. He wanted to cooperate, wanted it desperately. If they failed, there would be no more touching, no more loving; if they failed, no more . . . anything.

He closed his eyes tightly, demanding a respite from his runaway mind. He opened them to see her, take all of her in and remember it all. A hand out for her breasts, and his fingers brushed over the towel—it had loosened and was falling, and he tried to swipe it to one side.

"Hold," she groaned. "Hold, damnit, hold."

The faint sound of crackling, of rockets brightly dying.

He grunted and reached for her hips, determined to do as she'd bidden. He had to lift himself slightly, to get slightly closer. Cursed the shadows that threatened to veil her, that swarmed over his vision and made her breasts sag, gave a pouch to her belly, took the flesh from her thighs.

"Hold," she whispered between gritted teeth, and her head whipped side to side while Josh bucked to end it.

She sighed and her breath gurgled; she slumped back over his legs. Grinning. Mumbling to herself, brushing her hands softly over his chest. Josh helped her, massaged her, disengaged as she moaned and knelt beside her to kiss her, yanking the towel from beneath her head to lose himself in the cloud of her hair.

"Hold," she muttered.

"Hey, it's over," he said, laughing softly, poking at her shoulder. "Andy?" He kissed the hollows of her throat, her cheek, her forehead. Almost gagged as he backed away when he saw all the grey stiff as straw where there should have been black.

Hold.

He scrambled off the bed, trying not to vomit, pulling his jeans to his waist and fumbling with the buckle. In five strides he was at the door, and a slap of his hand turned the ceiling light on.

There was nothing about the woman that reminded him of Andrea; nothing, that is, except the mocking laughter in her black eyes. The rest of her was caved in, incredibly wrinkled, pocked with brown and sagging rolls of fat. She rolled agilely to a sitting position and calmly drew on the robe, all the while watching him, daring him to run. Her hair was matted dark with perspiration, the deep lines under her eyes giving a sadness to her expression. Her lips, once soft, were brittle and cracked; her cheeks, once round, were hollowed and boned. Wattles beneath her chin. Claws for fingers.

Sneeze and she'll crumple, he thought, fighting horror. Fighting, and losing, and dropping to his knees and retching in the corner. Tasting bile. Tasting salt. Grabbing for his stomach to force himself to stop. Standing again and leaning against the wall while she brushed both her hands through what remained of her hair.

"Well, Josh," she said brightly, "aren't you going to wish me happy birthday?"

He had little strength left to think it all out. He only knew what he was doing while he was acting.

She laughed and tossed her head, arched her back and offered him her breasts. Thrust her hips at him and laughed again.

"Stupid," she said. Then, "No, no you're not. A little young, a little foolish, and very much the romantic." Her voice, tinged with a shrilling whine, softened somewhat, lost some of its grating. "I do love you, you know," she said. "I have to. It's what makes this day more special than the others. The new cycle, the new energies, all fueled by love, and by love that's returned." She smiled coyly, grotesquely—all her teeth had turned black.

The breeze strengthened and she glanced toward the window.

"He's about ready, I guess," she said, as though she were talking about the weather. "A good man, Donald is. A very good man. He plays the father part very well, don't you think? He's been with me for ages." She laughed, nearly screamed. "Ages. My god, for ages!"

Josh took a step toward her. Lies. All of it lies. All of it manipulation.

"That night he was drunk he almost told you, you know. It's hard toward the end, for everything. I had to keep reminding him to hold on so he could keep his image, keep from . . ." She giggled, and ran her hands down her sides.

Hold! she had said; talking to herself, not to him . . . not to him.

"Hard." She lifted an eyebrow in a careless shrug. "You know, you could have gone to Boston, even to New York, and I wouldn't have been able to reach you." She looked down at herself and shook her head sadly. "I can't even be the way I look until it's over. Until we put it all together and drink the lives we've trapped down there in the ground." Another shrug, this time with her shoulders. "Ah well. Don's very protective. He has to be. He knows what will happen to him if something happens to me." She looked pointedly toward the door, then back to Josh. "He'll be back before you can kill me, you know. Why not be a stoic? Damn; and I wanted you all baffled and innocent right to the end. Ah well. Ah well."

He heard footsteps on the porch, let his shoulders sag, felt disgust and revulsion work his stomach again.

"And just think," he heard her say. "If you had listened to your friends instead of me, you would have realized you really did love poor little Felicity . . . and I would have been forced to start all over with some-one else. I don't think I would have killed you, though. Don's the one who likes vengeance, not me. It would have been easy. There was always poor Lloyd. You realize, of course, he told us about the wasps. He was trying to get on Don's good side, to get out of the deal." She grinned. Blackly. "Don wouldn't kill them. No matter. I had fun doing it myself. You should have seen Randy when she saw what I—"

Lies. Manipulations. Everything . . . lies.

He lunged. Andrea shrieked and scrambled backward across the mattress, too late to reach the other side when he landed hard on her chest and fixed his hands around her throat.

Claws raked at his face, gouging at the corners of his eyes; claws tore at his neck, pulled at his hair, stabbed across his shoulders; her knee rammed toward his groin, struck his buttocks instead; her mouth opened and she tried to snap at his arms, his jaw, his chest with her teeth. Her eyes rolled. Spittle whipped from her tongue. She bucked and nearly sent him over her head. Her screams subsided to an erratic rasping, and he could hear someone thudding lamely along the hallway. Could hear bloodsurf in his ears. Could hear her trying to talk to him.

"Joshua, please. Joshua, please. Andy. It's your Andy."

Wavering. Face shifting to soft, to warm, to cotton, to parchment. Hair darkening, glinting, greying, falling in rotten tangles over his wrists. Eyes wide, eyes narrowed, pleading and promising and sinking into hollows. Her breasts firmed, thrust, and sagged, her stomach flattened and stretched, and he compelled himself not to notice when flags of skin broke from her fingers to cling to his hands.

"Joshua, please. Joshua . . . please. I love you. I won't leave you. Joshua, please, don't . . .send . . . me . . ."

Blood seeped from one corner of her mouth; she had bitten through her tongue. He could taste blood in his own mouth; he had bitten through the inside of one cheek. Her nostrils flared and widened, the nose collapsing in bloodless flakes, falling inward, vanishing, while her blackened teeth began rattling down her throat.

The door. He heard someone pounding at the door. The knob turning weakly, the frame trembling slightly.

When he felt his fingers began to slip into slime, he yanked his hands away and leapt off the bed, wiping his palms hard on his jeans over and over while the ceiling's glaring eye outlined the robe that settled down around the corpse.

He fell against the wall, licking his lips and staring. Inched his way around the outside of the room, trying not to see, listening instead to the faint knocking at the door. He considered climbing out to the porch roof and dropping to the ground, changed his mind when he remembered there was still Murdoch left to face. The knocking stilled. He held a hand over his mouth and pulled open the door.

The hallway was dark. The light from the room spilled timidly over the threshold, over the crumpled bundle of clothes that lay huddled against the baseboard. A hand poked from a red plaid sleeve. A hand bunched loosely into a fist. A hand whose flesh lay in grey patches on the flooring.

He pulled himself to the staircase, climbing along the wall, and twice nearly fell as he used the banister for a crutch. A moment . . . an hour later he was standing outside and there were fireworks in the sky. Shivering, still naked to the waist and without his shoes and socks, he watched the display until it was over. Then he hoisted himself to his father's shoulders and walked slowly back to town.

By the end of the week he was done with the police. He had told his story as he had planned to do while Andrea was still . . . Andy. This time, however, he merely said he had no idea where she had gone. They believed him. They comforted him. They pitied him his ordeal so soon after his accident. His parents, at

Fred Borg's request, flew back from Colorado, soothing and urging, but he did not want to leave the
village, could not run from the place he still called his
home. He said nothing to anyone about the ceremony
in the hills; and when all the bodies had been ex-
humed, identified, were taken away to be reburied, he
drove out there the night his parents left and set fire to
the clearing.

By the end of the month, with Oxrun gossiping
about a new scandal at the college, he broke out of his
house to put an end to self-pity. Several jobs were
waiting for him when it was learned he was back in
business, but he only accepted those that took him
out of state. He traveled alone. He did his work.
He visited his parents, he saw dozens of movies, he
found some quiet beaches he had thought he'd forgotten.

And on Labor Day he returned, picked up his
repaired Buick from King's Garage, and drove home
smiling.

He did not expect that his life would change much,
though he knew now the supernatural was not something reserved for children. He suspected, however,
(and with brief surges of regret), that it would be some
time before he would be able to escort a woman again,
and some time after that (unless he were lucky) when
he could forget his last intercourse and resolve the
impotency that plagued him. A year or two, maybe
five, maybe ten, and his mind would somehow ration-
alize the farmhouse, the graveyard, drift Andrea to a
memory that was only faintly disturbing. On the
other hand, he knew full well it might never happen at
all, and he resigned himself to the possibility that he
could be forever alone, and haunted.

The thought did not cheer him, but it served curiously to calm him. It was something he could accept
—like Felicity's passing.

The one thing he would not do was let it drive his
mind away.

So he was grinning, sometimes whistling, when his

parents called on the morning of his birthday, to wish him well and reinstate their gentle urging for his moving.

And he was grinning, sometimes whistling, when Peter Lee treated him to dinner at the Chancellor Inn. With Fred Borg and his wife, Karl Tanner and his date, Dale Blake and her husband, Sandy McLeod and his girlfriend.

All right, he thought then, so I won't be alone.

And he was grinning when he walked home, and grinning when he went to bed.

He didn't mind, then, the dreams of Andrea as she'd been and the loving they had shared. The process of healing and continuing, he told himself as he stirred. Shaking his head in half-sleep, sitting upright and blinking.

A glance at his watch; it was just before midnight.

"Happy birthday, Josh Miller," he whispered as he grinned . . . as he turned to the open window . . . as he saw the wasps pouring in.